'Dan is a warm, wise, uncyn̲_____
qualities shine through in his writing. *The 14th Storm* is an immensely enjoyable read, a real page-turner, exciting, intriguing, and propulsive, and with a stark and salutary message at its heart.'

DONAL RYAN, **winner of the Guardian First Book Award and the European Union Prize for Literature**

'A howling keen of a novel that asks timely questions of us as readers and citizens – who will we want to be when the time comes, and what are we doing to become those people now? *The 14th Storm* places us in a world that is unsettlingly imaginable. Mooney creates a fully realised world through perfect, devastating little details.'

GRÁINNE MURPHY, **author of** *The Winter People*

'Dan Mooney writes the imagined aftermath of climate collapse in brutally vivid and disturbingly plausible terms, and the main characters, particularly Malley, really got under my skin. The book is unsettling from start to finish, but weaves a thread of hope throughout. I would recommend the book for the fight scenes alone, which are absolutely brilliant!'

JULIET CONLIN, **author of** *Sisters of Berlin*

'Rarely have I seen satire and dystopian literature combined to such compelling effect. Dan Mooney shows us a world mangled by catastrophic climate change, where the passage of time is measured in storm seasons, the political posturing of today's social media is literalised, and accountability is enforced at knife-point. The plot is action-driven, kinetic and gripping, but the best apocalyptic stories are those that also retain some poignant memory of how the world used to be; in *The 14th Storm*, the most darkly humorous elements of the setting are also the most heartbreaking. This novel is awesome – you owe it to yourself to read it.'

JACK FENNELL, **writer, researcher and author of *Irish Science Fiction***

# THE
# 14<sup>TH</sup>
# STORM

Daniel J Mooney

Legend Press Ltd, 51 Gower Street, London, WC1E 6HJ
info@legendpress.co.uk | www.legendpress.co.uk

Contents © Daniel J Mooney 2023
The right of the above author to be identified as the author of this work has
been asserted in accordance with the Copyright, Designs and Patents Act
1988. British Library Cataloguing in Publication Data available.

Print ISBN 9781915643667
Ebook ISBN 9781915643674
Set in Times.
Cover design by Heike Schuessler | www.judgebymycovers.com

**Daniel J Mooney** was born and raised in Limerick City. He is a member of a writing group with a number of other writers in Limerick, Writepace, which has been going strong since 2016.

Daniel's writing is inspired by the ongoing dialogue of current events and by the many brilliant writers emerging around Ireland and the world. His debut *Me, Myself and Them* was published in 2017 and *The Great Unexpected* in 2018.

Follow Daniel on Twitter
@danielmoonbags

*For Andy Curtin, Lesley-Anne Liddane and Danny McDonagh. Sometimes I like to imagine that you're all hanging out together at some cosmic gig for some cool band that I probably never heard of. You're all very much missed.*

# CHAPTER ONE

Sometimes they ran.

Mostly they didn't. She found that curious at first. That the majority would stand still, a lack of motivation overriding their survival instinct, holding them in place for her to kill them. Sometimes they wept when she killed them, sometimes they prayed. Some met her with defiant looks and heads held high, while some squeezed their eyes shut and held their last breath.

Malley thought it might be relief. That looking over their shoulders, always waiting for their punishment, had taken its toll on them and that finally being caught allowed them the peace of knowing they were paying their debt. She knew that was naïve. It was much more likely, she reasoned, that this new and relentless world had simply ground them down until there was nothing left and hearing her Proclamation, hearing their own names, their *old* names, was simply one thing too much for them to take. So they gave up and let her kill them.

But sometimes they ran.

Broderick, tall and hard beside her, had a sort of sixth sense for which ones would run. He was coiled so tightly that when they bolted, he unsprung, and the movements seemed simultaneous.

As she walked through the wide-open gate that was the main entrance to the Black Stair settlement, and along the wide dirt avenue that was its only road straight toward the solar-panelled 'town square' where the markets were held, she wondered if this one would run.

She knew this settlement not only because she'd been here before but also because it was every settlement on the edge of civilisation. Rows and rows of small flatpack homes in tight squares of fours and sixteens, mostly built by companies in Dublin on government contracts, intersected by little dirt streets that all radiated from the town square, such as it was. In the small clear Perspex windows of the huts, she saw adornments and homemade curtains, knick-knacks to add some individuality and relieve the unrelenting bleakness of this boxed living.

The town hall, the only building of substance in the town, stood above all others, towering at two storeys high, perched to look down the side of Black Stair Mountain across the bruised countryside of the lowlands.

The uniformity of the new camps was a comfort to her in changing and troubling times. The layout and straight lines were imposed by the Government to bring order to the haphazard nature of what were once refugee camps. As if by ordering them they became something different, something better. It only half worked. Those young enough to be raised among the seasons of the storms had known nothing else but the older ones knew a shanty town when they saw one.

Initially, no one noticed her or Broderick, despite their uniforms, but as they were recognised, the locals all stopped in their tracks, taking in the two agents – one short and sort of sad looking, the other tall and furious. She could feel their moods change as they looked at her. She could feel that shift, though she had never identified what they were shifting from, or indeed to.

Those who still hadn't noticed her remained engaged in their shopping, haggling over handmade toys and salvaged conveniences collected from what was left of the towns out west, soaking up the last of the pre-Storm Season fare and good nature. But their smiles and joviality seemed like brittle things, easily broken, and hard times were coming. Again.

Those who did notice her stood upright. A mere scattering of faces. A scattering of BlueArmbands too. Brave to be wearing those in public, but less brave here where the Government's long arm was less evident. In Dublin, a BlueArmband could get you killed, out here a BlueArmband could get *her* killed.

She reached into the folds of the leather jerkin she wore under her wax coat and pulled out the envelope stashed inside. The uniform of an agent of the Department of Environmental Justice was a thing of concealment. Camouflage to conceal the wearer, pockets to conceal the weapons.

Unfolding the paper in her scarred and ruined hands, she began to read:

'The fucking globalists want you to believe this sham, but it's fucking bullshit,' she intoned loudly.

Her words were a stone dropped into water, the silence rippling outwards through the packed square. It spread out from the ones who had already spotted her and stilled the ones who heard the words before they saw the agents. All faces turned toward them. All bar one.

He was a runner.

He took off as soon as she Proclaimed the very first word. He darted from the open market square into the cover of the flatpack 'homes' that sheltered the people of Black Stair from the coming storms. Broderick moved the very instant that the man did, bolting into a sprint.

Malley did not. She moved without haste and spoke without haste.

'The climate change hoax. Like the fucking vaccination hoax. Just another way for them to control us. And you fucking shills keep eating it up.'

Her words travelled to most of their ears. The wind in the pre-Storm Season pulled it away from a few at the far edge of the market stalls. It was hardly important. They knew what she was, what Broderick was. What they were here for.

They knew from the clothes. Layered browns and greens in linen and wax. Loose fitting around the legs and torso, but tight to the ankles and wrists and shoulders. The clothes must breathe but never encumber. They changed with the limited seasons. But in these days before the first of the storms would hit, when the wind pulled at things and the intermittent rain vied with intermittent sunshine in the otherwise unrelieved grey of the clouds, the uniform was made for weathering.

She changed direction unhurriedly. Her eyes following Broderick as he appeared and disappeared behind the low buildings, hunting his prey. She didn't need to follow the runner. Just track her partner in between reading from her Proclamation. They'd done this enough times already to know the drill.

'Resist the climate hoax.'

Some of the onlookers grumbled at that, their low growls heard over the whistling breeze. They wouldn't have done this twenty years ago. They'd have agreed with the sentiment. Or perhaps just sneered at the man who had written it down. She would have ignored him. Young her. Stupid her. Naïve her. Former her. She knew better now, and so did they.

Broderick turned sharply, ducking low as he darted through the gap between two flatpack shanties. In one hand his long-bladed knife; with the other he signalled to her which way to move.

She pivoted at his direction and drew her knife casually. The handle, clad in wrapping that was now fourteen storm seasons old, seemed to fit, ridges and bumps, into the scars and the pitted contours of her hands, completing her. A jigsaw piece. A part of her. A thing that made her whole.

Mostly.

Lately she had begun to feel something else…

The man became visible again as he doubled back. She could see the panic in his eyes. Broderick closing in over his shoulder. There was a light in Broderick's eyes. A dangerous light. Something close to pleasure. He was a man who loved doing his duty.

'The statistics are there. Why won't any of you idiots read? There's warm years and warm decades, that doesn't mean the planet is doomed.'

Outside of the town square, there were fewer people moving between the buildings, but she could feel the eyes of the locals behind her watching. Those with the BlueArmbands were likely statue-still, the rest moving in uneasy agitation. They knew what was coming for this panicked man they called neighbour.

It was unlikely they held any sympathy for him. Not after what they'd been through.

'David Sullivan, born Peter O'Sullivan, in Carlow Hospital in the year 2004,' she called out.

Thirty-nine years old. He wasn't even forty yet.

'These statements made in the year 2023 were made by you. Your location and identity have been a matter of investigation by the Department of Environmental Justice.'

She was closer to him now as Broderick cut the escape routes with each new twist and turn. Herding him. Shepherding him to her. She could see him dead ahead at the end of a long row of market stalls, unattended as the people cleared the way for justice.

'In the presence of the Minister for the Environment, you have been accused by two agents of Environmental Justice. The Minister pronounced your sentence.'

He stopped and turned, frantically searching for a way out, gulping in deep panicked breaths. He could see her closing. Broderick was too close for him to turn back, and she herself now blocked his last avenue of escape. There was nowhere left to run. He turned and looked at the other members of the Black Stair community but met only hard-eyed stares.

She wondered how many had lost their children to the storms. Or to the violence? Or to the deprivation that followed every Storm Season?

He tried one last pathetic ploy, rushing at her, hoping his size and desperation would count.

It didn't.

She pivoted on one heel as he charged, ducking low, spinning and slamming her foot into his midriff. He pitched to the floor.

Slowly, she straightened. He did not.

'Please,' he implored, on his knees.

The ones who ran always begged.

'You have been deemed guilty of betraying humanity and condemning it to catastrophe,' she told him. 'You condemned humanity and the planet, thusly are you judged and condemned yourself.'

Had he been standing he might have topped her height by half a foot, but crawling on his knees, she loomed over him, the regretful sadness on her face a contrast to the desperation on his.

'Please,' he implored again.

Broderick moved to stand behind him, one hand clamping on the man's shoulder, a vice grip. As usual he seemed to struggle to contain the furious energy that powered him. The energy visible in his fevered-looking eyes.

The village was silent. All eyes were on them.

'I have small children,' the man whimpered.

The words caught her. She didn't want them to. For a long time, no words could have stayed her. But lately some feeling had taken root in her mind. Something tugging at her. She remembered an old man's face. A face like her father's. A face full of gratitude, with tears in his eyes. Involuntarily, she looked around for signs of the children. She didn't see them. She saw no one who might now have to watch their father die.

The ridges of her scarred hands shifted slightly against the grip of the handle as she adjusted her stance, ruining the nice feeling of jigsaw puzzle completeness that usually came with holding the weapon.

'And how many don't because of you and your kind?' Broderick barked.

A rare moment of speech from the man, but it wasn't for

Mr Sullivan, or O'Sullivan as he had been. It was for her. For her hesitation. He'd known her too long. Seen her do this too many times but had never seen her hesitate.

She glared at him, clenching her jaw. He met her glare with one of his own.

'Daughters,' the man whispered, pleading.

She returned her regard to the man on his knees before her, now furious. As if their gender might somehow alleviate his sentence. As if he might manipulate her because she had also been someone's daughter once. No one knew better than her the sacrifices women had to make in the new world. Well, her sister Hilda did, but not this man.

'Thusly are you judged,' she said again, coldly, as she stepped forward and plunged her blade into his chest. It ran in smoothly. As it did every time.

The blood that spurted from the wound wet her scarred hands.

Broderick let a small sigh go through his nose. There was something in the sound it made. A type of satisfaction, though you'd never know from his face. The light of enjoyment that had burned in his eyes was gone. His duty done.

He slipped his own knife into its sheath and nodded to her before he turned away. Off to set up camp. To resume his waiting. She turned to give the villagers a look. She always did.

In every village, town, or city, there was always at least one who looked at her like she was the villain. In a town with too many BlueArmbands, there would be more than a few. She met that stare every single time she encountered it, though she had no idea why.

She cleaned the blade with the soft red rag she kept, and then wiped her hands with it. She rolled her neck. The sharp popping sound as she cracked it seemed loud in the breezy silence. Scanning them slowly again as she ran the rag across her rough skin, she dared them to judge her, to resent her.

For reasons she never understood, she was relieved when one or two of the faces did just that. They didn't move though. They stood silently. They wouldn't dare move. She waited another moment, to give them time to *realise* that they didn't dare, and then she nodded and followed Broderick.

David Sullivan or Peter O'Sullivan, or whatever it is he had been called before she executed him, lay unnoticed. Every community had different ways of dealing with corpses. She didn't care to be around to find out what Black Stair did with theirs.


She sat, cross-legged, at the small fire she shared with Broderick. They had camped just inside the walls of the settlement on a patch of hard rocky ground where the meagre handful of sheep and goats grazed. The palisade that surrounded the settlement loomed up by their campsite, double-layered rows of thick tree trunks lashed together with recycled plastic and caulked in mud-concrete.

Inside the town hall, two hundred yards away across the jumble of huts where the locals sheltered, the evening meal was about to be Shared. She knew from the noise and the small congregation of Christians standing outside the building saying their grace before their meal. Always outside now, never inside.

She reckoned that both she and Broderick would be tolerated at the meal, if not welcomed. The BlueArms weren't numerous enough here to turn them away. Technically their job counted as Sharing for the purpose of community, but she'd have truly done her Sharing in the chores, preparing vegetables, laying plates, ladling out the food, or washing up. They remained outside because of Broderick.

He'd frighten them.

In the flickering firelight, all the angles of his face were shadowed and then revealed, and the effect added to his menacing visage. She used to be afraid of him. Not just him, but anyone like him. She used to fear that aura of violence they exuded. It was in their very movements and the way they stood, vibrating with violence.

That was before she'd earned the scars on her hands, before her sister had made a dreadful deal for their survival. Back when some men had taken from her because they could.

That fear had made her strong in the end. Training. Self-defence. Exercise. She did it all, so that she wouldn't have to be afraid. She remembered the first moment that she caught someone looking at her the way she had once looked at men like Broderick. Trepidation and awe. It was thrilling and saddening simultaneously. She tried to crush the feeling of sadness. The world had no time for it anymore. The world rejected sadness. And it rejected fear. Things that feared or got sad were excised.

Her sister's eyes were sad the last time they had spoken. Pitying her. She resented that. There was much to resent in that last conversation. In almost every conversation since that first Storm Season.

She tried not to sigh bitterly as she ate her rehydrated soup and thought about those inside. Sharing. Singing. Some places still allowed people to Share by singing. In the pre-Storm Season, it would be welcome. During Storm Season, Sharing had to be of significantly more value. Skills. Food. Shelter. Electricity. The tools and means of survival. Important things. In the aftermath of the storms, there would be little to sing about.

She heard the voices drift over from the town hall.

A song about a winding road to a bay, where communities shared in comfort and joy. She recognised it from Before. She never enjoyed recognising things from Before. They were a link to a soft woman, in a soft land, who had let things be taken from her. The cheerfulness of the song overrode her distaste, the warmth of it seeping into her, and she smiled across the fire at Broderick. If he noticed the smile, he showed no sign, stirring his small tin suspended over the fire. And she went back to examining the ridges and folds of her palms, idly tracing her thumbnail along the trenches where the knife had bitten them.

She had a friend who was a singer once. She had no idea where the woman was now. Maybe dead. Maybe not.

The song floated through the night, twisting occasionally on gusts of wind, making its way to them from the Black Stair's town hall, the only building that felt real, solid. This close to the edge many of the settlements didn't have town halls. They were too far from safety for such permanence. Out in the west of Ireland were the lands that Government couldn't control where need was stronger than law. Black Stair itself sat right on that knife edge between the two.

It was the same as the last time she'd been here, nestled on top of its hill where flooding and shifting rivers couldn't touch it. Where the hand of climate change wasn't so destructive. Where they could see the threats coming before they were on top of them. The palisade walls and ditches offered a measure of protection to the small, tidy rows of flatpack homes with their low doors and single windows, as well as the workshops where people built, then rebuilt year after year. But she knew it was a sham. The uniformity and organisation were a trick. A means of convincing people to feel safe and comfortable between Storm Seasons.

The reality was that here, like almost every place outside of the cities, the dangers were many and the protection flimsy. Clans who occupied the lowland towns raided, desperate bands of refugees with nothing left to lose came to claim for themselves, crops failed, the summer sun slowly baked the life out of people, or viruses ran rampant. And at the end always, always the storms returned.

Thirteen Seasons so far, and the fourteenth not far off.

She let her gaze linger on the little homes – she'd seen sheds bigger than these in Before – and wondered how safe these people really felt, and how many more times their strength would be tested before it snapped.

Broderick finished his meal by rattling his spoon against the inside of his tin, loudly.

Meaningfully.

She looked at him across the flames and his eyes flickered, barely.

*We're being watched.*

She narrowed her eyes at him, slightly in reply.

He blinked at her, and his head tilted, a fraction of a fraction to indicate *behind her, on her left-hand side.*

She twitched an eyebrow at him.

*How many?* The gesture asked.

He let that sharp nose-whistle go again. Not quite a sigh. Barely a noise.

*Unknown.*

That was the way of them. Side by side. Silently. Shoulder by shoulder. Silently.

And in those silences, all the meaning they needed.

That he hadn't moved told her the danger wasn't imminent, that he'd called her attention to it said it was a danger, nonetheless.

She looked at him for a long moment, then nodded and as one they rose to their feet, not quickly. In a slow and deliberate action, they turned in the direction of the watcher, hidden in the shadows of the flatpack sheds that now passed for homes.

For a moment nothing, and then a flash of movement as a young woman bolted away.

In that flash, she weighed the little thing. Young. Dressed as the young people did now with form following the function of their storm-prepared clothes, decorated here and there. Her long, curly hair blowing out behind her as she darted away.

Malley retook her seat calmly. Broderick was slow to follow, still tense.

*Are we doing something about that?* His reluctance asked her.

Malley let out a long sigh to show how little she thought of the possible threat.

Broderick scowled back at her.

*Everyone's a threat.*

Malley turned her hands over, letting the light from the dancing flames play across the scars as the sound of singing struggled to reach out from the town centre, struggled and eventually died on the quickening breeze.

She nodded.

*Everyone's a threat.*


Fionnuala had slipped out in the darkness, creeping through the town's locked gate, held open by another BlueArm who would watch for the return of their compatriots. The memory of the agents' cold eyes searching the darkness from their fireplace still chilling her every bit as much as the wind did.

They hadn't even spoken, the two agents. Not a word said between the man and the woman who had killed her neighbour only hours before. But somehow, they knew, and they moved as one, the air about them charging with violence.

They frightened her. And the fright was slow to die in her chest.

She thought of them as she crowded into the small building at the bottom of the eastern slope of Black Stair, fifteen people of varying ages, their BlueArmbands on display. Fionnuala wore hers too, but it felt stupid – a showy gesture of defiance that served no purpose in a room full of people who agreed with you.

Her father would have called it 'preaching to the converted'.

She disliked the room. Disliked the swirling anger it contained that dissipated once all her fellow rebels walked back into the winds and the rains outside.

She wanted more from them. More from herself.

The BlueArms' modest headquarters had been some kind of office for the forestry service once upon a time, before the first Chain of Storms fourteen years ago. It was a pathetic sort of a place for a meeting of rebels who jostled each other gently as they crammed into the musty-smelling space with its dirty windows and meagre furniture.

The four outsiders in the room didn't jostle. They didn't wear armbands either. Why should they? They needed no proof of their loyalty. They ran with Gibson and Kelly. They were the Children of the Storms. The 'military wing' of the BlueArm movement, such as it was. Hard types who ventured out west, beyond the arm of Government, to gather supplies, to recruit, to coordinate with the BlueArms in what was left of Limerick, Cork, Galway, Sligo and Donegal.

Their youthful features were marked by signs of premature ageing. The four of them were older than her, falling into the category of people who had real memories of Before, but only as children, who could look back on that time with the bitterness of knowing what the cost of losing it was. And that was the reason for their early grey hairs and the hard lines about their eyes. Too much asked of them when they were still too young to carry the weight; caring for smaller siblings as they moved from place to place seeking refuge, watching elderly relatives give up and die in the process. For the ones from the cities, they'd remember the riots. And the ones from the countryside would remember the desperate isolation as their tight-knit communities dissolved in the winds and the rains and the starvation.

Hard folk. All of them.

Douglas called for silence by raising two hands up in front of the group. It all felt so performative – his serious face on his youthful features, his dramatic gestures, his armband bigger by half than all of theirs.

'They've Pronounced both Gibson and Kelly,' he told the room.

His theatricality had the desired effect as the room erupted with groans, complaints, and protests at the announcement.

Fionnuala felt it too, like a ball of ice forming in her stomach. A tightening in her chest. Gibson and Kelly Pronounced.

Douglas shushed them with his upraised arms again.

'The Minister himself Pronounced him in the Dáil. Kelly and Gibson have both fled Dublin.'

'Where are they going?'

'They can't expect us to believe that?'

'What's going to happen to the deal with Europe?'

The voices talked over each other, the anger and indignation rising.

This was what they loved. The same thing Fionnuala hated. They loved to gather and be angry. They loved to wear their armbands and swagger. They loved the appearance of action. For Fionnuala, it wasn't enough.

She'd spent her life moving, running from storms and from people. Three settlements before Black Stair. Including a filthy refugee camp in Dublin City Centre. Always running from one impermanent thing to another. But she was younger than the Children. She couldn't remember the home they'd left behind on the northwest coast when the first Storm Season had destroyed the country, but knew it was bigger than the capsule she lived in now, and she could remember the *feel* of it. The feel of a home. Not a box.

She ached for that feeling. Yearned for it in her soul. The feeling of permanence, of security. A place that gathered smells and memories that you could look back on when times were tough. She yearned for a thing she never remembered having. These were things all the BlueArms wanted.

'It can't be true,' someone shouted behind her.

'Of course, it's not,' Douglas snapped. 'The Government falsified some newsletter they claimed was written by Gibson and Kelly. They printed it themselves two weeks ago. Now they're circulating it to disgrace us.'

'So, what do we do?' Fionnuala asked loudly, cutting through the pointless denunciations.

'*We* don't do anything,' Douglas told her. '*They* do.'

He jerked one hand in the direction of the Children standing by.

So, more *nothing* then.

'Fine,' she snapped. 'What do *they* do then?'

One of them stepped forward. Handsome in a sort of battered way, though his nose was slightly too long on his weathered face, patches of grey showing on his dark stubble.

'The less you know the better,' he told her in a low voice, 'but to put it briefly, they can't hide here anymore. Not with those two agents here. Gibson is gone to Galway. The evidence of the Government's bullshit is there. Kelly is gone to Limerick. The BlueArms there are massing, getting ready.'

'Ready for what?' she asked.

'We know what's coming. The moment is any day now, but we have to wait. For orders,' Douglas told her calmly.

Of course. Wait for orders. Even more nothing.

'What if they don't make it out of Dublin?' she pushed him.

'They're already clear. With luck, Kelly must be in Limerick already and Gibson is collecting the evidence of the Government conspiracy. They're smart, resourceful men. You know that better than anyone.'

Of course, she did. To everyone else in the room, they were Joe Kelly and Frank Gibson, political leaders and revolutionaries, but to her the former was simply Uncle Joe. Not that he was really her uncle. He had been friends with her father and mother. They'd been on the front lines of the protests against the Government since the movement started.

Uncle Joe had built the BlueArms, unified the anger at the Government into a cohesive force determined to reject the abrogation of responsibility, fixed on the goal of a new government that built for the people, that didn't use the storms as a means of dividing the country and pitting people against each other in the scrap for the meagre resources their leaders deemed to share with them. And more, Kelly and Gibson promised them Ireland again, and a reconnection with Europe and the rest of the world that they'd lost when Ireland had become an international pariah.

'Then we have to help them,' she demanded of the room.

'How?' Douglas asked, trying to inject a note of command in his voice.

'Anything is better than the nothing we've done. If the Government are moving against us, we should move against them.'

There was a murmur of agreement within the room.

'Let's hit the grid?' she suggested. 'We can disrupt supply to Dublin from one of the turbines or mills up the country?'

The murmurs of agreement died down somewhat. Anger replaced by trepidation.

Interfering with the electricity grid could get you killed as fast as denying climate change.

'What about the Doejays?' another voice challenged her.

The Department of Environmental Justice agents, or Doejays as they were known, were the cause for concern. It seemed she wasn't the only one thinking about the two cold-blooded monsters sitting by their fireplace inside the settlement.

'You leave them to us,' the leader of the Children told her. 'We've got something in mind for them.'

There was about him a supreme confidence. Arrogance even. She'd seen the agents at work. Fast and cold and brutal. This man with his handsome features and long nose seemed soft by comparison. They all did.

She recalled them again, standing in unison, not quickly, but slowly, as though there was no threat powerful enough to move them to alacrity. That their slow, measured turning, achieved in complete silence, would be sufficient to cow whatever was waiting for them.

She nearly shuddered at the thought. The silent terribleness of them.

These four Children would be mere appetisers to the wolves she'd seen by that fireplace.

'There's only four of you,' she told them. 'You have to let us help.'

That was the end of their shared anger.

The room became quiet as all the other BlueArms shifted uncomfortably. Taking on the Doejays was not something they were prepared to contemplate. Talking and shouting and agreeing with one another was one thing, opposing this terrible arm of the Government... well, that was something else entirely.

The smile the leader of the Children shot her was amused. And patronising.

'We know where they're going,' he told her conspiratorially. 'And when they leave, we'll be waiting for them.'

The others nodded together. Their confidence all consuming.

But they hadn't seen the two wolves by the fire. They hadn't witnessed the terrible quietness of them. They had no idea what they were getting into.

'We wait for orders,' Douglas insisted, his word the final word. 'The day is coming. When it finally happens, we're finally going to be free.'

She heard the note of hope in his voice, and the fear that underlay it.

# CHAPTER TWO

Malley woke early as she always did now. It had been a long time since she would wake at noon and spend hours in bed scrolling on her phone before she rose. It was, she always reminded herself whenever she recalled the embarrassing excess of her previous life, a different time. Nowadays, she rolled from her bed, whether it was in the apartment block in Dublin, or in this pokey little tent, and began moving. Always moving.

Outside, a bright, windy day had already dawned. Pre-Storm Season at the heights of the hills that wind was ubiquitous, but it pushed small puffy clouds across the sky rather than the dark ones that threatened something terrible. There was a freshness to this air that everyone enjoyed. Not the relentless heat of the summer that wilted people and hammered them into the ground, nor the implacable heaving and battering of winter when the storms came.

A perfectly peaceful freshness that renewed a body.

The sun poured across the fields below. In the distance, small towns could be seen, too far away for their destruction to be visible and spoil the stunning view. You could almost have tricked yourself into thinking that you were looking at Before, and those towns would be carrying on their existences, some bustling, some sleepy, blissfully unaware of what was coming.

She watched the people of Black Stair make their way to

their Sharing. Burlier types, stripped of their heavier layers ambled alongside one another, axe handles slung across their shoulders. Smaller, slimmer ones moved in groups – some would fish, some would gather, some would be off to pull the last of the vegetables from the ground, the hardier types that grew late, for storing and dehydrating, and making soup. BlueArmbands were visible here and there, symbols of something Malley didn't fully understand. A movement that demanded something that could no longer be given to them. They demanded the past. For these people, her sister had left her. She scanned them one by one and wondered what they were like. Strong? Violent? Soft? Enduring? They just looked like people.

Among them a young woman walked. Something about her marked her out, or perhaps it was simply Malley's instincts, sharpened to a fine edge. Though the young woman moved among her neighbours, she didn't move with them. She glanced Malley's way as she walked, her face serious, trying not to be noticed, watching Malley as she moved, so slight among the broad, muscled types, but her head swivelled to look back as she followed, the wind whipping her long, curly hair.

Malley remembered the blur of movement at their fireplace the night before. A watcher. This watcher, she now assumed. Still spying? Or on her way to the Sharing?

The Sharing was important for them all now. Within days, the first storm of the season would be observed swelling in the Atlantic, shaping for the west coasts of Europe. As soon they spotted it, they would name it, and that name would hound and torment the country until the Storm Season ended. Preparation was everything in these moments before the storms.

Every settlement would Share as one: stacking, collecting, building, fixing, making themselves as prepared as they could be for the violent weather that was to come.

In the cities, it was different. In Dublin, Belfast, and Waterford, employment counted as Sharing, the unemployed had to Share in other ways, their tasks issued on a day-to-day basis. Industry still ruled in its warped capacity. Manufacturing for a changed landscape, jobs a symbol of status so that the lives of those in the cities were far removed from those in the settlements and towns of the countryside.

Broderick might object to Sharing, but as far as she was concerned, if there was one – only one – thing that might be worth celebrating in the relentless battering of the modern world, it was the Sharing.

A small part of her yearned to join them. To chop the wood, to fish, to hunt, to skin the animals, and prep the meals. The part of her she considered soft.

She pulled on her stout boots, adjusting the clasps until they were almost too snug around her calves. She smoothed the front of her lightweight T-shirt, salvaged from some pile of communal clothes a long time ago as she tucked it into her combat trousers. The fabric, as always, too smooth against her scarred palms.

For a moment she considered her knife.

That was a new thing for her.

Like the feelings she'd felt stirring before she'd executed the man yesterday. The knife was a part of her. A symbol of her work. A totem of the office that she held to anyone who still obeyed the laws of the Irish Government. More than that, it was a symbol to her, a hard thing, with sharp edges, like herself. A thing she once feared, but no longer did. She often played with the handle, running her rough, ruined hands over it, feeling it slide into her grip, the oneness.

Sometimes, when she was on her own, she'd even hold it gently by the blade. These were her most private moments. There was no more perfect sensation of oneness than the feeling of the blade finding the ridges and valleys in her skin that had been caused by its kin. That still frightened her a bit. Then sometimes it would make her think of her sister Hilda, and that would sometimes even make her cry a little.

These days though, these days she felt more and more like

there might be a different her. A her without the knife. The same soft part of herself that she tried so hard to ignore.

Only sometimes she didn't. And so, when she was safely in community in Dublin, or feeling adventurous in the field, she'd leave it behind her. And the feeling of that was liberation. An incompleteness that was somehow fulfilling. She didn't know why.

If Broderick saw her, he'd make a face. Or give that snort he was so fond of. A fool he'd call her, without saying a word. She was older than him. Eight years older. Yet his almost impenetrable silence gave him an exaggerated 'wisdom' that seemed to level the playing field.

She looked at the handle of the knife, protruding from under her pillow where it stayed while she slept and chose to leave it behind her.

She looked across the campfire at Broderick's curiously empty tent. Already up and about.

Down the hill the people kept moving, snatches of chatter floating on the breeze that moved clouds quickly by them in the otherwise steely blue morning sky.

She let them walk away. There was work to be done.


Across the town square where the solar panelling caused her footfalls to echo as dull thuds, two men stood at the door to the town square. Younger men than her, with hard-looking faces that showed signs of ageing too early. They had speckles of grey in their hair and the kind of hardness about the eyes that added years to them.

One stood indolently against the door frame, casually picking at his fingernails, the other, like a pointer dog, long nose thrust forward, scanning the town. Scanning her.

Security for the town council, she assumed. They had to have some kind of status not to be out Sharing with the others. Whatever their jobs were, she outranked them.

She almost smiled at their attempt at looking grim.

'Cummins, Malley,' she introduced herself pleasantly to the long-nosed one. An imposing man, six foot two or more.

She had to look up at him as she said it, her hand briefly missing the feeling of her long blade. The oneness of the wrapping and her scars soothed her when she was confronted with men like this one.

His glance brushed by her empty sheath, and the scars all over her hand.

'Lynch,' he grunted at her.

His recalcitrance immediately bothered her. This was the way with security types and men she'd met during Before and since. They didn't like her authority. They resented her. She didn't much care usually. Their resentment was their business and it only bothered her if it got in her way.

'I have business here. If you don't mind…' She gestured for him to step aside.

The look he returned her was pugnacious, and for just a second, she thought she might have to beat him around the square to put manners on him. Big men, with big egos and big muscles, often mistook their bigness for dominance. She once did herself. But the time when that was something that concerned her was long gone. She no longer feared that bigness. In fact, she welcomed the notion of disabusing him. He knew only the half of what violence really was and would only go half as far as she would to exercise her authority, so he'd lose. And maybe die in the process. For a long moment, the words hung in the air, and his life in the balance.

It floated there between them, him staring down his long nose belligerently, her offering him her most withering look.

He thought better of the exchange before it became a problem, and reluctantly stood to one side.

She held his gaze, so that he'd know how close he'd come. Until he looked away.

As she walked into the town hall building, she let the feeling of anger slide off her, just as she had done the day before when she'd murdered a man whose name she could no longer remember.

Remembering those who had destroyed the world was as pointless as regret for the world they'd never see again.

Inside, the building gave a lie to the rustic nature of the settlement outside. The feeling of electricity and comfort reflected from the walls. It felt like buildings used to feel. Automated and warm and firm. Substantial things made of permanence in a way that few things felt like anymore. Through this building, the town got its rations of electricity and charged their batteries, cooked their meals, taught their children, watched their movies, and navigated what remained of the internet that the Government permitted them to access.

Here they learned about what was happening in the rest of the world, when they could bring themselves to watch it collapse around them. But they also learned about how to care for themselves. They learned cooking and sewing and horticulture and relearned skills that they had thought lost.

It was almost enough to make her sentimental again.

At least it might have been if not for the presence of Broderick in front of a monitor, in the 'chambers' room of the local council, glowering at the Minister for the Environment, Garrett O'Neill, who in turn glared right back.

A confrontation of some sort then, though the fact that they'd started the meeting without her was a cause for more than annoyance.

She cocked an eyebrow at Broderick as she crossed the room to the end of the long table where he stood, tightly wound as ever, as if on the verge of movement at all times.

*What's going on?*

His reply, in the form of his tension and furious glare, was something she'd never encountered before. An unknowable reply. And in keeping something from her, he cracked the wall that was their joint resolve, marring the years of solidarity and solidity between them.

She narrowed her eyes at him a smidge and bit her teeth. *What aren't you telling me?*

He blinked at her in reply. *Nothing.*

She held his gaze for a long second. Angry all over again at the lie.

'Agent Cummins,' the monitor interrupted her. 'I'm glad you're here. There's news.'


Fionnuala watched, from behind a wall, as the woman faced down the Children outside the town hall. It was mesmerising. She hadn't done anything. She hadn't changed her stance, or drawn a weapon or even frowned, but somehow, something in her body language went from a casual, smiling, pleasant woman to something different and terrifying. In an instant, she'd transformed. And what she had turned into frightened anyone who looked at her.

Fionnuala enjoyed watching the Child drop his eyes and the agent hold her ground for a moment or two after he'd spoken. Salt in his wounds. And proof of what she already suspected; these Children would be less than useless at protecting Uncle Joe and Frank Gibson. The agents would eat them without salt.

As the woman left to go inside the hall, Fionnuala scurried forward, hoping that no one noticed her – a small woman, hardly more than a child, off on an errand somewhere.

She had doubled back to the town on her way to the Sharing, determined to prevent the Children from getting slaughtered pointlessly. If they let the rest of the BlueArms help, they might stand some chance. Perhaps all of them together...

But now a fresh chance presented itself.

She tried to look casual, but busy. A woman with somewhere to go who was not to be bothered. Striding across the square, she imagined she could feel the Children watching her, following her. As if some part of her radiated the words 'rebel' or 'traitor'.

She held her head until just out of sight, when she gave

a furtive glance and was annoyed, somehow, to find that they'd ignored her. It always annoyed her when people underestimated her.

Hoping no one would notice her absence at the Sharing, she unlocked the boiler room door and slipped inside. The little passageway that led into the main building was just large enough to fit her. If she was careful, she could position herself in the public gallery, behind the partition, and hear everything that was being said. It was risky, she knew, but she'd accepted those risks when she joined. And whatever was being discussed inside, it might well involve the lies that might get the BlueArms' leaders killed.

On silent feet, she crept through the corridors.


The headache crawled up from the base of Broderick's skull, enveloping his entire head and squeezing him. It started the minute the man on the monitor started talking. It always happened every time he felt the need to wrap his hands around someone's throat and squeeze.

O'Neill had that effect on him. A hypocritical rat. A career politician. Broderick could picture him as a teenager in his button-up shirt grinning like an idiot at some young political party conference next to the leadership that let the world burn, standing by and letting it all happen. Now they preached 'sustainability' and 'justice' as if those words weren't ashes in their mouths.

He was about to tell the little weasel to go fuck himself when she walked in.

He bit off the words, clamping his jaw shut around the throbbing in his head.

'What news?' she asked.

Her voice was deceptively mild. Almost pleasant even. Her entire persona was deceptively mild. At first glance she was by no means imposing. But her shoulders were broader than her frame should have allowed, and her forearms rippled whenever she dry-washed her hands, betraying the hardness of the ropey muscle beneath. That hardness went to the core of her, however soft she appeared.

They'd been paired together for six years now. At first, he resented her, hated her a little even. She was old enough to have been part of the problem, as he saw it: a generation of lazy, entitled, selfish, narcissistic scum, all of them, who'd let the world burn so they could have Christmas crackers stuffed with crap. He loathed them. And her.

Every time she'd opened her mouth to him, the headache swelled up to consume his head, crushing his brain until only quick, decisive justice eased him.

But he'd grown to respect her. Her work was methodical, and typically ruthless. She spared no thought for those who deserved to die. She had no philosophy about her. No politics. He couldn't abide the philosophers or the politicians.

There'd been enough of both when the world was being allowed to burn.

At least, he *thought* she had no philosophy. Lately there had been something in her. Something reluctant. He doubted she knew what it was any more than he did, but she had hesitated before she had killed Sullivan the day before.

He tried to remember all of their names. He *needed* to remember them. If it were possible, he'd have burned their names into his soul for what they'd done. He'd have built a wall and immortalised their names if he could have. He'd engrave the top of it: 'Remember: They died for what they did.' He bitterly resented their anonymity. They hid behind new names when they lived, and their crimes were forgotten when they died. It wasn't fair.

He studied her for signs of weakness, for the early warning that she was becoming soft. The first seeds of doubt creeping in. He saw none. He hoped he never would. He couldn't tolerate another apologist.

The little weasel let his gaze greasily linger on her. Broderick fought the urge to massage his temples as the pain flared.

If she noticed his lechery, she didn't let it show.

Her knife wasn't in its sheath on the belt that hung at her waist.

He scoffed slightly in spite of himself.

She noticed that alright. Her eyes swinging to regard him. Dangerously mild again. He didn't meet her glare. Sometimes he struggled with that. There was something about the way she looked at him, at a lot of people, as if she was measuring them for butchering. Every time she did it, he felt a little thrill of fear. He wasn't afraid of her all the time – he wasn't really afraid of anything – but if anyone could have been said to intimidate him, it was her.

He'd faced big men, he'd faced gangs of toughs and mobs of refugees and little raiding parties determined to take what they could, and he'd met them all with a towering rage and watched them scatter before him, but her...

'There have been certain developments,' the weasel told her, snapping Broderick back into the moment.

Her eyes settled on O'Neill as the thumb of her right hand traced the tracks of the scars in her left palm. Even that lazy dry-washing was somehow compelling to look at.

The council room they sat in, empty now with the Sharing taking place on the lee side of the hill, offered a place to talk, and a place for locals to watch movies or have parties or Share meals. Versatility had become a virtue in the new world.

'Two men have been judged,' O'Neill informed her.

He tried to make the comment seem casual, a throwaway thing, just as he had done moments before when he told Broderick who he wanted dead.

'That's not how things are done,' she replied quietly.

'Who's the Minister here?' he asked, a mocking twinge on his lips. 'Me or you?'

It was the wrong tone to take with her.

She went cold, instantly. A deep freeze. Her face no longer mild, but impassive and terrible.

'Are you suggesting you're above the law?' she asked.

Her tone was ice. The temperature in the room plummeted.

'No one is above the law,' O'Neill replied placatingly, but Broderick reckoned he'd caught his mistake already.

'We investigate,' she snapped at him. 'We bring you evidence. You judge them. We Pronounce them. *You* do not bring *us* lists of dead people.'

That's what they surely were. O'Neill may as well have offered them a hit list.

'Special circumstances, and it was too late for you to travel all the way back to Dublin. Winter will be here literally any day now. The meteorologists are preparing to name it. This job must be done before the storms start.'

He'd modified his tone. It sounded reasonable. It sounded much more like the tone the man had been using before she came in, when he was issuing his confidential orders.

'Who were the investigators?'

'Proper protocol was followed,' O'Neill assured her, using his weasliest voice.

'Who?' she asked, relentless.

So cold. And so hard.

'Jameson, Shields, Nduku, Alraheem,' he listed them off.

Broderick hated all of them. Philosophers and politicians and career men.

'Four long-tailed rats,' she dismissed them.

'Four agents of the Department of Environmental Justice,' he rebutted, still using his weasel voice, still unsure of his footing.

The sound of his voice grated on Broderick's teeth, and he had to almost grunt with the effort not to massage his temples.

'Then why don't they go do it themselves?' she asked.

Broderick knew why. O'Neill had told him before she arrived in. It was a job made for tougher than the likes of them. Now the Minister hesitated for a moment.

She caught the hesitation, her eyes narrowing. She was too sharp for his gamesmanship. Men like O'Neill thought themselves clever, until they came up against someone like her. She was putting it together in front of him, and he knew it.

Broderick grunted his respect at her. Fucking politicians. Fucking greasy, sneaky, hypocritical politicians.

On the monitor, O'Neill picked up a small folder containing a meagre handful of paper sheets.

'Joe Kelly and Frank Gibson have been judged and Proclaimed as climate change deniers. They've fled justice. I need you to go after them.'

Broderick wanted to smile at the look she gave him. He could almost see the fear creeping up in the man.

'Kelly? Gibson?' she asked with scorn.

Broderick grunted.

'You want me to murder your political rivals?' she asked him.

'No,' O'Neill protested, his weasel voice morphing into mousy desperation. 'You don't understand. Things... certain things have happened.'

'Things have happened?' she asked sarcastically. She had so little fear of him, it was almost funny to watch.

'Look at this,' he said, his busy hands reaching and clicking until a document showed on the screen in front of them.

It looked old, like it was from Before.

'They had a newspaper,' O'Neill told them. 'Them and some others. In University. A little thing. They called it *Liberal Tears*. It was a small thing. But they did it. They said it.'

Broderick's headache intensified with each line he read, his fury manifesting as a physical pain that obliterated thought.

It was damning stuff. The essay on the front page was enough to have Kelly killed. In fact, the first paragraph was enough that the Government wouldn't have to do it, his own people would kill him for words like these.

Broderick tried not to gag with the rage.

*'They're lying to you and if you don't resist them now, we'll pay the price later. The Green Agenda, the whole Climate Hoax, is merely a means to make money off the backs of the people. Resist. Now. Burn the electric vehicles, boycott the 'green energy' companies. The only way they'll know fear is to hit them where it hurts.'*

The settlement they sat in was testament to the price people had to pay, a town that had grown out of a refugee camp.

'I still don't believe it,' she scoffed. 'Your only political rivals since your former parties merged, both of their leaders, just happen to be deniers?'

As if the minister cared who was a denier at a time when his party was burning the world to the ground even as people begged them to stop. He was an opportunist and a sneak. Broderick watched him closely trying to make out if he was lying or not.

The sweat on his brow under her steady gaze seemed real enough.

'Someone broke into my office to steal these,' O'Neill protested. 'If that's not guilt...'

'Someone failed,' she replied, but her tone was not quite so sure.

'We received these two weeks ago. From a source out west. We barely had them when someone came to steal them. Why else would they want them except to cover their guilt?'

It was, on its merits, unbelievable. In the fourteen years since the first Chain of Storms in the winter of 2026, since the leading political parties had amalgamated to form The Fianna, an emergency government, there had been no credible opposition.

Years of government-imposed rationing of food and electricity, orders banning the movement of people from the settlements into the cities, the fact that the government was refusing to cooperate with European and world leaders on best practice for dealing with an environment that was increasingly murderous had created an opposition.

Not just an opposition, but a groundswell of support for change, and with that growing support, the first whispers of rebellion.

Now the leadership of that movement was apparently up for execution.

But it was plausible. And that was its charm. Broderick,

for all his rage, didn't like being led around by the nose. And if he didn't like it, Cummins despised it. Her eyes narrowed dangerously as she adopted that where-shall-I-make-the-first-cut look that terrified people.

There was more to this than simply killing two alleged deniers. More than political chicanery. There were more lives on the line than the two men named.

The BlueArmband crowd would surely revolt if their leaders were executed. There would be riots in the cities, maybe even a full-blown revolution. The streets would run red for this piece of paper, and they'd be stacking corpses by the time the Storm Season ended.

It didn't weigh on Broderick. They were dead men to him anyway. His code said so.

They weren't innocent, and they weren't him, that only left one option: guilty.

The silence extended, with Cummins considering, and O'Neill waiting expectantly.

'It's true,' he eventually insisted.

'How convenient for you,' she replied.

'I'm not asking you to kill without merit. We have evidence. He wasn't always called Kelly. We believe that was his mother's maiden name. His name, we think, was Trench. And Gibson was a first name. Gibson Waters. We think.'

'You think?' she replied sardonically. 'Where's the proof?'

'They fled when they knew we had that letter. The two of them fled the capital rather than face the accusation. We suspect that they have destroyed the evidence, or that they're on their way to. One of the old technology hermits out west has servers from the hospital in Galway. One of them has gone there.'

Servers. Solid gold now. Little mines of information. Sometimes the kind of stuff that might mean the difference between life and death. Most banks of servers had been in coastal cities or huge sprawling data centres. One third of the world's population had once lived on the coast, before the weather had driven them inland. Now they huddled on the hill tops. When the coasts flooded, so too did the servers. The stuff and makings of the internet.

The tech hermits were just people who managed to eke out a living outside Government control by tapping into what was left of the internet and commanding just enough control of that to offer leadership in their communities. They bought loyalty with electricity and information.

'Ha,' she spat her laugh contemptuously, 'so you have no evidence, just a flimsy story about a break in and some servers in a city that's mostly underwater now?'

O'Neill blinked at her. His miscalculation was glaring now. He had missed the measure of her by a good distance. He had mixed up who was really in charge. Broderick laughed, the sound a whistle from his nose more than anything else. It was as much as he could muster through the throbbing pain.

'Is my word as Minister not good enough? The word of four fellow agents?'

'The word of four long-tailed rats...' she barely paused before adding, 'and a short-tailed one too.'

'I could have you fired,' he told her angrily, realising suddenly that his only power was political.

There was a stillness to her then, a dangerous stillness as she peered at him through those narrowed eyes. And for a moment, she looked on the edge of moving.

Broderick moved himself then, just a shift, and she looked at him. He blinked at her, tilted his head a fraction.

*Don't do something stupid.*

Her nostrils flared a fraction.

*I don't like this.*

He blinked at her and his lips pursed. Slightly. Ever so slightly.

*Neither do I, but we have a job to do.*

They held that look for a moment before she sighed in resignation and turned her face back to the monitor.

'I'm not your hired hand,' she told him eventually as she took a seat. 'I'm no paid assassin.'

He nodded, swallowing hard.

'I don't kill people for the love of killing, or for the love of my government or for the love of anything. I serve justice because justice is what these people deserve. No one asked for this, to live like this. I kill the people responsible. End of.'

She glanced at Broderick as she spoke. Just a flicker of her eyes. He knew part of that was meant for him. Because he did love killing. Not the act of taking a life, but the act of taking *those* lives. She spoke to him because she knew he didn't care about justice. He cared about revenge.

'If they're guilty, I'll Pronounce them,' she continued, 'if they're innocent they live. I'll go to see this hermit in Galway. Where in Galway is he?'

'We don't know.'

'How very useful of you,' she replied sarcastically.

Broderick snorted again.

'We've done a deal, with Digital,' O'Neill told her, half relieved, half embarrassed. 'He knows where this Galway hermit is. And he has something for you. Go to him first.'

'What deal have you made with that particular devil?' she asked.

'It's confidential, but…'

He hesitated for a long moment.

'But?'

'We don't believe they're both in Galway. We think Gibson is gone for the evidence, and Kelly is hiding in Limerick.'

It hung in the air. No one went to Limerick. Anywhere out west was bad, but Cork and Limerick, the last of the cities outside of Government control, they had their own councils now, their own laws. And the agents weren't welcome there. Limerick was especially dangerous. All the electricity from the nearby hydroelectric station at Ardnacrusha kept them in clean power. And clean power was power in every sense of the word.

Broderick had no fear of the place. He'd grown up there.

He knew it inside and out. Some of his family might still be there. Maybe his mother was still alive. He knew his father wasn't.

Her sister Hilda was there too. He wasn't supposed to know that, but it was a poorly kept secret that her sister was a BlueArm. He'd even gone to her house once, just to see her, to see if she was as intimidating as Malley.

'Why Limerick?' she asked after a long moment.

'We found out that he'd been contacting them only days before the break in. It's where his allies are.'

The look she offered the minister was a flat-out threat of violence. And for a second, her hand toyed with the sheath where her knife should have been, before going back to tracing the lines of her scarred hands.

Sending her into the city her sister now lived in as a rebel against the Government. Treating her like a paid assassin. These things impugned her honour.

She was touchy about her honour, and her justice.

Her thumb still traced her scars, but now the motion was forceful, her anger contained in it, no sign of it showing on her face.

'Fine,' she said, standing so suddenly that the weasel started in his seat. 'If a thing must be done, let it be done. I'll get the evidence. If it exists. And if it does, he'll die in Limerick. If it doesn't exist, he lives. End of story.'

The council at Limerick might disagree. Her sister might too. It was a bold statement. And it was the reason he followed where she led.

Broderick smiled at her fearlessness, and his own. Let them go to Limerick. Let them leave behind the weaselly politicians and the coddled Settlements. The pain in his head began to subside. He let the smile slide off his face as he nodded at O'Neill.

Outside the building, two men stood by the door. Broderick followed her out. The biggest one, the one at the front, hesitated as she walked by him, stepping out of her path.

Broderick's smile returned. She feared nothing, but they at least had the sense to fear her.


Back at their tents, he packed his things neatly. Life on the move was an ordered and structured thing, and it demanded a certain discipline. Careful consideration had to be afforded to what went where.

Out of the corner of his eye, he spotted someone watching them again. Perhaps the same little thing that had watched them the night before.

She stood at the edge of the line of houses that surrounded the main square, a distance back from the clearing by the defensive walls where they'd made their camp. She tried to hide herself behind the corner of one of the flatpacks, but the tightly ordered towns were laid out so there was nowhere to hide. Her eyes were locked on Cummins. Her face unreadable.

Broderick grunted for Cummins' attention.

When she looked at him, he nodded in the direction of the young woman.

*Same as last night.*

The little thing slipped behind the wall fully.

Malley grimaced dismissively.

*Not a problem.*

He scowled at her reproachfully.

*How do you know she's not a problem?*

'She was watching me this morning too,' Malley told him out loud. 'I don't think it's anything to worry about.'

Broderick wondered if she might be related to Sullivan. He'd had to kill relatives before. It wasn't common, but it wasn't unheard of for them to try to avenge their climate-denying family members. To Broderick, that made them guilty by association.

He cocked an eyebrow at Cummins.

*Related to the one from yesterday?*

'Too old to be a daughter,' Cummins told him. 'And too young to be a lover, I hope.'

She was right. Far too young.

Too young. Too naïve. Too silly.

He remembered people like her from Before. He was nineteen when the first Chain of Storms hit in 2026, so his memories of Before were mostly those of a child, but a very different child to the man he had become.

He'd seen her likes on the marches. Every Friday he'd march. He'd make banners and posters and join the other children from schools around the city, as well as the students from nearby universities and colleges, along with a handful of politicians, desperate to be seen to care while doing sweet fuck all to actually help. They'd march on city hall, demanding real action and real change to protect the climate.

He remembered the boy he had been then, but bitterly now. So sure they were helping. So sure that it would work.

Little things like her would be there too. Students from university. Dressed up for the occasion with posters and banners that had clever slogans. So pleased with themselves. So full of energy and enthusiasm that waned and vanished when they found causes that didn't involve walking in the rain. He hoped those types liked the rain now. The rain that lashed the country, driven by winds that scoured the infrastructure from the earth like it had had enough of tolerating it. Winds and rains and lightnings that drove landslides and floods and hounded the people into the hills. He hoped they liked their fucking rain now.

The ache at the base of his skull flared.

He directed a furious glare at where the woman had been standing, but she was gone.

His glare attracted Cummins' attention.

She scrunched her face a touch, the light in her eyes speaking of scorn.

*She didn't do it, Broderick. She's a damn child.*

She was right in that respect. The girl was a child, and if he had surrendered everything else about himself, he kept to his own rules for the sake of what was left of his soul.

44

The code was simple: there were only three types of people in the world – the innocent who were too young to blame; the guilty, which was everyone who wasn't innocent; and the last group was a group of two. Just him and Cummins.

He looked askance at her as he thought about that. The last group was subject to change.

If she was getting soft.

# CHAPTER THREE

Fionnuala threw a furtive look over her shoulder as she walked through the large western gate of Black Stair. Her eyes scanned the low, rude homes as she moved, taking in the bustle as the residents of the settlement moved about their Shared duties. To the side of the grazing paddock where the animals wandered, she could make out Douglas, watching her leave, his eyes following her out the gate and on to the rocky path that led outside, a place she had never been.

That thought held no great fear for her. She hadn't even been born there. Her parents told her that she was born in Letterkenny. A town they said was hilly and beautiful and whose people were kind and hardworking. It was abandoned now, by all accounts. It had the misfortune of being in the red zone, the stretch of Ireland along the west coast that bore the brunt of the Chain of Storms every year. A place that meant nothing to her. She had no memory of it and so her identity was in no way formed by it, though her father and mother both used to sing songs about Donegal. She could remember her father's voice: *And I wish I was in sweet Dungloe…*

They'd lived in other settlements too. Scrounging for food and materials in Dublin. Enough to eat and build a slipshod roof for your family. Back when it was dog-eat-dog. And sometimes people-eat-dog. A chaotic and troubled place back then, before the Government had managed to take it in hand.

Brutally. People said it was a lovely place now, but her early memories of it were of a massive sprawling refugee camp. Refugees in their own land.

They'd moved down the country piece by piece from the scenic tops of Djouce to the rocky outcrop of Mulla, always moving when the settlements became too full, too dirty, too smelly, or too violent, always moving further and further from the Government's long arm, until they finally landed in Black Stair. She'd spent the last six years in the small settlement. She'd burned the corpses of her mother and father in that small place that felt too small for their lives and too large for their deaths. One winter after another. Father and then mother. And now, with a decision born out of impulse and duty, she had abandoned her 'home' in pursuit of the cause.

It couldn't hold her. A battered town on the edge of civilisation and a lazy on-off relationship with a man who was too old for her were not things that would keep her. The memory of her parents could be left behind too, because it had to be done. For the chance at having a future. For something more than filthy settlements and boxes for homes.

'We have our orders?' Douglas had whined at her as she stuffed her belongings into her bag. 'The Children can handle it.'

'Those two will murder the Children. The fella could do it on his own. The woman could do it with her fucking fingertips,' she told him.

'And what are you going to be able to do that they can't?' he pleaded.

She knew what she could do. The woman had offered her a chance. In her own words, she'd said it: She wouldn't kill them if they were innocent. A hint of a chance. So all she had to do was make sure she could prove that they were.

And she might have shared the plan with him if he wasn't so clearly afraid. Of the agents – the Doejays as they were colloquially known. Afraid of the outside. Of the storms. That fear was why she had to go – that pervasive fear.

But the woman said it straight to the Minister's face… She wouldn't kill the innocent.

She'd been raised in the cause, her father's daughter, furious that the society that they'd wrought for themselves could be reduced to such ignominious circumstances as these. Joe Kelly was there when she'd taken the oaths. Uncle Joe had always been in her life. He had saved her father in Galway hospital during the first Storm Season, performing surgery on him even after the power had gone, cutting and sewing back together until he'd stitched a life into one piece. After that he was welcome into whatever roof they were calling home. Always with a smile and a wink for her. So gentle the man on whose shoulders she'd placed her faith, but strong enough to face down the totalitarianism of the Government.

And now he needed her help.

'You'll have to get word to him. They said he was in Limerick,' she had told Douglas before she left, trying not to sound contemptuous.

'I could order you not to go,' he told her in a low, sulky voice.

And, technically, that was true. He was the leader of the BlueArm movement in Black Stair. A leader unsuited to the role, and only in his position because he had been the first one. He could order her. She wouldn't listen though, and he probably knew that.

He was eight years older than her. Old enough that he would have a child's memory of Before, but he didn't give that impression. His sulkiness and his all-talk-no-action attitude toward activism spoke of someone who fell between the cracks; not knowing enough Before to have felt like he'd lost something, not young enough to be able to leave it behind and look to the future they desperately needed to start building.

'I'll pass on word to any settlements we get to west of here,' she told him, 'if there are any, but you'll need to get word to Lugnaquilla and to Dublin.'

He looked at her for a long moment. She'd known what it felt like to have his eyes on her. She knew what it felt like to have his body on hers too, truth be told, but there was nothing about Douglas that she liked. Their romance, such as it was, was a matter of convenience. Their bodies pressed together in the dark when the winds and the rain and the thunder and lightning made it so that feeling anything besides fear was a type of freedom... She thought she might even miss it.

But he was cowardly, and she was determined not to be.

She made a point of ignoring him as she stuffed her rucksack. The sooner he let her go, the sooner she could be on the road behind the agents. They were moving away from her by the minute, heading down the hill and into the wild.

'I'll do what I can,' he told her, his voice full of resignation.

And she left him behind, for the chance to save Gibson and Kelly.


The track she followed bended and twisted as it plunged down the hill, with each step moving her further from safety, closer to danger. And it wasn't just the Doejays that were dangerous. The lowlands were full of refugees and exiles, those who refused to Share, who wouldn't or couldn't follow the rules of the settlements that made coexistence in terrible times possible. Like all the other so-called clans that had made their homes in ruins of long-abandoned towns or in the shelter of the high-standing motorways. They preyed on those foolish enough to leave their places of safety, a source of re-supply and of protein, if the rumours were to be believed.

She forced herself to think about the agents instead.

They were compelling in a way she didn't like. Something about them froze her, frightened her. A permanence. A sense of terrible endurance. Storm Seasons could scour society from the land it tried to live off, and those two would somehow still be standing.

In Black Stair, as with everywhere else, the little box homes and the workshops felt so temporary. They'd done everything they could to anchor them, to make them feel real, but Storm Seasons made a mockery of permanence and in her admittedly limited experience, society was malleable, shaping itself around the conditions that dominated. Besides the community hall, the buildings were flat pack. Just large enough for a small room or two, and a tiny common area, insulated with repurposed car tyres or rubber stripped from manufactories that had no place in the new economic and technological landscape. They couldn't afford to build towns to last, since the storms would see to it that they didn't.

Impermanence was the way of life and having been born just six years before the first Storm Season, she had known no other.

If everything was collapsible, there was no need to mourn when something collapsed.

But those two felt different, they were not collapsible. There was something almost mythical about them. Frightening and mythical.

They had left almost immediately after the meeting she had spied on, even though the nights began closing in early this time of year, they stayed closing in for longer and longer so that twilight was a long, extended thing that allowed darkness to sneak up on you. She hurried after them, keen to cut the gap their head start had given them, conscious of not getting caught alone at night.

No one travelled outside the settlements at night. The roads were treacherous enough, having been ravaged by winds, rain, and neglect for all of fourteen years, and that danger was amplified heavily by the possibility of ambush.

She was halfway down when she saw them in the distance. Moving carefully but confidently, winding away from each other for stretches, but always finding their way back to one another, travelling with their shoulders almost touching at times.

Fionnuala kept them in sight, even as she slipped on her way down, biting off curses as she wheeled her arms to keep her balance, but the wind caught her words and whipped them back up the hill, so the two almost indistinct figures ahead didn't hear as they made their sure-footed way down the western road.

At the bottom of the hill, she briefly lost sight of them and for a moment, a flare of panic took her. Looking back up, she could no longer make out the relative safety of the walls of the Black Stair. She'd always fancied herself as tough and fearless, and now in the failing light and down in the low country beneath the settlement, she knew that to be a lie. Now she was just exposed.

The temptation to turn back was stronger than she might have liked.

A flicker of movement in the distance caught her eye. A light: small and almost hidden. It was them. The light of their tablets giving a low blue glow. She suppressed a sigh of relief and began picking up the trail again, stepping carefully over branches and roots as quietly as she could.

There was still, she knew, every reason to be afraid, but their permanence, ahead of her, increasingly difficult to follow, drew her on. Where they could go, she must go.

They moved silently. Like ghosts in the distance. The wind would surely carry the noise of conversation back to her but there was none, just an unrelieved silence in between the whistles of the gusts. She longed to close the gap, to be closer to the people and out of the darkness that might be hiding anything, but she didn't dare get too close, lest she give herself away. She could feel herself trembling and cursed herself for her weakness again.

Then they were gone.

One second in front of her, then somehow vanishing.

She twisted and turned in the now near-blackness seeking any indication of them, but all she could make out were some shadows on a small hill that might have been the remnants of the buildings that made up the town of Ballymurphy and the remnants of a welcome from Before. '*Fáilte go Baile Uí Mhurchú.*' The battered sign had survived, clinging to life through thirteen Storm Seasons, it now moaned when the wind pushed it too hard.

Of the agents, there was no sign.

The panic engulfed her. She was under-prepared and it was dark and it was pre-Storm Season and she was alone in the night.

Desperately, Fionnuala tried to settle her thoughts, to soothe the panic. They must have gone into the town? They must be in front of her? Slow, careful, step by step she followed the road, the low wind hiding the sound of her tentative footfalls.

It looked like it was asleep. A large shadow of a dog sleeping on the side of a battered overgrown road, but a dog that might kill you if you woke it. Into the darkness she peered as she moved, hoping for signs of them, but fearing sounds of any kind.

Ahead in the distance, by faint handheld lights she could make out four shapes. One, taller than the others and broader in the shoulder, she knew instinctively was the Child with the long nose from the meeting the night before.

The four of them stood on the road, assuming that the agents would take this path on their journey into the wake of Gibson and Kelly, and now they stood, stupidly, in a clearing on the road holding lights that would mark them out.

By what little natural light remained, she saw something else: a flicker, a shadow moving low across the grass to the side of the road and the same instinct that had identified long nose recognised the agents, re-joining the road together from either side, renewing their pattern of winding out and back to each other. Only this time their coming together was happening directly in front of the Children.

She also knew it was deliberate. Like the slow rising to their feet, like the way she'd seen them hunt Sullivan through the market square, each step they took was a deliberate decision, a premeditated action that brought them inexorably closer to violence. They were springing the trap but doing it without giving the Children time to ready themselves.

Without thinking she called out, to warn the Children that they were doomed, that it was already too late...

'Look out,' she roared into the last embers of daylight and four heads snapped in her direction. Two did not.

The sound of violence was shockingly loud in the night air, bursting forth from the middle of the road in a tumult and carried by the wind in every direction. The man roared his fury, the woman left screams of pain dying in her wake and in seconds it was over. Just as she had predicted it would be.

The Children for all their confidence and size and the fact that they outnumbered their opponents two-to-one, had lasted mere seconds against the agents. Their lives snuffed out in the darkness. Their last breaths stolen by fingers of wind that brushed over their corpses as they fell.

Then they were walking back to her, the agents. The man taller and moving with a military bearing, the woman with a sort of swing-hip swagger she could only barely make out.

In the last of the light, she could make out her hands. Scarred all over, hideous-looking things, muscle and bone wrapped up in destroyed flesh.

'The girl,' the woman said.

Fionnuala hadn't realised how scarred her hands were when she'd seen them back in Black Stair.

'Looking for us or looking for them?' the man asked. His voice was exactly what you might have expected from someone like him – a guttural sounding thing ripe with the promise of violence.

The warning she'd called out. They thought it had been for them. Not for the Children.

'What are you doing down here?' the woman asked her, almost pleasantly.

There was something terrifyingly impressive about how casual they were. Neither of them seemed to be even breathing heavily, though they'd just mown down four people. Fionnuala tried to match their nonchalance.

'Thought I'd take a stroll,' Fionnuala replied tightly, amazed at how steady her own voice sounded.

The man grunted. It might have been a laugh.

The woman didn't laugh. She simply stared for a moment, and for all her casualness, her eyes were hard. Harder than his.

'Was he your brother? Your father? Your lover?' the woman asked finally.

'Who?'

'The man we Proclaimed.'

So that was it. She thought Fionnuala had been following her out of some sense of vengeance.

'Sullivan? He was none of those things. He was just a man who lived in the settlement. I don't care that you killed him.'

She said the words. She knew them for what they were. So did the woman.

'Liar,' the agent whispered back.

Fionnuala tried to make her face unreadable. She did care. Not because of anything Sullivan was, she frankly found him weak and spineless, like Douglas, but without the political convictions. She cared because she knew it was wrong. Wrong to kill someone for what they once were.

'Alright,' she replied. 'I do care. About seeing the deniers punished. I'm on your side. I followed you here to warn you that there was an ambush. I heard some of them discussing it at the Sharing earlier.'

They regarded her for a long moment.

'I want to be an agent,' Fionnuala lied again.

The man grunted again. Another hint of a laugh.

Quite the sense of humour he had, she thought bitterly.

The woman didn't look at the man. She held Fionnuala's gaze for a long moment.

And this was the plan. It hinged entirely on this woman, this scarred and terrible woman before her who killed silently and remorselessly and apparently effortlessly. It hinged entirely on this woman's sense of justice.

That she wouldn't kill the innocent.

After an eternity standing in the darkness, the agent looked down at her own ruined hand, and then she sheathed her knife.

'Don't make me have to kill you,' she said finally.

Fionnuala held back a sigh of relief.

'You'll make camp with us tonight. Tomorrow we'll decide what's to be done with you.'

The man grunted again. This time it definitely was not a laugh.

# CHAPTER FOUR

A barn, a large thing with a repaired door and wall, was their home for the night. Inside, a collection of rotten, old furniture was strewn about the dirt floor in a grim approximation of a kitchen. A dining table with mismatched chairs, rotted and broken. Malley wondered who might have loved these things once? What moments those chairs might have once been party to before being relegated to this terrible place? Someone had tried to live here at some point. Sheltering from everything, they had tried to make this place a home. They had failed.

Broderick had gone out earlier with his hydroflask. The utensil filtered all manner of water, making it safe to drink. Even the cleanest-looking water might be hiding something. It was impossible to know what might have died upstream.

Water was handled with care everywhere these days.

Now Malley watched the girl-child sitting on one of those rickety chairs at the edge of the fire, hoping to absorb some of the meagre heat. The girl drank their rehydrated soup and tried to look casual. Her pose too forced, her posture too rigid. Malley could measure things such as these.

Accustomed to a living in the confines of the flatpack modules, the girl kept glancing up at the space that loomed above her, the ceiling too high, the room too spacious. Too much nothing, and too much failure in the damp air.

The crackling of the fire was loud in the dark room where

Malley gently probed at her scarred hands with one thumb, the long shadows silent as they flickered across the walls and the high ceiling. Like their shadows, neither spoke. The long silence between them extending and extending.

She didn't want to interrupt it. She had learned long ago that silence was her friend. Broderick and herself had found communication in their lack of words, and for strangers, the silence of the lowlands was a sharp contrast to the constantly whistling winds that were ubiquitous at the top of the hills where the settlements sprawled.

Malley let that silence swirl about the girl, assailing her, until her bravado faltered.

'Well, this is cheery,' the girl announced.

The wind whistled a little at her joke. Malley allowed herself a small smile. All she needed to strike was that opening.

'Why are you here?' Malley asked her bluntly.

'I came to warn you.'

'Bullshit.'

'Why would I lie?' she asked, shifting in her seat.

'I don't know why, but I know that you are.'

'Why would you think that?'

'Because no one voluntarily leaves safety.'

'You do.'

She was quick. Malley had to give her that. There was something about her. Something familiar. And charming somehow. The innocence of her. A little thing, unspoiled by the world around her.

'I leave to search for things.'

'Like what?'

'People mostly.'

'Like Sullivan.'

'Like Sullivan,' Malley agreed.

'And you kill them.'

'Usually.'

'Not always?' the child asked.

Malley remembered the old man again. Standing in the

sunshine, soft eyes, too soft. Eyes should be harder than that. Especially now. She remembered the relief that had swept through her when she'd decided not to kill him. As though her body needed her to make that decision to be comfortable with itself.

'Not always,' Malley agreed again.

'I want to be an agent,' the girl told her.

There was something in the sentence that bothered Malley. Something she couldn't quite put her finger on. Too wrong coming from this little whip of a thing. But then, she had once been a little whip of a thing. Before the men came. Before they gave her scars to remember them by. Before Hilda had stopped them from killing her. Before she had learned to be hard.

'Why?'

'Because I hate the climate deniers,' the girl told her in an obvious lie.

'What's your name, child?'

'I'm not a child. I'm twenty years old.'

'I asked you your name, child,' Malley pressed.

'Fionnuala. Fionnuala Regan.'

'Good. I'm Malley. Cummins. Broderick is Broderick. He used to have a first name. He gave it up in case he's the last person to carry the name.'

Malley watched the slight widening of Fionnuala's eyes. So she'd heard then. Heard of the trend. Zealots giving up their first names. Carrying the burden of their surnames in case they were the last. In case the storms came and scoured away every other strand of their family.

'Now,' Malley continued, 'don't lie to me again, Fionnuala. Why do you want to become an agent?'

The girl sat still for a moment. Her eyes first glancing back at the ceiling and around the shabby 'room' they now shared before settling on Malley's own eyes.

The look was not so childish. Almost stern.

'Justice,' she told her. 'I want to see justice done. Nothing more than that. Let the guilty be punished. Let the innocent live.'

The sensation of familiarity intensified as Fionnuala's gaze and her words settled into Malley's broken skin. No, this was no child. Small, she may be. Innocent too. Naïve perhaps. But there was an iron in her, at her core.

Malley could detect no lie in the words.

'Very well then,' she told her.


Fionnuala and Broderick slept as Malley kept watch. Such a small thing, this woman. She felt an urge, some instinctive thing inside herself, to protect the woman. To shield her somehow.

Perhaps she was becoming soft, allowing feelings and doubts to slip through the cracks. She didn't even know this person. It was a worrying thing, a symptom of a problem that had begun manifesting in her decision making. She remembered the face of the old man. He had been harvesting the grid illegally. Anti-government or just an opportunist looking to get rich, she couldn't tell, but it didn't matter. The man should have been killed on the spot. Stealing electricity from the grid was stealing from the whole world.

And yet she'd let him go. Something in his demeanour. Something in the softness of his eyes. And something inside herself had told her it was the right thing to do.

Likely, Broderick would kill her for that if he ever found out. He'd consider it betrayal. Broderick killed people who betrayed him.

Not that she'd allow him.

She survived. She endured.

The bond between her and Broderick had been a long time in the forging, and she hoped it was stronger than this new softness that seemed to have crept in.

Hilda.

Her sister.

That's who the girl reminded her of. The same curl in her hair, the same blue eyes. The same steel hidden inside her, buried so it was hard to see unless you went looking for it.

She wondered if her sister was still soft.

She thought back to the moment when they had begun to diverge from each other, her and her sister. The scrape of blades destroying her hands, the desperate need to fight… the humiliating moment when it was no longer necessary.

The months after they had been attacked had shaped them both. Malley had become hard, and then harder again. Because that's what this new world demanded. Her sister had not toughened appreciably. Instead of hardening to meet the new order, she instead demanded that the world change to suit her. She demanded peace, and togetherness.

The world, as you might expect, ignored these demands.

Their arguments had become bitter, fuelled by their diverging views. When she'd come-to in their basement, the men were gone, her hands were in tatters, the bleeding was profuse, but that was all they had damaged in her. In Hilda the damage they'd done was deeper. Worse than any ruined hands.

There was still food. Not much. But not nothing. The food taunted her. Her sister's soft tears that trickled down her otherwise steely expression… Malley would never forget those tears.

She was useless then, her hands ruined, nerves severed so she could barely move her fingers, needing help to remove her trousers when she needed to go to the bathroom. Even after the storm, it was her sister who had to forage for their food. And when she brought it back, Malley hadn't the courage to ask how she had come by it, and in the silence that grew, Hilda perceived judgement: the truth was it was self-flagellation.

The world had become something in those weeks and months, and they were both too soft for whatever it was.

And now Fionnuala Regan, this aberration. This thing of concealed steel. The walk out west would be tough on her. There'd be trouble along the way, certainly there'd be violence. She'd have to protect the girl. Protect her from the dangers on the road and maybe even protect her from Broderick. By all accounts, they should turn her out. Send her home.

Yet Malley knew that she wouldn't.

She'd already left Hilda behind. She wouldn't do it again.

She mulled over her inconstant mind as she toyed with the handle of her long knife. Outside, the wind picked up.

They broke their small camp the next morning. Storm Season had begun to show itself, carrying thick clouds that dumped rain on them in bursts that went from light to downpour and back to light in minutes.

The wind pushed those clouds, driving them overhead at pace, and flattened the grass before them, tossing the tops of trees from left to right.

Fionnuala followed behind them a pace or two as they moved through the fields, skirting around Ballymurphy and re-joining the road at the far side. She'd dealt with rain before, but the discomfort seemed to be affecting her more than them. They paid the rain no mind whatsoever as they moved. As if they were somehow above the trifling problems of feeling water run down their backs underneath their clothes.

They walked at a decent pace, not too fast, but by no means slowly. A pace meant to last. The pace of long walkers. When side by side, their shoulders nearly touched. They didn't speak. Every now and then one of them would break into an easy jog, opening up a goodly distance, scouting in front. For what, Fionnuala didn't want to know.

They skirted around the towns, first Ballymurphy and then another Malley called Borris, passing an ancient aqueduct as they moved. There were sounds coming from the town: sounds of people, noises that both Malley and Broderick seemed to ignore. Their vigilance picked up though, heads moving constantly as they scanned their surroundings for danger. They stopped at the entrances to old houses, probing for traps and offering each other dead-eyed glances of reassurance.

The homes themselves were a curious mixture of grand

and pathetic in equal measure. Even the meanest looking of them had a feeling of permanence to it. Despite smashed windows, empty door frames and the licks of black soot that showed how fire had gutted some of them, or the long grass that peeped out from inside, nature making a place for itself, they still stood, but whatever magic had once made them homes had long since dissipated. Driven out by wind and rain and people. Fionnuala could see why the Befores longed for these places. They hinted at something possible, something she'd never known before.

The sounds of people were familiar, and somehow scary too. The lowlands were dangerous, and everyone living within them was tainted by that. Either as desperate aggressors who took from others, or as dangerous defenders who killed anything that might be considered a threat, regardless of how remote that possibility.

It was a mark of the uniforms the agents wore that they moved around down here. A threat they might be. Their equipment, the electronic pads, the weapons, and the hydroflasks would all be valuable bounty, but the cost might be entirely too high.

They moved for hours in that silence, ranging out in turn, stepping off the road then back on at seemingly arbitrary moments. Fionnuala worked to keep up, her footing nowhere near as confident as theirs as she struggled through soft terrain. She was grateful when they stopped for lunch.

Not a word had passed between them and yet they seemed to be in constant communication. Something in their body language suggested questions being asked and answered. These wordless conversations were fascinating to her. The decision to stop for lunch, the decision on where to set up their mini-camp were all made without a word spoken, information conveyed in looks and nods and soft grunts from Broderick, whose face still remained impassive.

'Where are we going?' she asked Malley as they sat around their small meal in loamy clearing at the side of what was once a road, now an overgrown ditch.

'Bloom and Athlone.'

'Why?' she asked.

'There's a man outside Athlone. He trades information. We need it.'

'Why?'

'We're investigating some people.'

'Who?' Fionnuala asked, as if she didn't know.

'Two men who helped to break the world,' Broderick told her bitterly.

Still angry, with a hint of an accent she couldn't quite place.

'They've been accused of climate denial,' Malley told her. 'It's our job to investigate that.'

'They've been found guilty of denial,' Broderick corrected her. 'It's our job to execute them for that.'

Malley paid his correction no mind, stirring her dried beef into her tin of beans.

'The man in Athlone collects servers,' Malley told her 'He has a little fortress there and some information we need. A lot of the social media companies had server banks here long before the first Chain of Storms. He's collected them.'

'What if the men you're investigating are innocent?' Fionnuala asked, trying to keep her voice casual.

'They're not,' Broderick answered her.

'How do you know that?' she ventured, knowing the ice she walked was thinning.

The look he offered her was poisonous. His face hadn't changed from his near permanent scowl, but now his eyes were on fire.

'No one who lived during Before is innocent to Broderick. They're all guilty. If you're old enough to have been part of the problem, then you're as much to blame as anyone else.'

It was what she suspected. The man would kill Uncle Joe and Gibson without bothering to find the truth. He'd kill her future, all of their futures, without hesitating.

'Oh absolutely,' she agreed sarcastically, 'that seems fair and reasonable and not at all psychotic.'

Broderick made the noise that she now understood was his laugh. A grunt that came out as a sharp exhalation from his nose.

Fionnuala was starting to hate that noise.

'Well, I just don't think that's very fair,' she told him.

His mouth twitched. You couldn't call it a smile, but she reckoned it was the closest thing he had to one.

'Look around and point at all the fair things,' he told her.

The wreck of a car sat in the ditch, tyres stripped from it, glass removed, likely painstaking work. Anything salvageable carried off so that the husk of what it once was looked pathetic.

'What about all the people who tried to help Before? They say lots of people tried to help, but Governments and corporations wouldn't do their bit, so it was for nothing.'

'Weaklings and fools. I know all about the people who "helped" Before.'

'What about the people who are trying to help now? What if someone who denied is changed and now they want to help? And you kill them?' she asked.

'Well, good for them,' Broderick retorted, leaning forward on his log-seat. 'They weren't good when it counted.'

'You don't know that!' she bit back.

'Yes, I do. Do you know how I know? Because every year a new season comes and it tries to kill us. There was a time when we might have stopped that, but these *decent* people were too busy telling everyone not to help. So now we live like this… And all the nice little boys and girls tell me I'm the villain.'

He spat the word decent as he said it.

'We're never going to survive if we don't start to work together,' Fionnuala replied.

Broderick leaned further forward. Now his face was angry, not just his eyes. He opened his mouth to retort but a word silenced him.

'Enough,' Malley told them.

She didn't shout it or snap it. She just said it. But it worked.

Broderick sat back, his face resuming its standard blankness. Fionnuala took a long deep breath. Cursing herself inside for her impulsiveness. Her politics would give her away.

Neither of them seemed to notice. Broderick retured to his tin of beans. Malley swirled her hydroflask and watched the silt separating at the bottom. Through the clear plastic, her scarred hands looked even more warped than usual.

'We have to cross the Barrow,' Malley told her, still watching her water purify.

There was something in her tone that suggested this was momentous.

'Okay,' Fionnuala replied, waiting for more.

'We'll be at Goresbridge shortly. There's an old bridge there that's been extended somewhat to make space for flooding. After we've crossed it, there's no turning back. When the Storm Season arrives, they'll dismantle the bridge to stop it being pulled away by floodwater. You can still turn back now, but once we're passed the bridge...'

She turned her gaze on Fionnuala then. A weighing, measuring look that seemed to see right into her thoughts. Going back? Not really an option. Her only chance, the only thing left to her if she was truly better than those who talked instead of taking action, was to go on.

Broderick was looking at her too. His face impassive but his eyes burning with barely contained zeal.

'I'll keep going...' she began.

'No,' he interjected. 'You need to think about this. If you want to be an agent, there are sacrifices you have to make. And no room for politicking and philosophising. It's hard out here. If you come, we train you. You'll learn what it's like out here. But once you start that training, like the roads, there is no way back.'

They both looked at her, to make sure she understood.

She wondered if they could see the fear in her eyes.

Once, she had gone fishing with Douglas miles away from Black Stair out in the open where anyone could have been waiting. He'd told her then that her impulsiveness would be her downfall. She thought of the BlueArmband tucked away in her rucksack. She thought maybe he was right.

But Gibson was out in front of them, and Uncle Joe, with his gentle ways and firm leadership, was counting on her to be brave enough.

'Okay,' she told them and hoped that her voice didn't sound as weak as she felt.


Water was pooling in Gibson's boots as he stood at the edge of the treeline, staring across the dip in terrain from which Digital's 'fortress' reared up. It was, in reality, a manor house. Albeit one surrounded by high fencing and patrolled by wary lackeys.

Funny how words could change meaning like that. This home, this edifice, once a thing of decadence, a symbol of largesse, had transformed, though every single brick remained exactly where it had been during Before. Its solidness, its permanence, its ability to endure had morphed it into something formidable, so that each Storm Season it weathered, added to its fierce reputation. A fortress. A thing to be in awe of, to fear.

For Gibson other words had changed shape too, taken on new meanings.

Leadership. It weighed heavier on him than it ever did on Kelly.

Behind him, in the trees, six BlueArms. They'd been dubbed Children of the Storms. A stupid name, in his opinion, but in adopting it they had made of themselves something totemic. Something bigger than themselves. And he was responsible for them.

'What now, sir?' the boldest one of them asked.

A baby. At least, a baby compared to him, with eyes too soft and a smoothness of skin under his sandy stubbled chin that granted him an innocence of presence.

Likely this young man had been four, maybe five years old

when the first Storm Season hit: when Gibson and Kelly had worked – frenzied – through the days and nights in Galway Hospital, even as the windows gave out and crashed in, and floodwaters crept up hills and ran down through ceilings.

Gibson had been born again in that moment. Born in a seemingly never-ending storm.

And what leadership had meant then began to change for him.

The lives that weren't saved meant more to him than the lives that were. And that was the difference between him and Kelly too. The reason his friend had become the charismatic leader, while he had become the morose philosopher.

'Sir?' the boy tried again, interrupting his reverie.

Gibson ignored him, turning his eyes back to the fortress across the little valley.

The people there did what they had to, too. They defended their patch because it was theirs now. Likely with a ferocity that had cost lives. Because this place, this community into which Digital had gathered them was a rock to which they could cling. Did they regret those killings? Did they seek forgiveness? If so, from whom?

Who, Gibson wondered, was left to forgive them? Who was there left to even ask the question of? And if the answer was nobody, did they seek absolution from themselves?

'Sir,' the boy insisted once more.

'What's your name again, son?' Gibson asked him, still staring across the distance between himself and the absolution that might be waiting for him inside the fortress.

'Phelan, sir. Dominic.'

'Dominic, from here I go alone.'

'I can't allow that, sir.'

'I'm afraid there's no other option.'

'Sir, with all due respect, I was entrusted with keeping you safe. We don't know what's inside that house, and we don't know what's waiting in Galway…'

The innocence of the creature. The naivety.

'I know what's in that house, son,' Gibson told him calmly. 'Dinner. Maybe some answers. Not much else.'

'And what about Galway?' Phelan demanded.

'There? Maybe nothing. Maybe something.'

He couldn't help being cryptic. It was a thing he did when his leadership required him to do more than he was able to. More than he could cope with.

'And what about us, sir?'

A nice young man. A nice young man who was about to be robbed of the future he thought was stretching out before him.

'I don't doubt that there are agents following us, Dominic. If I know the Minister at all, he's sent them to kill us. I need you to take the BlueArms and go back and stop them. Logically speaking, they'll be stopping in Bloom on their way. I need you to see that they go no further. Can you manage that?'

He hoped his voice didn't sound as hopeless as he felt. As helpless as he felt.

'Yes, sir,' Phelan assured him.

His soft eyes lit up, eager to be at his job, grateful for the direction someone had pointed him in, the purpose he'd just been granted.

And Gibson knew no matter how strongly Phelan believed it, he was wrong.

They'd be eaten alive.

He watched the boy gather the others around him and wondered who might be left to forgive him for what he'd just done.


They dragged Joseph Kelly into Limerick, his BlueArms surrounded by burly locals armed with a menacing array of weapons – studded, sharpened, spiked, and brutal looking. He didn't resist. At his age, they'd manhandle him either way. So he bore their ministrations with a calm demeanour.

He hadn't exactly been expecting a welcome wagon, but he wasn't expecting this.

So, they knew. They had heard he'd been Proclaimed. Likely they'd seen or read the 'evidence' the Government had sent out to the world. The paper they'd printed just two weeks beforehand.

He tried to take measure of the city as they marched him through the streets; the wind racing up the long avenues flanked with their old Georgian buildings, the rain spitting at him as they hauled him forward step by step.

He had been in Limerick before Before, at a medical conference when he was still young and stupid. He had found it to be a tough place then, with a certain grimness to it that he found off-putting. He welcomed that sensation now. Tough things survived.

The people seemed to epitomise that. None of the coddled softness of the city folk to the east. None of the air of communal geniality and subservience that were the hallmarks of the people in the hillside settlements. They were one and all stern looking. Their movements purposeful and direct.

If he could keep them from killing him, they'd be valuable allies.

Through the streets and up to a massive building that loomed above the racing river Shannon below. Easily ten storeys, maybe more, he was surprised to find a functioning elevator in the place, testament to the hydro-electric station at Ardnacrusha that kept the city in clean power.

As with much else in this life, it was something of a double-edged sword. The waters that powered the turbines also flooded the city, so that the lowest streets on the waterfront had been eaten by the river, and the upper floors now had makeshift sky bridges linking buildings to one another.

In the room to which they dragged him, a single window dominated one wall, allowing for a breath-taking view of the Shannon. The river the locals called a Goddess was a furious and powerful thing carrying the detritus of storms and people's lives on its surface, flinging them out into the ocean in a temper that none could resist.

Present in the room was the local 'council'.

If the people on the street could be called stern, these were statues in their austerity.

'Is it true?' one man bellowed, barrelling toward Kelly in a rage.

He was a big man, old for the times, with streaks of red still showing in the iron grey of his beard. For all his age he was still terrifyingly large.

'Carney,' a woman barked at the bigger man, stopping him in his tracks.

She was smaller. Much smaller. A slip of a thing really with curly hair and too-large eyes. But looking at them, he could see a steeliness there. A reservoir of strength that surprised him.

'Easy now,' a third man said, stepping forward to take the larger man by the elbow. Short and powerfully built, a patch covered one eye and a sledge hung from a loop in his belt.

'It's a legitimate question, mind you,' the one-eyed man said calmly, as the larger man still seethed.

'I'm not disagreeing with that,' the woman told him.

Kelly checked the room. All eyes pivoted from these three to him. So this was where the authority came from. These three leaders. There might be a council of twenty but if these three spoke with one voice…

'Is what true?' Kelly asked calmly.

The woman laughed. The large one, Carney, presumably growled. The one-eyed man allowed himself a small smile.

'Did you deny the climate change?' a new voice asked.

Kelly looked for the new voice and was surprised that he'd missed the man who hovered at the side of the one-eyed soldier. A small man. Old. He stood with a sort of hunched posture. He had all the appearance of a weak man, and yet he spoke here among these hard, unbending people.

'No,' Kelly replied firmly.

'They have evidence, you fucking liar,' Carney growled at him through his thick moustaches.

'The evidence was printed two weeks ago on Government

computers by the Environment Minister O'Neill,' Kelly told them matter-of-factly.

That softened them. One and all. The air of violence dissipated somewhat, the hard-eyed stares softening as doubt and confusion entered their thoughts.

The small old one smiled to himself.

'Can you prove this?' the one-eyed man asked.

'Yes. At least I'll be able to when Gibson gets here. He's on his way to Galway to fetch it.'

The last vestiges of doubt evaporated, replaced by a type of angry confusion.

'You didn't do it?' the woman asked again. Pressing.

'If you'll lend me some help, I can hand you that proof.'

'Hilda,' she introduced herself, offering a hand. 'What is it you want from us?'

'Gibson is almost alone out there. He has a small cadre of BlueArms with him but they're young and inexperienced. He should be near Athlone by now. A fortress outside the town belonging to a man who calls himself Digital. If I know O'Neill, he'll have sent his best Doejays...'

He left it hanging in the air.

'Rook?' Hilda asked the one-eyed soldier.

Carney still stood fuming, though he seemed to have lost a focus for his anger, so it swirled about him. The soldier looked to the small older man beside him.

'Mahony?' he asked.

This was how they communicated. Short, sharp questions implied, threats hiding in those implications.

The older man nodded, a small sad smile on his face.

'I'll go then,' Rook replied. 'I'll take Mahony and a double handful of volunteers. We'll cut them off in Athlone.'

His single eye glittered threateningly as he eased the sledge from the loop on his belt.

# CHAPTER FIVE

The gates of Bloom, sitting on the lee side of Slieve Bloom, stood open as they approached, slowing as they did so, to show that they weren't a threat.

The wide-open space around the settlement showed, even in the night time. Signs of careful maintenance where trees and shrubs had been cleared to offer clean lines of sight and space for the locals to defend their patch should the need arise.

The wind had followed them over the bridge at Gorestown, playing alongside them as they walked up the long hill, rustling trees and tugging at their clothes. Now at the top of the hill, the darkness had added a tone of menace to it and it whispered threats as it moved across the hill.

A small congregation stood in the entrance, campfires inside the compound throwing long shadows and silhouetting the welcoming committee. Malley could make out the tell-tale handles of makeshift weapons protruding from shoulders and sticking out from hips.

'You're a long way from home,' a voice called out to them.

'And we've a long way to go,' she called back, forcing some joviality into her tone.

It didn't take much effort. She liked Bloom. At least she had before. Though the political landscape of the lowlands changed often, she doubted the hardy types who had held the settlement for as long as she'd known it were likely to have fallen in the interim.

'Two wolves and a kitten,' the man's voice called back.

His tone was equally jovial. And familiar too.

'Three people on a long walk. We'd like to Share for a night's lodging.'

'Everyone Shares,' the man agreed.

'We have a small amount of fresh fruit, dried soups, spare batteries, and tampons if you're interested.'

There was a small, huddled conversation. For a moment, Malley wondered if they just might say no. Or worse, decide that what they wanted was worth the risk of trying to take.

She could feel Broderick on her left, slowly widening his stance, preparing to turn on whatever lookout or sentry was inevitably hiding behind them.

She could feel Fionnuala too, reaching for the knife they'd given her on her belt. Only two days out in the wild and the young woman's instincts were sharpening, as she tensed up, preparing for fight or flight.

'Welcome back to Bloom,' the man called out, and the thin crowd at the gate made way to allow them in.


Malley peeled and washed small potatoes, her hands numbing in the fresh water of her basin. A fresh spring somewhere nearby poured it from the ground cold.

The trading had been brief. The people of Bloom obviously had enough food to turn down the chance at beans or dehydrated soup, but batteries were always welcome and tampons were gold. Access to Government stores gave agents a steady supply of tradeable goods.

The communal kitchen had expanded since she'd last been here. At some point in the last year, the community had found building materials and a person with the knowhow to put them to good use. Now the room was wider and longer than it had been. Stuffed with the people of the settlement, it hummed with activity.

She swapped her potatoes for carrots and began peeling them. She made piles out of the skins: they'd be dehydrated for soup. Nothing wasted.

To her surprise, Broderick hadn't stomped off to make camp and now stood between her and Fionnuala deftly peeling vegetables with his long hunting knife. They had fallen into step with the man who had greeted them at the gate and she'd allowed him to usher her into the town hall.

He was a priest. The least priestly man she'd ever seen, and almost alarmingly young for his collar. She suspected he was somewhere about Broderick's age. The spiked club he carried over one shoulder was also unpriestly, but he handled it with the ease of a man who had swung it more than once. His collar was obviously not issued by any diocese, but crudely made from some old, shredded cloth, and worn with a black shirt, though the rest of his attire was decidedly clannish – well-worn leather boots, faded jeans, and a coat with layers that could be buttoned on or shed as the weather demanded. It was patched and sewn back together in places, the top layer having lost much of its wax.

He made space for them near him, and that proximity seemed to give them a status among the community, for this man was surely their leader. He peeled and chopped with him, talking affably to her and smiling as he did so.

For her part, Fionnuala stood in a sort of awe. The familiarity of the settlement, so like Black Stair in its layout, would be welcome, but there was an edge about these people. The Gardai didn't come here, and if they did, it was to fight. Young and naïve as she was, she was unlikely to have missed the fact that most of the people here kept their weapons close by but was surely taken aback by the incongruity of those weapons on people so free with themselves.

All about the room they moved in a sort of chaotic rhythm, young to old, salvaged clothes reclaimed from the lowlands. Overalls from some factory or other, old replica GAA jerseys with shin-guards, and bits of helmets re-appropriated into makeshift armour that might have been fearsome but for the sound of laughing and singing that wafted up into the rafters of the tall roof.

'They all seem so happy for a people who wear weapons to dinner,' Fionnuala observed.

'It's because they are happy, little kitten,' the priest told her.

'Storm Season is coming, Father,' Malley reminded him, surprised by his gregariousness.

'Ah, but Joseph's not here yet, is he?'

Joseph. The Season had been named. And over the weeks that would follow, the name would become that of a serial killer. The whispered threat in the wind earlier became all the more ominous in the naming.

'You can call me Papa Smurf, or just Smurf if you like,' the priest told her. 'No need for formality here.'

'Papa Smurf?' Malley asked, smiling in spite of herself.

'I'm a priest named Murphy. Took my parishioners all of about two minutes to jump from Father Murphy to Papa Smurf.'

He laughed as he said it.

'I hope you don't mind me saying,' Malley said, enjoying the feeling of Sharing and people and the sounds of community, 'but you don't seem very priestly.'

'Laughing too much? I really need to work on being taken seriously.'

'I was talking more about the weapon actually,' she said.

'Shepherds must protect their flock.'

'What would Jesus think of that?' she asked with a wry smile.

'Ah that's the thing you see, he'll forgive me for what I've done, and for what I will yet do.'

What he will yet do. For all his joviality, this was a pragmatic man.

'A comforting thought,' Malley replied, trying but failing not to sound dismissive.

'It actually is, you know,' Fionnuala admonished her.

'Thank you, little kitten,' he told her. 'We'll have you at mass first thing in the morning.'

He grinned at her as he spoke. And Malley felt a jolt of familiarity with him. She'd seen him here before, though he wasn't a priest then.

There was a thing that flickered in her life from time to time. A feeling that at some point Before, her path had crossed with some stranger. She felt it looking at him. They might have been in the same university, or shared a friend in common, or perhaps they'd known each other in the refugee camps in the city before he'd made his way here.

As with every other time she felt that familiar feeling, she ignored it. Why bother to find out who a person was before? Who they were now was the only thing worth knowing about a person.

The door to the hall opened before either Malley or Fionnuala could reply, the wind rushing in to announce the arrival of more guests.

There were ten of them. Varying in size and age from mere pups to thirty-something veterans. One and all wore their blue colours on their arms, material stretched from shoulder to elbow.

Broderick dropped the vegetables, his knife now a weapon instead of a tool. Malley dropped the peeler and pulled her blade clear too, the oneness of wrapping fitting into scars so familiar, so comforting.

The BlueArms saw the agents as her knife came clear of its sheath and they pulled their own weapons clear and fanned out.

That instantaneous threat of violence brought the locals to their feet and suddenly the singing and laughing was done and the noise was that of chairs scaping back and tables being pushed clear.

For a moment, a tiny moment only, the air seemed to charge, electric with the violence now imminent.

'NO!' the priest roared.

He didn't reach for his spiked club, but instead raised his hands in a sort of supplication.

'Not here. Not in Bloom.'

Broderick's eyes drifted to hers, then flickered to the BlueArms, then the priest, then Fionnuala, and then hers again, silently asking for her permission to attack.

Malley lifted her chin slightly, still staring across at the BlueArms in front of her.

*Nothing yet. Hold.*

Broderick grunted. His jaw clenching with his impatience.

Malley narrowed her eyes and ran her tongue across her teeth.

*Stand fast. Hold.*

'You're all outnumbered. You BlueArms and you agents. The people of Bloom will enforce the peace. You put down those weapons now.'

The joviality was gone, the softness of him. The genial, joking priest replaced now by a fierce shepherd of a fierce flock.

The moment stretched. She could feel Fionnuala's fear, a vibration from the young woman that seemed to pass through Broderick. She could feel the grim determination of the people all about her.

Slowly, she lowered her knife and sheathed it at her hip.

Broderick grunted again.

*Bad idea.*

She turned to him and stared, her eyes locked on his.

*Not here. Not now. Stay the knife.*

He let a sharp exhalation out and slammed his blade down on the table.

The BlueArms stood for a moment, their leader in the middle. A young-ish man with sandy blond stubble on a pleasant face. With an unexpected smile, he looped the long-handled axe back on his belt.

Somewhere in the room someone laughed. A nervous reaction no doubt, but it was permission of a sort, and the low murmuring of conversation took up again as the locals regained their seats.

They ate to the sounds of comfortable chat, sporadic laughter drowning out the sound of Joseph outside who knocked on doors and windows begging to be let into the warmth.

Papa Smurf sat with them, his geniality restored and a small, pleasant smile on his face.

Malley watched Fionnuala and Broderick sitting side by side with no small amount of surprise.

Her partner looked... comfortable. The young woman showed none of the signs of revulsion or fear that she might have expected. A cooling between them.

She was half-way through her meal when the BlueArm walked to their table.

'You mind if I sit down?' he asked.

Broderick tensed and Fionnuala placed a gentle hand on his arm.

Malley tried not to look shocked.

'You're more than welcome,' Smurf told the man.

But he didn't sit immediately. Instead he looked questioningly at Malley. Waiting for her permission.

His smile was a small, pleasant thing – little gaps between his teeth worked in his favour, adding a certain strange attractiveness to him as he grinned through his sandy stubble.

Malley nodded at him and ignored the pleased smile on the face of the priest by her side.

'Phelan,' the BlueArm introduced himself.

'Malley,' she replied.

'So,' he asked, 'what brings you fine folk to Bloom?'

'Do you really want to know the answer to that?'

'Who's the misfortune?'

'A dangerous question.'

It was too. If the aim of the game was keeping the peace, certain topics needed to be avoided.

'I understand that your people killed a man the last time you were here,' the BlueArm pressed.

'I'd hate to have to do it again,' she replied, but she smiled as she said it to take away the threat.

'And I'd hate to be the fella you killed. Though I have to say, if anyone was to kill me…'

He trailed off, the suggestion heavy in his voice. It was a most disarming smile.

She laughed softly at that suggestion, but she didn't look at him.

'Play your cards right,' she told him instead, 'and I won't stick a knife in you.'

He laughed softly too.

'You know, I like the name Joseph,' Smurf announced to them. 'Good name for a Storm Season.'

The priest was angling for something. Word games. She could play if she had to.

'You think?' she asked.

'Biblical. Like the storms themselves.'

'You prepared for this one?'

'As well as anyone can be.'

He wasn't boasting, the room was packed with readiness, bustling with a sense of togetherness typically absent in the settlements in those last days, hours, and minutes before Storm Season. There was none of the typical shifting eyes and lines of taught worry on foreheads. It was impressive.

'The lowlands seem quiet,' she said, playing his game, words that meant many things.

'More and more clans and refugees moving to Limerick and Cork. They'll take anyone there. As long as you follow the rules. Little like Dublin I suppose.'

She smiled at that. He was a clan-man himself, but somehow they all thought they weren't.

'You think Limerick and Cork are like Dublin?'

'Different Government, same rules.'

He was smooth. A quiet way of telling her he wasn't a

BlueArm. Not that she trusted him. Trusting people was a recipe for getting killed.

The BlueArm, Phelan, looked at the priest. This was the game then. Between the three of them. Her an agent, him a BlueArm, and somewhere in between them a curious priest with a spiked club.

'Not all Government types are bad,' she noted calmly.

'No,' Smurf agreed. 'We met a good one not too long ago.'

She cleaned her hands on a napkin, trying not to look too interested.

'Oh?'

'Came through here a few days back. Very much a man looking over his shoulder.'

Gibson. It had to be.

'Any idea where he was going?'

'I know exactly where he was going,' he told her with a smile.

'And what'll that information cost me?' she asked, no longer sure if he was trying to be cute or not.

He was aiming at something here, she could feel it, though what it might be was still beyond her.

'What will you do if you catch him?' Phelan interjected coyly, as if he didn't know.

'That depends on whether or not he's innocent or guilty.'

'If he's guilty?'

'We'll kill him.'

'Will that stop Joseph coming to get us?' Smurf asked, unfazed by her bluntness.

Across the table, Broderick grimaced at the question. Malley tried to keep her face still. Fionnuala smiled broadly at the two men opposite, her naivete projecting onto this priest a reverence that he may not have earned.

'No, it won't. But we hope that the justice means that people can sleep easier knowing it was done.'

'Storms are loud and bad for sleeping,' he replied. So jovial. She was beginning to find it irksome.

Broderick was looking down at his dinner now. No longer eating. Fionnuala's arm still resting lightly on his forearm.

'And whose fault are the storms?' she asked him evenly.

'Lots of people,' he replied, 'maybe even his, but I have to ask, on the Lord's behalf you see, what if he's sorry?'

'Sorry?' Broderick practically spat the word out.

'Yes. What if he's sorry? What if he's a changed man? What if he's the world's nicest man now? What if he saves children for a living? Can you kill him still, for what he used to be, when he's something else now?'

So he knew then. He knew who Gibson was and he wanted a say for this man. She felt her muscles tighten, her hands gripping the small peeling knife. It wasn't her knife. It didn't complete her.

'I don't give a fuck if he's sorry,' Broderick barked at the priest.

'Well, we know *you* don't, my furious friend,' Phelan replied calmly.

'I already know he's sorry,' Broderick snapped. 'I know they all are. They're sorry now. When it's too late. They're all dreadfully sorry. None of them wanted this bla bla bla. But they did it. So, they get what's coming.'

'Can no good deed ever make up for what they did?' Smurf asked blandly.

She tried to remain calm. Perhaps it was a double-act. The priest in cahoots with the BlueArms. If the priest knew, if he was trying to protect Gibson, had they mis-stepped by coming in here? To what lengths would he go to save his man?

The chances of having to fight their way clear suddenly grew.

Oddly she felt that as a type of fear, the source of which sat at Broderick's side. For her and her partner, it was one of the risks of doing their job, but for the young woman with the unruly hair, curly like Hilda's hair, this was not a situation she was trained for. And the most likely collateral damage.

Malley couldn't allow that.

The spiked club was still by his side. He had hefted it as a man familiar with its weight and balance. A man who'd swung it in anger often enough. In defence of his flock. And Phelan's axe was still by his side too.

'How could it?' Malley asked softly, working to keep the anger from her voice. 'When you live with a weapon by your side at dinner, when the Storm Season is over, someone in this room will have died. Is there a deed big enough to put the life back into the dead?'

Broderick was looking at her now, grim approval stamped on his face. Their bond tightening in their shared anger.

'There has to be hope for everyone,' Smurf replied calmly. 'I just want you to think about that, okay? Just think about it.'

'There has to be justice for everyone too,' she retorted.

'Is this what you call justice?' Smurf asked gently.

His voice was pitying. As though he felt sorry for her, like Hilda had fourteen years ago. It made her skin crawl. They were soft and easily beaten. She was hard. They were the ones to be pitied, not her.

His words landed in the softening part of her, the part that had let an old man go, the part that was still somehow, inexplicably, sheltering Fionnuala.

*'Is this what you call justice?'*

Suddenly the camaraderie of Bloom and its residence, the optimism of them, was difficult for her to take. A small part of her would have welcomed the violence, and that was saddening.

'I think I'll make my camp outside,' she told the priest.

Broderick stood abruptly too. Violence they could both deal with. Pity, on the other hand...

'He's gone to Athlone,' Smurf told her resignedly.

Phelan moved as if to protest and then thought better of it. She stopped.

'You're sure?'

'I'm sure.'

'Why are you telling us?' Broderick asked suspiciously.

'Because she said she'll give him justice and I believe her when she says she won't kill an innocent man. And maybe when you get back to Dublin you'll tell them? Maybe we all learn to live and let be? For my flock, you see.'

She scanned him again for signs of aggression, or duplicity. He simply sat there peeling, with Fionnuala beaming at him.

'I can't make any promises,' she warned him.

'These days nobody can. He's less than two days ahead of you and he's moving slow. I doubt he's been outside of Dublin since Before.'

She continued her appraisal of him for a long time. She resented the part of her that wanted to like this place. She resented the part of her that resented that. She felt that struggle in her rise again, still not knowing fully what it was. But in her mind's eye, she saw Hilda and Fionnuala and that old man with the soft, grateful, terrified eyes and knew that somehow they were part of it. And so was the pity.

'Please sit down,' Smurf told her, gesturing gently. 'I want to share a meal with you. Please.'

She looked at Broderick, silently asking for his opinion. He hesitated for half a moment before his eyes flickered to Fionnuala and he retook his seat.

She sat back down. Hoping once again to find the joy in the bustle and the noise, and wished she had her hands on her knife that she might feel the oneness with the handle in the cracks of her palms.

'I can't let you go after him,' Phelan told her as she sat down.

'Can't let?'

'I'm sorry.'

'Not now, you're not. But you will be if you try to stop me.'

'Perhaps. Perhaps not.'

'Not here,' Smurf told them both firmly.

'Not now,' Malley agreed as she looked straight at the BlueArm sitting opposite her.

He didn't seem fazed. He was still smiling and the way he looked at her suggested a man seeing a woman, rather than a BlueArm seeing an agent.

She had forgotten that feeling too. It had been so long since it had meant anything to her to have a man look at her like that.

'We'll see in the morning,' she told both the priest and the BlueArm.

And there was no way she could say it without it being a threat.

Fionnuala watched the meal being Shared in low key awe. They were different here than they were in Black Stair. There were weapons by the door and some of the people sitting at their table, laughing and smiling and singing in little snatches, wore their weapons on them. None of the dread, all of the community.

She had expected Broderick to spend all night in his tent outside, eating his soup noisily as he had done the night before and the night before that at Black Stair. But he had come inside instead. For just a moment, she thought someone might ask him for his weapons, but they had thought better of it. When they had argued with Papa Smurf, she was sure he was going to storm out. Both of them. But they didn't. He stayed.

Now he sat next to her. And minute by minute, she almost felt him softening. His shoulders had been hard and set when he had taken his seat on the long narrow bench they shared with fifty others, but almost imperceptibly, they were easing into her so that her right shoulder now rested against his left.

Somewhere someone struck up another song, and the sound of it was haunting in its own way, somehow beautiful. The singer was benches away and she strained to be able to see her, without wanting to break the tiny contact she had achieved with Broderick.

As she strained, she turned to him, to see if he was craning his neck for a look just as she was, but she found the man staring straight at her. His eyes were hot like they always were, but for a moment she wondered if it might not be anger, but something else in them.

She smiled in spite of herself, and his lips twitched so slightly that she might have imagined it.

# CHAPTER SIX

They were waiting at the gates the following morning. Ten BlueArms arrayed in a thin line, blocking the western exit to the settlement. The wind, sensing the moment picked up, as if Joseph could feel the potential for violence and would come to witness it.

Broderick stopped when he saw them, thrusting an arm out to halt Fionnuala in her tracks. She was such a little thing. Barely a scrap of a woman. But she had steel in her. He could see it in her eyes. She had argued with him, refusing to be cowed by him. There were fewer and fewer people capable of that.

He was aware, without having to look, of Malley moving out to his right, giving herself space, knives blossoming in her destroyed hands.

The BlueArms carried themselves like men who knew their work, the array of makeshift weapons about them held competently.

He wasn't afraid. Experience counted, and his had taught him that these men would fight fiercely, as they had no doubt done before, but they'd fall short. A lack of something – will or determination or simple ruthlessness.

He had no such lack. Nor did Malley.

His only concern was the small woman by his side. A target now for being in their company and without the training, skill, or experience to defend herself against them.

This would be her first lesson. She'd learn the hard way. Just as he had promised her she would.

For this lesson, he would be her shield.

She was too young to be guilty, and the innocent should be protected.

'You don't move,' he told Fionnuala as he stepped wide.

'No,' she told him, her hand pawing at her belt for the knife he'd pressed on her. 'We don't have to do this.'

We. She said we. He liked that.

'They won't budge.'

'Let me talk to them,' she pleaded.

Before he could answer, the priest emerged from the town centre, his face a mask of concern, his arms raised in peace.


'The peace,' the priest shouted at them over the growing wind. 'The peace of Bloom.'

Fionnuala watched him rush across the ground between the town centre and the gate. He had been such a pleasant host. A kind man. Now his concern was evident.

'Just don't do anything,' she pleaded with Broderick.

The look he returned her still burned with its usual fervour but there was something else there she hadn't noticed before. It looked like hesitation.

She weighed up the men standing at the gate. Ten of them. They seemed harder than the Children she'd seen in Black Stair just days before. Harder and more willing.

There were signals she could use. Small identifying gestures known among the BlueArms operating in dangerous territory. If she could get them to look at her and not at the agents, she might be able to get them to stand down.

It was a risk… if she was discovered…

'We're leaving,' Broderick told her. 'They either let us, or they don't.'

There was an implacableness to the statement. As though the BlueArms were mere obstacles. Go around them or go through them, Broderick didn't care. He wasn't looking at her anymore. He was staring at them. She could feel the terrible energy of him as she pressed a hand against his broad chest.

For all that, the knives in his hands were rock steady.

The priest placed himself in between the two groups, hands extended out as though he could hold them in place by force of will alone.

'Bloom keeps its peace. Hold to that. This is a place for everyone. A place of safety in the storms.'

'Then ask your guests to move,' Malley demanded.

Her voice was steady, cold, and hard. It cut through the wind.

'We've got nowhere to go, my dear,' the leader called out. He was smiling as he said it, but the tension in his voice was palpable.

She had to stop this. Stop it from becoming what it might be.

'Then you won't mind waiting inside and letting some travellers out for a walk be on their way,' Malley called back.

Her voice was winter cold now. No sign of the dry smile she'd shown the night before.

'Put down your weapons,' the priest told them. His tone was desperate.

Fionnuala turned to face the BlueArms. The signal for 'all is well' was a small thing. Like all the signals. If she could just get them to look.

'I'm afraid I can't let you go. Couldn't just have you walking out of my life after we've just met,' Phelan called out to Malley. The words were jovial. The tone was not.

Malley looked at him. A stupid boy to be standing in her way like that. She watched the way he held the axe. Competent.

It wouldn't be enough. Not to stop her and Broderick.

All bar one of their weapons were long handled. Just the one with a hatchet, short enough for close-in fighting. She'd close with them, so would Broderick. Their numbers might count, but not spread out like that. They may as well have been queueing up for her...

'I'm begging you,' the priest shouted at them.

She looked at him. Standing between the two groups.

She could feel the softness in herself. The hesitation. The feeling that had been creeping up on her lately.

She wanted him to have his peace. She didn't want to bloody the ground he'd worked so hard to make peaceful. Peace broken was hard to win back. She'd learned that.

His pleasant nature. His easy-going camaraderie. His forgiving world view. It was all appealing to her. And if there was a way out of this, she'd take it.

But the BlueArms stood. And in Phelan's eyes, she could see a man determined to do his duty. To stop them from reaching Gibson or Kelly.

She looked to Broderick with slight tightening of her eyes and a pursing of her lips.

*Not yet. We don't move first.*

He scowled. And then his eyes flickered at Fionnuala's back.

*Fine. What to do about this one?*

Malley looked at the young woman facing the BlueArms, her hands twitching at her sides. Then at Phelan. He looked from Fionnuala to Malley.

Around them a crowd of locals gathered, their weapons in their hands, but standing by. One wrong move and this would get bloody. Phelan lowered his axe.

'Thank you,' Smurf sighed with relief.

Malley lowered her knives and frowned at Broderick.

*Lower them.*

He snarled at her in disgust. She scowled at him.

Grudgingly, as though it was paining him, Broderick lowered his blades.

And then someone made a mistake.


Fionnuala watched the leader of the BlueArms lower his axe. Then Malley lowered hers. Behind her, she heard Broderick snarl in disgust before lowering his.

For a glorious moment, it seemed as though he'd seen her message. That everyone would walk away.

Until a BlueArm, sensing his chance, hurled his hatchet straight at Malley.

Fionnuala watched it turn, end over end, as it flew across the space between them.

Malley moved like she had liquid bones, simply altering her stance so that the axe sailed by her. Someone behind screamed, and suddenly they were all moving. All at once.

Broderick let loose an animal scream, a noise born of pure rage, and sprang forward knocking Fionnuala from her feet as he moved.

From the ground, she saw Malley gliding forward with alarming speed, her knives held in front of her, extensions of her ruined hands.

She didn't scream, she moved silently, wraithlike across the muddy ground.

That was how they worked. Malley – cold and deadly. An arctic wind that left bodies in her wake. Broderick – roaring wordlessly. A tornado tearing through the melee.

They bounced and careened off the BlueArms, never planting their feet, always moving, terrible in their ferocity.

The first man Malley encountered dropped to his knees, clutching at his neck, blood pouring over his fingers. Broderick's first target collapsed backwards, already dead before she hit the ground with a hole in her chest where his blade had punched in and out.

And still they moved.

Fionnuala picked herself up from the floor and stumbled forward, headfirst into the maelstrom, determined to do something, anything, to stop it.

It was seconds, painfully long, eternal seconds, but by the time she reached the scrap, there were only three BlueArms still standing. She watched uselessly as the agents mowed through them. One broke, making to flee only to find her in his path, swinging a spiked hurley aimlessly in front of himself.

Paralysed, she stood watching the bloodied man bear down on her.

Then the dervish that was Broderick was by her side. The BlueArm's hurley bit into the agents shoulder, and he died with a knife in his eye.

And then it was over.

Silence save for the wind, Joseph playing among the corpses.


Malley pulled the blade out of Phelan's chest. He had been the last one she'd killed though that was not by design. He hadn't pulled his punches. He'd clearly been trying to kill her and she was grateful for that. That in the end, whatever bridges he'd tried to build between them the night before were torn down in combat. It was easier for her that way.

They'd all tried, and she had marks to show for it. A slice across one thigh, a long scrape up one forearm, and a bruise forming on the side of her face from where one of them had punched her.

But they lacked. And she didn't.

She glanced at Broderick to make sure he was okay.

He stood before Fionnuala, blood leaking from a wound on his arm, and the smaller woman stared back at him, her face a mixture of horror, pity, sadness, and shock.

Malley turned to the priest who stood, tears forming in his eyes, surveying the damage.

She wanted to go to the man. To comfort him. To say sorry for the broken peace he'd worked so hard to keep.

His was a soft soul. Too soft for this world.

None of the locals moved, save for those attending the man who'd taken the hatchet in his thigh that had missed her.

Malley stood her ground, and as she plucked the red rag from the pockets of her cargo pants, she looked at them all, taking them all in, daring any of them to say anything.

They stood in silence looking at her. Some in judgement. Some in awe.

She nodded at them, and after sheathing her knives, she looked down at the ruination on her hands for a moment, just a moment, before making for the western gate, feeling Broderick ushering the young woman out behind them.

# CHAPTER SEVEN

The first winds of Joseph's storm season played all about them as they moved down the hill. Little shoves and jolts before running off to pull at the shrubs and the branches of trees.

The early season brushed its hand over the land, still gently, almost fondly. Soon, Joseph would begin to scrub it, cleaning away the damage done, freshening it so that he could sign his name on it the same as his siblings had done year on year for fourteen years. From Storm Season Abraham, when they'd abandoned the idea of even trying to name the individual storms, all the way through Gertrude, who had drowned hundreds of people, up to Joseph who was now waking to wreak his own havoc.

As she moved, Malley found herself wanting to spit out the sour taste of the morning's violence.

She liked Bloom. The warmth of the fires and the sense of community was welcome. The Sharing and the eating together. The sound of laughter. She had found her way back to that feeling of belonging again. Though never fully, it was enough to enjoy those occasional moments.

A soft thing to think, but there it was.

And then Phelan had planted his feet.

She tried not to think about the soft grey of his eyes, the broad smile he wore only hours before she stuck a knife in him.

Instead, she surreptitiously studied Broderick and Fionnuala.

The latter first, keeping pace behind her on overgrown road that wound between the low hillocks of the midlands.

Her hands had flickered. Twitching nervously? Or was she signalling to the BlueArms? The rebels liked to think their coded language was a secret but every agent she knew was aware of it.

To her own alarm, Malley found that she didn't care if the young woman was among her enemies. After all, her own sister numbered among the BlueArms in Limerick.

Hilda. Again. The parallels between the two women continued to haunt her.

The stubbornness of them. The fierceness of them in spite of their stature. As though sheer willpower might overcome all odds.

Fionnuala had run into the fray. Holding the knife Broderick had pressed on her. No training. No concept of the danger she faced. The embodiment of Malley's younger sister. Who had sacrificed everything for her. Who had sacrificed a part of herself that she would never get back. And all either of them had to show for it were the scars on Malley's hands.

Broderick was a different matter.

He ranged out as they moved along the route to Digital's Fortress. Winding to the left when the road bent right, to the right where it twisted left. By such movements he would come up behind anyone hiding on the far sides of the curves, out of sight.

This was standard for them, but when he found his way back to them, it was Fionnuala he stood beside.

Malley felt a pang of something at that. Not jealousy. Broderick had never inspired in her any kind of feeling besides resolute determination. He was a blade she could point at things just like the long knives that hung at her own belt. His fury and righteousness made him less than human, more animal.

The pang was worry for Fionnuala.

His protectiveness over her, the softening of him as he sat by her in Bloom… that would evaporate quickly if it turned out that she had been signalling the BlueArms. If she was one of them, Broderick would cut her throat without hesitation and feel no more remorse for that than he did for the likes of Sullivan back in Black Stair or Phelan in Bloom.

He'd cut Fionnuala the way a man had once cut Malley.

That, Malley decided, she could not allow.


Along the grassy tracks they walked, Fionnuala found herself staring at Malley's back. The older woman moved with a kind of grace Fionnuala wished she could replicate. Smooth almost, as if the cut-up ground and divots and debris were known to the soles of her feet and there were no obstacles.

Fionnuala felt clumsy behind her, stumbling as the ground seemed to shift beneath her.

And she felt afraid.

Malley hadn't spoken to her since they'd left Bloom. Offering occasional enigmatic glances and little else. She'd been a horror in the scrap. The silence of her, the depth of coldness. The previous night during the Sharing, the woman had seemed almost convivial, but pushed even a little, the agent showed her implacability and her ice-cold ferocity.

The silence was the most unnerving part.

Had she seen the signals? Did she know now that Fionnuala was a BlueArm. If so, why had she not confronted, or even just outright killed her yet?

She was relying on this woman, to still Broderick's hand when the moment came to Judge Gibson and Uncle Joe. Broderick's fury wouldn't be stilled by things like innocence or guilt, only Malley's determination might stop him.

And now Fionnuala feared the woman might be contemplating killing her.

Broderick, on the other hand…

She watched him as he re-joined the path, back from another scouting expedition. His face was still granite with two fires burning in his eyes.

But there was something new about him now. Something almost protective. He took his place at her side. Not Malley's. His shoulder close to hers. He didn't look at her. He didn't say anything. He just walked. And, in that pace, kept with hers, there was almost a shelter from Joseph's wandering hands that pulled and pushed her along the path out west.

Broderick could almost feel the woman's eyes on him as he moved. Funny how she'd changed like that. From child to woman.

He didn't like it. But at the very least, it didn't set off the pain in his head that seemed to flare up whenever he found himself in the company of certain people.

Wrong people.

Ahead of them, Malley moved. He watched the tiny twitches in her head that revealed her scan to him. He knew, instinctively, that she was counting on him to protect Fionnuala, and watch their six.

That was the way between them. It was the immutable fact of his life. The code. Malley and the code.

And yet...

She wanted 'justice'. She wanted 'truth'.

It was borderline philosophical.

He had a job to do. Several jobs actually.

Soon they'd be upon their quarry. Soon they'd be at Digital's Fortress and there a test waited for them. A test of their bond. Soon they'd have Gibson or Kelly in their sights. And when that moment came, would she try to stop him doing his duty? Would she try to spare the man because of what she perceived as 'innocence'?

He pondered that, and watched her back, and a small headache started to grow at the base of his skull.

*** *** ***

The man called himself Digital. His actual name was Aidan.

A leftover from Before. He'd been a conspiracy theorist and a doomsday prophet back then, as well as an IT engineer of some note. His expertise had brought him money, and his proclivity for doomsday preparation had bought him a manor house outside Athlone town, on a hill-site with its own well and a clear view of the surrounding terrain.

That manor house was now a Fortress in every way in which that word could be understood. He had guns, water, power from solar panels and wind turbines and, most importantly, a band of desperate people who sheltered from the storms in his benevolent protection.

That protection had earned their zealous loyalty. As it did all over the island of Ireland. Whoever could keep you safe...

Over the years, Digital had collected servers, hard-drives and personal computers. In an age when the internet remained a spotty thing, given to failure and controlled tightly by Government, a man with information, independent information, was his own sort of king.

They watched his kingdom from a tree line on a hill opposite the compound. He'd cleared what walls had once surrounded the manor house and replaced them with high fencing for better line of sight. It was incredible to Malley in many ways, how the old houses, well maintained, weathered the Storm Seasons better than anything built in the last fifty years.

The cloudy and threatening sky had brought the light down quickly and for the second time in two nights, they faced the dangerous prospect of seeking entry when they might well be mistaken for a threat.

Standing in the darkness with Joseph tossing treetops above them, they could make out the electrified fencing and the outline of the spotlights that were mounted all around the property, activating, no doubt, when the fences did. Just about visible at irregular intervals were the shadows of movement that confirmed the presence of Digital's personal bodyguard.

Broderick looked at her, a question in his eyes.

*What now?*

'Walk up and knock?' she asked him with a smile.

His lips twitched in reply. A momentary flicker only.

As good as a laugh from anyone else.

'Anyone any good at building wooden horses?' Fionnuala asked.

The wind rustled the trees above them, sprinkling them as the wet leaves stirred, adding to the occasionally spitting raindrops that found their way down the back of her neck.

'Why not let them come to us?' Fionnuala eventually tried again.

She'd shaken off the worst of the road to Athlone with a grim determination that became her. Malley had stolen a glance at her as they'd approached Digital's fiefdom. Her face was set, tinged with anger, that overlaid by resolution. The world taught lessons and this little one learned them fast it seemed.

'Say again?' Broderick asked flatly.

'Settle down here. Light a fire. Talk loudly. Make sure they know we're here. Then let them come to us?'

Broderick grunted.

As good as a belly laugh from anyone else.

Malley smiled at her. The girl had wits and intelligence. Both of those things made her more and more threatening since Malley couldn't decide if they were hiding something else.

They lit their small campfire and began heating their meals. The fire wasn't even buried, and big enough to ruin their night vision. They'd be unable to see anything beyond a couple of measly feet.

It was anathema to her.

'What should we talk about?' Fionnuala asked innocently.

Malley found herself almost laughing, swallowing the impulse to guffaw.

Years and years with Broderick. Travelling what was left of the country and, in all that time, they never once had to worry about what to talk about. Since they never talked at all.

Broderick's eyes said that he too felt almost startled.

The man rarely offered a word that wasn't spoken in fury or *absolutely* necessary.

A laugh escaped Malley, surprising and welcome, and when Fionnuala joined in, it seemed to double her laughter. Broderick did not laugh but he didn't grunt his disapproval either. He simply sat there, the fire-drawn shadows on his face hinting oddly at a smile.

'You don't talk a lot,' Fionnuala told them when the laughter died down. 'I know nothing about either of you. Where are you from?'

Malley studied her battered hands, the smile still on her lips, but she said nothing.

'I'm from Limerick,' Broderick announced softly.

It was so unexpected that Malley nearly laughed again. She hadn't known that about him.

'You live there all your life?' Fionnuala asked.

She was looking at him in a curious way, a soft look for someone who had argued so passionately with him only a day before.

It was the look a young person might give to a handsome man like Broderick. She'd never considered his looks before. When they'd met, all she'd seen was his violence, and the terrible silence of him. She saw the things in him that she herself had worked so hard to be.

But underneath that there was a man – a man who some women might have found attractive.

'Two tours abroad with the peacekeeping force,' he said.

His face was still hard and cold, it likely would be that way always now. He couldn't possibly change it. But his eyes, hazel and usually on fire with his rage, were softer looking now. Almost human.

'You've been outside Ireland?' she asked him wistfully, the concept alien to her.

'Twice. We were called back early to help with the relief effort after the first Storm Season. After that, every time I went to Limerick, it was to kill someone.'

'How many times have you been back?'

'Five.'

That was news to Malley too. Five times he'd walked through Limerick since the first Storm Season. She'd been there only once. To collect Hilda and bring her home to Dublin.

A task she'd failed to complete.

'How many people have you killed?' Fionnuala asked him. Her face was sad.

'No idea,' he replied, 'but they all deserved it.'

He meant that too.

Another part of that increasing gap between them was what exactly constituted 'deserving'. To him, everyone was deserving. To her, there was, she hoped, still a sliver of honour and humanity left, and that 'deserving' threatened to cross that line.

Malley had also lost track of the number of people she'd killed. Weapons didn't count their victims.

That rapidly disappearing line was her humanity.

'Do you have family there?' Fionnuala asked him.

'Probably,' he replied, still looking into the fire.

'What about them?' she asked.

He looked like he might answer her, his eyes still reflecting flames, but before he could open his mouth, a flash in the dark evening sky, distant, but bright, was soon followed by the crack of thunder rolling across the shallow hills.

Joseph speaking for the first time, his voice demanding their attention.

Fionnuala's face looked frightened. Storm Season for her was spent behind walls, inside a flatpack, hunkered down. Warm. Comfortable. On the exposed hillside as the first fat drops fell, Malley felt for her. Alone. Out of her depth.

For her own part, Malley welcomed the new Storm Season. It always seemed to arrive on time.

She didn't comfort the child though. Instead, she listened as the faint rustling of broken branches and the squelching of sodden leaves drew closer bringing with it the dangers she faced over and over. People.

Broderick didn't look at her. He stared into the fire as the fat raindrops hissed on impact with his hearth. She knew he heard it too though. The zeal was back in his eyes. He rested one arm casually across his thigh, where he could draw the blade at a moment's notice.

'Well, don't you all look comfortable?' a voice asked from behind them.

Her hand closed on her knife just as Broderick's did on his.

'It's okay,' the voice told them. 'Simi is only here to offer you a room for the night.'


'Spotted you on the cameras some time ago, agents,' Digital told them, reclining in an armchair, cocking one leg over the armrest.

He was a man of average height, with long lank hair and an untrimmed beard that gave him a look of something almost feral, except for his clean and comfortable clothing. It wasn't outdoor wear; it wasn't multi-layered and designed to protect against the elements. It was cheap suit pants, a clean but wrinkled shirt, and a fancy but ill-fitting woollen coat that wouldn't have been out of place twenty years before.

The wild, unhinged look of him over the fine clothing was an incongruity that marked him out as different from the world around him.

He had more weight on him than people normally carried these days. There was a time when his body type would have been regarded as average, but now he looked overweight. Overfed. Too comfortable.

Simi, the bodyguard, did not look overfed or soft. He was tall, lean thing, sinewy somehow, but broad at the shoulders. A hyena, his fixed smile as he stood behind Digital's chair was a grim thing in the tallow light of the candles.

The furnishings were comfortable, borderline luxurious.

Soft and old. They would have been considered high quality and expensive before the first Chain of Storms, but now they were jarring in their decadence. Long, plush curtains hung in the windows, the effect of comfort only slightly ruined by the reinforced bars on the outside of the glass. Besides the candles dotted here and there, a fire burned in the fireplace, crackling pleasantly and filling the living room with a warm glow.

It was a room that belonged to another age. Another life. It had no place here and it put Malley and Broderick very clearly on edge.

Fionnuala looked at it with something approaching equanimity. She didn't recognise it as a room that might once have been common. It was too large, too permanent.

'I should have guessed you'd have cameras,' Malley replied.

'When the whole world is out to get you, it just seems prudent,' he replied, spreading his arms.

'Where did you even get cameras these days?'

'These days?' he laughed, 'I've had these things since before the fall of Rome.'

There was something in his tone, and a shine in his eyes that somehow didn't match his face. As though they didn't belong in his head. She'd seen it before. He was obviously touched with just a little madness.

Isolation would do that to a body on a long enough timeline.

'How long have you been here?' Fionnuala asked him, trying to inject some authority into her voice.

'I'm curious about you,' he told her, ignoring the question. 'A little tiger cub? A young wolf? You haven't the look of these two yet. I don't think I could use your face to hammer nails.'

'I'm in training to be an agent,' she lied.

'Oh, I don't think so,' Digital told her, laughing. 'I don't think that at all.'

Malley stilled her face to hide her surprise.

What did he know? Or was this grandstanding? Pretend omniscience?

'We're here for information,' she told him.

The effect on him was a startling change.

He sat bolt upright in his seat, his face furious.

'DON'T BE SO RUDE,' he roared at her.

Broderick moved instantly, placing himself between the two of them, his knife appearing in his hand, while Malley spun to face Simi, her hand whipping her blade free even as the hyena of a guard reached to drag his small gun clear.

The agents' movements were practically simultaneous, and they both froze at the same time, in that split second before launching killer blows. Simi stood with his hand on the butt of his gun, knowing she had the beating of him. He still smiled at her.

Digital tipped his head back and howled with laughter.

Fionnuala had pinned herself against the wall, frightened, but she'd drawn the knife quick enough.

Sharp and getting sharper.

'Oh my, oh my, but you two are good,' Digital told them mirthfully. 'They told me you were good. So fast. It's uncanny.'

Simi let his hand drop away from his side, with a nod that might have been respect.

Malley slipped her knife back into its sheath.

Broderick didn't. For a moment he held Digital's gaze, the knife still in his hand. A threat.

'Oh, he's a terrible one, isn't he?' Digital giggled at Malley. 'O'Neill talked about him. Half wild he called him. I think that was generous. He's almost all the way there.'

'Been speaking to the Minister a lot lately, have you?' Malley asked sceptically.

'We talk when the need arises,' he informed her pompously.

Malley guessed that they did speak from time to time, but doubted highly that there was much real communication happening. She surmised that Digital had an almost pathological need to be regarded as omniscient.

If they did speak often then something was seriously wrong. Why were they even here?

'And what is it you talk about?' she asked calmly.

Between Fionnuala's obvious fear, Digital's fevered madness, and Broderick's white-hot rage, the room was in desperate need of some calming.

'We talked about you too. Cold he called you. Cold as winter.'

'I'm sure you did,' she drawled back at him. 'At any point, did you talk about what we were coming here for?'

'We did actually. He's a terrible little liar, isn't he?'

Malley forced herself to be nonchalant. He had the information, but this was how he wanted to play things out, with little hints on his side, and some begging on their side. He gave nothing away for free and even after he was paid for it, he doled it out as and how he pleased.

'Do you think?' she asked.

'Oh yes. Don't you? Terrible liar.'

'I told him I didn't believe him the last time we met.'

'Because you wouldn't be anyone's hired hand or paid assassin?' he quoted.

Those were the exact words she'd used when talking to O'Neill.

'Interesting choice of words there,' she told him, still forcing her nonchalance.

'Bet you didn't know that you had someone peeping while you were talking,' he told her with a grin.

Out of the corner of her eye, she saw Fionnuala flinch.

Her heart twisted at the sight, and her stomach turned.

Fionnuala had been spying on them. The flinch was as good as an admission of guilt.

'Is that so?' she asked, her eyes keeping Fionnuala in her peripherals.

'Wherever there are cameras, I can peep,' he smirked at her.

Cameras. Not her. But she had flinched. So she had spied. Had Broderick noticed? Was he so focused on Digital that he'd missed the tell-tale sign? She was afraid to measure his reaction in case that was the confirmation he needed. The woman had spied. If he tried to kill her, why should Malley try to stop him?

Yet she knew she would. She knew that she wouldn't allow the young woman to die. For Hilda, she'd fight for this frightened little thing.

'So, what makes the minister a liar?' she asked him, still looking at Digital.

Digital struck a nonchalant pose.

'His "evidence" of Kelly and Gibson's climate denial.'

'What about it?'

'It's fake.'

'Fake?' Broderick snarled incredulously.

'Completely contrived,' Digital told them.

Malley narrowed her eyes at him in confusion. Broderick shook his head, his knife still in his hand.

'Start talking,' Broderick told him angrily, 'start talking plainly and start talking now.'

'The document he showed you was printed two weeks ago from a Government computer.'

He sat back enjoying his revelation, proud of himself, preening in his seat.

'You can prove this?' Malley asked him.

'Liberal Tears, their little right-wing newspaper *was* real though,' Digital told her, ignoring her question, drip-feeding the information. 'It was online and in print. It was out the same time that Kelly and Gibson were in university there together. So maybe it's a fake, or maybe it's a copy of the real thing. The only person who knows if they were involved is hiding on the top floor of a hospital in Galway.'

Fionnuala flinched again.

'If it was real, does that make them guilty or not?' Malley asked him.

'Not necessarily, I suppose,' Digital replied with a shrug, 'but the changing names thing is always a bad look, isn't it? He's not Joe Kelly, he's Joe Trench and Frank Gibson is actually Gibson Waters.'

'What are you saying? Did they do it or not?' Malley snapped. 'If they did, is there *real* evidence?'

'It's enough for me,' Broderick told her putting up his knife.

'Oh, I don't imagine it takes much for you, does it Mr Eoghan Broderick?

Digital was taking a risk now, though surrounded by his guards and his guns in the kingdom he'd reigned in for over fourteen years he likely thought himself safe.

Broderick might well disabuse him of that notion.

'My name is Broderick.'

'It wasn't always,' Digital replied with a chuckle.

'It is now,' Broderick told him and the look he gave the man might have killed someone else on the spot.

Digital paid it almost no mind.

'If you want *real* evidence, I know where you can get some.'

'Galway?' Malley asked.

He was posturing still, desperate to look smart and powerful.

'Omega lives there. On the top floor of the hospital. That's where you'll find everything you need.'

'They didn't do it,' Fionnuala asserted, daring to speak again.

Malley felt for her. The young woman's whole life was in the balance. If they were guilty, she'd wasted her years on them.

'Honestly,' Digital told her, and for a moment he looked sane, 'I don't know. All I can say is that the one who goes by Omega has been in touch with Kelly and Gibson and O'Neill and me, and that person says they know it all.'

Galway. Best part of a day and a half if the weather and the roads held. Both increasingly unlikely as one headed west.

'What about Gibson?' Broderick asked suddenly.

'I stalled him as best I could,' Digital told them. 'But he's on his way to Galway. A poor traveller that man. I imagine seasoned types like you could be on him before he gets there.'

'O'Neill told us you have something for us?' Malley prompted.

Digital motioned Simi forward with a gesture and the tall man moved to a side cabinet. On the old, polished wood, a small box sat. He picked it up and passed it to her.

Opening the box, Malley saw two simple-looking, blue, circular pins.

'Keys to the city of Limerick,' Digital told her, clearly delighted with himself. 'Wear them and you can pass any checkpoint without their codes or any troublesome questions.'

She looked at them for a long moment. This was what they'd come for. The information and these little keys so that they could kill a man who might yet be innocent. The plump little hermit truly was playing all sides.

'What are you getting out of this?' Malley asked the kinglet.

'Same thing everyone wants. Power. Electricity. My generators run when I need them, but they're for security mostly, the fencing, the lights, etc. But if I was on the grid... and you're to bring her servers to me. All of them. Whatever she has is mine now.'

His smile was unctuous.

'And what do Gibson and Kelly get for your help?' Broderick asked.

'Same thing,' Digital replied smugly. 'You'll beat them or their BlueArms will beat you, but in the end...'

He spread his arms expansively.

Outside the wind moved from a loud moan to a shriek, almost triumphant, as Joseph introduced himself to the world.

There was something wrong about it all. About Kelly and Gibson, about their being here. She was being manipulated somehow. The simple facts of justice, of punishing the wicked, were blurring as players moved in ways she couldn't quite see yet.

'We stay tonight,' Malley told them eventually. 'We leave first thing in the morning.'

'You're more than welcome. It's always a pleasure doing business with the agents of the Department of Environmental Justice.'

She was surprised when Broderick didn't object. It should have been a warning to her. She thought he'd be keen to cut the gap to their quarry. But Digital was right. The roads out west were no place for the inexperienced on the edge of Storm Season.

Still, it stuck with her. Too many players in this game. The black and white of her duty was beginning to blend into new shades of grey she found unpleasant.


The One-Eyed Rook watched the fencing and the men patrolling it as the rain sluiced down from the bent boughs of trees above him. The jumble of people nearby were hunkered down under the branches at the top the hill, waiting for his signal. The burden of leadership still weighed on him, all these years later, a one-time barman commanding the militia, but they followed. Because he was hard enough for them.

They had gone looking for local BlueArms at Ferbane, but only found corpses. Someone had decided the people of the small town had something valuable, something they needed for Joseph's extended visit. And they took it.

Same as every year outside.

His people had discovered something else though. A functioning tractor. The beast had been modified. Rook watched with approval as the BlueArms prepared it. A perfect battering ram. Electrified fences might be excellent at stopping people getting by, but they were no match for an armoured vehicle.

The wind and the storm, Joseph's first infantile outburst, hid the sound of the tractor rolling around the bends on the small road that led to Digital's compound.

The orders were simple; kill the agents, save the girl. The request from Hilda was less simple; save the women, kill the man.

That she didn't want her sister killed didn't surprise him, that she thought the one-eyed Rook had it in him to save her did. By all accounts, the sister was an agent beyond compare, fast and cold. In combat with one like that, it was usually kill or be killed. Saving her might be beyond him.

Still, he understood the motivation. O'Mahony wasn't far away, he never was. Shrugging uncomfortably in the rain and driving wind. This was no place for the likes of him, but the older man couldn't be left behind. He was too naïve, too soft, too easily exploited. In a word, he was too kind for this world.

A man too kind to be left alone, and a woman too hard to be kept alive. Rook cursed himself for getting caught up once again in other people's games.

The rumbling of the tractor as it rolled into sight snapped him out of his reverie.

'Stay close,' he shouted to O'Mahony as he ran, still crouched low, across the grass and into the wake of the battering ram his people drove.

Someone was about to die. If it had to be her, so be it.

# CHAPTER EIGHT

Fionnuala sat on the bed, in the room she was to share with Malley trying to pretend she was calm as she looked at the older woman. Broderick had been given the room next door.

She was concerned. Had either of the agents noticed her flinch? It was the not knowing that was the worst. She knew she'd been caught for spying the moment the crazy man downstairs had mentioned it. And now she might be about to die.

The agent sat on the floor with her back to the door, blocking the only means of escape from the room. Not that it would have helped for her to get out. The house was crawling with bodyguards. They'd passed half a dozen of them on the way to bed alone.

Malley just sat there. Slowly, reverentially, she ran the tips of four fingers up and down the palm of her other hand. She didn't look at Fionnuala, she just sat there, staring into space and running her fingers up and down, over and back across her hands.

There was no proof Uncle Joe had done it, nor Gibson, his soft-spoken friend and fellow rebel. Nothing. Memories of her father and mother came back to her whenever she thought of Joe Kelly. Their faith in him. He had saved her father. He came to their home. He spoke gently to them, but with a wry smile, and he said little swear words and winked at her when he said them, a secret communication between them. A man surely not capable of climate change denial.

What person could deny the existence of climate change and then lead this revolution? An uprising of the people who only wanted the best for the planet and the future? A chance to let go of the age that had built people like Broderick and Malley. It simply wasn't possible.

The room itself added to her nerves, it was too large. It felt like a bedroom should feel like, but oversized. The bed was twice as big as anything she'd slept in for over a decade. The empty spaces in the room were crowded with nothing. The bedside lockers, the wardrobe, the door itself were all too large, too much. Malley fitted in this room, but Fionnuala felt that she did not.

Outside the window a young Joseph, really finding his feet for the first time, began to stomp across the land. The sound of him was howling and screeching and clattering as he began to pick things off the ground and dash them back down again.

'Who did you tell?' Malley asked her, softly, quietly, barely audible above the rising wind.

Fionnuala didn't trust herself to say anything. Instead, she transferred her gaze to the window at the flashes in the night sky and the booming sounds that accompanied them.

Malley sat and waited, swapping hands around, right for left, so that no scar would go untraced. Fionnuala wanted to ask about them, but the near holiness in the act of brushing those scars spoke of a personal battle too terrible to tell of.

The silence extended. Malley still didn't look at her.

The agent's face was too hard to look at when she went cold like this. As though nothing human lived underneath it. It was the face she'd worn in Bloom when she'd cut through people as if they were brambles in her way. The face she'd worn after she'd murdered Sullivan. Fionnuala had watched those hard eyes even before she'd known the Doejay, watched her turn her head and challenge every person in the square at Black Stair, daring them to denounce her.

What must it take for someone to become so hard? So slowly they revealed themselves, a little at a time. The more she saw, the more she recognised herself as soft. And with that recognition, she began to fear that the world was too far gone for anyone to change it back. There was no future in the dead eyes of the agent, just a terrible past.

Joseph filled the silence that stretched between them with his screams and howls, with the ping of hail striking the bars on the window. Malley still didn't look at her. Still she stared into space and her fingers delicately probed the crevices of ruined hands.

Fionnuala couldn't take it.

'I'm sorry,' she whispered. The sound mixing with the wind.

'Who did you tell?' Malley asked her again.

Her face didn't change, her eyeline didn't move. She still stared straight ahead.

'What do you mean?'

'When you spied on us in Black Stair. Who did you tell?'

The question wasn't a surprise and yet it still gut-punched her.

'I didn't,' she replied. 'I never got the chance.'

'Liar.'

'No, I didn't, how would I?'

'Don't be a fool,' Malley barked at her. 'Who did you tell?'

She didn't bother controlling her volume, the storm drowned out the noise anyway.

Fionnuala tried to hold her tongue, but the agent's face swivelled toward her and her eyebrow raised in that same grim challenge she had offered the world.

'Something is happening here,' Malley told her. 'Something I don't understand. What are we doing here if that man can speak to the Minister whenever he wants?'

'To collect those pins?'

'Nonsense. Broderick's been in and out of Limerick multiple times. He didn't need them. They're useful, no more. I need to know who you told. I need this to make sense. Tell me, Fionnuala.'

Near as she could tell that was the first time the agent had referred to her by her name and not as 'child' or 'girl'.

'I sent word to Kelly. We have a computer stashed in a boiler room at the back of the town hall. I got in that way, and when you were done, I sent word to his people in Limerick.'

She waited for the woman to move. She held her breath for the whisper of the knife being drawn from its sheath. Instead, the only sound was the soft sigh Malley emitted as she closed her eyes.

'Fool,' she whispered as she leaned her head back against the door.

There was something human underneath the concrete of this woman's exterior. She wondered if the same human centre waited underneath Broderick's hard surface. Something for Fionnuala to appeal to.

'I can't let you kill him,' Fionnuala told her, her voice small and full of fear.

'Brave fool,' Malley told her with a soft bitter laugh.

'I need you to see,' Fionnuala replied. 'There's been enough killing. There's been enough controlling. It's time to build now. We have to look forward, not back. There's nothing back there for us anymore. That world doesn't exist—'

'No,' Malley cut across her bitterly. 'It doesn't exist. It's gone now. But it didn't magically evaporate. It didn't vanish. We didn't wake up from a dream. It was taken. It was torn from us. And the people who stole it are walking among us.'

'No, they're not.'

'I see their words. I read the things they said. The things they did. They're real. They exist. And every winter we get to see exactly what they've done to us.'

Was there a hint of resignation in her voice? Was there a crack in the concrete into which Fionnuala could slip?

'No, you don't understand me,' Fionnuala told her. 'They don't exist anymore. Even if the people are still alive. Whoever those people were, they're not that anymore. It was real when it was real, but it's gone now. They're different people, because this is a different world.'

She felt the truth of those words, Kelly's words really. He'd said them countless times. He was even brave enough to say them in Government. She felt their truth and hoped she could plant that truth somewhere in the agent.

Malley laughed out loud, before looking Fionnuala dead in the eyes.

They weren't hot like Broderick's. They were deep and cold.

She turned her palms up so the ruination was clear, the criss-crossing ridges, the jagged streaks of white.

'We are what we are,' Malley told her. 'This is what we are.' Ruined and scarred. This is how she saw the whole world.

'You weren't that during Before though, were you? Your hands weren't always like that.'

The older woman dropped her eyes back down to her palms and looked at them for a long moment.

Somewhere in the house something smashed. The crash startled them both.

At first Fionnuala thought it was the sound of the squall outside scattering something across the driveway, but the next noise was the muffled scraping of furniture and a dull thud.

Then a roar, cut short as someone died.

Malley was out the door.

The speed of her was still something extraordinary to behold. One second, she was sitting with her back to the door, the next she was outside the door, her knife in her hand, her short ponytail whipping behind her as if she'd simply deleted the space in between.

Fionnuala sprang from the bed after her and into the broad corridor of this surreal house.

Malley was already pulling her knife from the chest of one of Digital's bodyguards on the landing. He slumped off the blade, crumpling and tumbling down the stairs with the agent bounding after his corpse, following the sound of the roar.

Fionnuala followed after, impulse driving her down after the body that tumbled lifelessly before them onto the floor of the foyer with its myriad doors.

Two men burst into the hallway, guns drawn. Fionnuala saw them before Malley did and, with a scream, she dived at the two men.

It was an instinctual action, born of desperation and well short on timing or dexterity. The men sidestepped her clumsy charge. She sprawled across the floor.

It was enough to slow them though. And that was enough to get them killed.

A knife appeared in one of their eye sockets, blood spurting from the wound. The crunch the man made as his head hit the floor next to Fionnuala was a sickening thing.

She flipped on her back, twisting on the ground even as she did to move away from the corpse leaking blood beside her. From the ground, she saw the second man attempt to engage the agent.

Malley kicked out at the hand holding the gun. It went off wildly and inaccurately, strafing the walls and sending chips of stone in all directions.

The agent's fist connected with the man's throat, her knee then catching him in the midriff and as he doubled over, she took a handful of long hair and slammed the man's face into a side table. Then a second time. And a third.

The fourth time, the man went limp.

Malley didn't stop, didn't hesitate. The second her hand pulled the knife free, she was moving again.

Through a library, then onto another corridor, through a kitchen, a huge room with the surfaces dusty from underuse.

The corpse of another bodyguard lay on the floor, a pool of blood spread all around its neck where the throat had been cut.

They zigzagged through the huge house.

Fionnuala's heart raced. She kept herself as close as she could to Malley while still fearing that her proximity would activate the woman's reflexive killer instinct.

So much for bodyguards. The corpses were a testament to their effectiveness against the agents. She assumed Broderick was ahead of them. The dark corners and winding corridors were perfect for a man like him. A fury moving from shadow to shadow.

Malley's hand stopped her in her tracks, startling her.

The agent silenced her with her eyes. Still dead, unhuman. *Wait. Don't move.*

Fionnuala understood the look as if the woman had spoken the words.

They were standing in a shadow on a corridor by a door, looking across the narrow anteroom that led to Digital's audience chamber.

Inside, a mumbled conversation, too low to be distinguishable. The only discernible voice was Digital's, but there was a clear line of sight to the man he was talking to.

Through the open door, a portion of Broderick's broad back could be seen.

From the right side of the room, a man moved into view, creeping on silent feet, his weapon drawn, the conversation pulling him toward his quarry.

With Joseph's screams to mask the sound of his passing, Simi crept across the floor with his gun. In the half light of candles and lightning, Fionnuala could see that the creepy smile he had worn was gone, in its place a rigid determination.

Quietly, Fionnuala marvelled at the instinct which had made Malley stop in her tracks. Had they walked straight into the room, Simi would be behind them instead of the other way around.

She watched in muted surprise as Simi stepped into the doorway behind Broderick and raised his gun.

She shouldn't have been surprised to see Malley move then. Silently but quickly, the woman stepped up behind the gaunt man and with casual aggressiveness, reached around, slammed the knife into his jugular, pulling it clear to tear out Simi's throat.

The fury on Digital's face was clear. The fury on Broderick's just as clear. He clearly hadn't heard the man sneaking up on him.

Malley stepped over the body casually and looked back at where Fionnuala hid, still standing in the shadow.

With a slight tip of her head, she beckoned for Fionnuala to join her in the room.

*Come, child.*


Digital was a cornered rat, standing behind his elaborate desk, a small handgun in a shaking hand pointed at Broderick.

To Malley's eyes, that cornered rat might have been facing a mountain lion, such was her partner's casual disregard for the danger he faced.

Broderick's face was its usual combination of hard and impassive, though the light in his eyes, that fevered heat, lent to a sense of mania about him.

What was he after? Why did he want to kill Digital? For using his old first name? That really might be all it took for him.

A voice told her she had to stop him… another voice disagreed.

'We both know that gun doesn't work,' Broderick told Digital.

'What makes you so sure, Mr Broderick?' Digital drawled back.

To his credit, his voice didn't waver. Malley was more than a little surprised. Slightly impressed, even.

Not that his calmness would do him any good.

She was behind Broderick. If she wanted to keep Digital alive, she'd have to step between them somehow.

If.

She'd never put herself in direct conflict with her partner before. Doing so now would surely widen the gap between them beyond repair.

Could she do that for the likes of Digital?

Could she abandon six years of partnership for this greasy, unctuous man?

She needed answers, and corpses talked even less than Broderick did.

'Because you'd have shot me when this one distracted me,' Broderick replied, his foot nudging Simi's corpse.

She'd done it without thought. Like the three others that she'd killed on her way here. Obstacles. No more, no less.

It was a measure of Broderick's disregard for Digital's gun that he looked down at the body as he nudged it.

'There were others,' Malley told him, closing the gap to him slightly.

If she wanted to stop him, she'd have to be patient. Move slowly.

'I thought I'd gotten them all,' Broderick replied.

'How many?' she asked him.

'Ten,' Broderick told her.

Fionnuala gasped at him.

To Malley's surprise, he swung his eyes to her and for a brief, tiny moment, she thought he looked sorry.

Unless she was imagining it.

Fionnuala returned his look with one of horror. Tinged with pity. They held each other's gaze for a long moment.

'How many did you get?' Broderick asked her, his eyes still on Fionnuala.

'Three and him makes four,' Malley told him.

Digital groaned his disappointment.

Malley took the opportunity to edge closer again to Broderick. If she could get close enough, she could stop him if she needed to.

'Fourteen people,' Fionnuala gasped in horror. 'And you don't care? Neither of you?'

No. She wasn't imagining it.

The look in his eyes was sorry. It was the first time she'd ever seen him look anything but frightening. The young woman was under his skin too, somehow.

In his moment of weakness, Malley saw a chance to manoeuvre herself into position between Broderick and Digital, but there was no way to do it casually...

She fluffed it, her subtlety undone by their shared bond and his keen sense of the room. He spotted her moving before she'd taken two steps.

That would teach her for underestimating him. Everything was a threat to him. Even her.

His eyes flashed as they narrowed. That hot, feverish look that was so often the closest thing he had to emotional display.

Casually, almost contemptuously, he sidestepped, keeping himself between Malley and Digital, but opening his body up to cover her advance. It was a defensive step that put the two of them in direct conflict. If she wanted to stop him now, she'd have to attack, and now the change in his position meant that he knew that and was willing to fight her.

His lips twitched too. A hint of a rueful smile, if you knew him well enough to know what that twitch meant.

*Really?*

Fionnuala and Digital both seemed to notice it too. Digital's eyes scanning the room for possible egress. The sweat still standing out on his brow.

Fionnuala looked petrified.

They stayed locked in that moment for a long minute, like four cardinal points. Fionnuala, back against one wall, directly opposite Broderick, her eyes locked on his face.

Digital, his back to the large, barred bay window, still holding his placebo gun, eyes darting around the room for a way out, directly opposite Malley, who now had Fionnuala on her right and Broderick on her left.

The air in the room sharp with the smell of freshly spilled blood and thick with tension.

Malley looked at him questioningly, shoulders taught.

*Why are you trying to kill him?*

He blinked at her and shrugged slightly.

*Why are you trying to stop me?*

She let a small laugh go at his reply.

'It's my job to kill him,' he told her.

But she knew it was for Fionnuala. Because he felt guilt.

Somehow, Broderick was capable of guilt. It was an almost astonishing admission.

'No, it's not,' she told him forcefully. 'Your job is investigating, charging, and Pronouncing. This man is a sideshow.'

'This man impeded an investigation. He also aided and abetted a man convicted of climate change denial.'

'There's no proof of that…' Fionnuala interjected.

'He's been Pronounced. By the Minister. This man let him go.'

'I couldn't stop him,' Digital pleaded.

The layer of condescension and pretend-omniscience was gone now, replaced with pure terror.

'A terrible little liar you are,' Broderick mocked him, mimicking his condescending tone.

It clicked with her then. Terrible liars everywhere.

'You have orders I don't? O'Neill gave you other names?' Malley asked him.

Broderick looked at her for a moment then grunted a bitter laugh.

*Nothing gets by you.*

He had been talking to O'Neill before she arrived in. He had orders she didn't. Who else was on his list? How far could she trust him now? The gap between them widened by the minute.

'You don't have to kill him,' Fionnuala pleaded.

'Why do you care?'

'Fourteen people are dead already. Isn't that enough?'

'No,' he told her.

'Why am I on the list?' Digital almost cried. 'We had a deal!'

'This one worked for a tech giant,' Broderick told her. 'Server farms that ran on coal or oil, day and night. They diverted rivers from their course to cool them. He burned the world while he quietly built himself a little fortress so that he could survive the damage he'd done to us.'

He gestured around the room taking in the furnishings and the finishings.

'He gets to live here off the profits he made destroying the planet. He hides behind these walls while people starve and kill each other and die of diseases and viruses. He did that to them. Hospitals stand in ruin up and down the country, but this man...'

His sneer said everything he wanted it to say.

'Even if he hadn't already been Pronounced, I'd be killing him. He deserves to die.'

In its own brutal manner, his logic was impeccable. His code. The guilty, the innocent, and them.

Broderick was right. If Digital had been Pronounced, why not just let him die? He lived in luxury while people suffered. The scars on her hands were evidence of how little she owed him. What else did he deserve but death? Why was she straining, looking for reasons to save his life?

Fionnuala was the answer. Her face was pure sorrow and pity. She had none of their anger. None of their bitterness. She had survived hard winters and seen more death than a twenty-year-old should have, but she didn't carry their deep and abiding resentment.

In that generosity and humanity, there was something tremendously pure and admirable. Her strength was the capacity to let go of the past and forgive. Like Hilda had done.

Fionnuala didn't care what this man had taken from the world. She didn't want him to die, and the part of Malley who remembered what caring felt like, that secret part of her that had manifested when she'd let an old man live who had been sentenced to die, that part of her wanted to live in the world Fionnuala lived in.

But she didn't live in that world. She lived in a world where weakness and sadness and pity were soft things that could get you killed.

For this wretch? There would be no weakness.

The alarms that suddenly blasted through the house startled them all, the floodlights outside activating simultaneously, flaring in the living room like a small explosion.

Broderick recovered first, his reflexes kicking him into action, moving before Digital had time to fully compute what was happening. Malley saw him move. Instead of stopping him, she closed the gap to Fionnuala and wrapped her in place, in case the fool woman tried to intervene.

Broderick vaulted the large, ornate desk, one hand propelling him over the top, the other brandishing his knife.

Digital had a second to utter a scream that died in a gurgle as Broderick's knife sank into the man's chest, the force of the charge bringing the two together up against the large window.

Fionnuala struggled ineffectually in Malley's arms, writhing to get loose. Malley held her in place as she watched the light go out of Digital's eyes, his last breath taken as he looked disbelievingly at the handle of the knife sticking from his chest.

'Thusly are you judged,' Broderick told the body as it slid to the floor.

'We have to move,' Malley told him, all too aware of the noise of alarms blaring, drowning out the storm, and the light that now filled the room.

Someone had decided to attack the house.

Shadows and flickers of movement streaked past the barred windows.

It seemed that the message Fionnuala had sent hadn't fallen on deaf ears. The BlueArms were here for them.

Broderick looked at her for a long moment. Weighing her. She could feel him calculating in his head. Were they still partners? Could he trust her? She was wondering the same thing about him. With his secret list. How long before that trust killed one of them?

Eventually he nodded at her, and the two of them bustled Fionnuala out the door.

# CHAPTER NINE

Broderick took up the rear with Malley moving on point, dodging through the house quickly but carefully. Fionnuala was in the middle, her fright tempered with an obvious resolve that Broderick found admirable. Shadows were harder to find with the floodlights from outside streaming light into the manor, but those they did find were darker and deeper. The loud blare of alarms shattered any attempt at thought, and so he operated almost by instinct.

The noises outside, a mixture of people moving and fighting, and the sounds of Joseph running amok reached them in between blares of alarms. Doors closing, furniture being knocked over, calls from one room to another existing only in the second between each horn. Broderick worked hard to keep his concentration in the din, head always moving as he covered their backtrack.

The sound of violence was prominent too. Those who had breached the fence and activated the alarm were now clashing with those members of Digital's personal bodyguard patrolling his fortress.

His disjointed thoughts kept drifting to Malley.

It couldn't be a coincidence that the house was being attacked now. It had to be for them. So how did anyone know they were here? If Digital really could communicate with Dublin, had he been communicating with someone else? Or, had Malley or Fionnuala betrayed him to the men who now stormed the house?

She surely wouldn't. They had grown too close over the six years of their partnership. As for Fionnuala... he killed the thought as it formed and then cursed himself for doing so. Weakness. Weakness he thought he'd seen in Malley, now eating at him.

They moved through the house as adroitly as they could. In the lobby, Broderick noted the collapsed skull of one of Digital's men, the remnants of grey matter on the edge of a side table, the signs of Malley's silent rage.

Grabbing their gear, they struck out again, no words between them, stepping from shadow to shadow. Malley led them on a circuitous route, avoiding rooms where men might be waiting and hiding. The loud hammering of the alarm was a tricky thing, hiding some noises, the silence in the beats between amplifying others.

At the back door of the house Malley stopped in a small laundry room. A service part of the old manor. There was no hint of the indecisiveness that had crept into her. No sign of the weakness she'd shown lately, the hesitation that made him suspicious. She was every inch the agent he'd worked with for more than six years. Hard and determined.

'Stay close,' she told them in a voice she only dared to make as loud as she had to. 'We make for the back outhouses. From there, we figure a way out.'

'Why?' Fionnuala asked, though he understood her only from context, her words drowned out by the noise.

'We don't know how many they are or how well armed. Let them fight it out. If someone tries to stop us...'

Malley jerked open the door and moved out into the storm. She didn't need to finish that thought.

Heavy rain and some hail peppered them as they crossed the wide-open yard, the errant wind pushing them this way and that as it rampaged across the hillside. The alarms blared and floodlights illuminated the elements as they poured down to slicken the cobbles in the middle of the outhouses. In the centre of the yard, by an upturned sundial, three men grappled with one another on the ground. Even in the bright false light, it was impossible to make them out as more than shapes.

Broderick could have despatched all three and they'd have hardly noticed, but the distant shouts and noises of combat between the loud blaring were being carried on the wind, deceptive as it changed direction, suggesting there were possible attackers first here then there.

Malley dashed across the courtyard purposefully, throwing her shoulder against the door of one of the outbuildings and barrelling into the room. Fionnuala sprinted after her, but her legs went from under her as she slipped halfway across.

Broderick barely had to break his stride to scoop her up with his free hand, his knife still grasped in the other. She allowed herself to be hauled up and clung to him as the two of them followed after Malley.

Inside the outbuilding, a former stable Broderick reckoned, there were cots spread out haphazardly among the signs of a people's living quarters. Hydroflasks and little wireless chargers, battery recharging packs, and even a television. It was more comfort than most settlements had, even if they were all crammed in together.

The soldier in Broderick recognised it for what it was: a garrison room. The place where those not on duty in the house would have slept and spent their time. A smattering of small children's toys suggested that it was a family room too.

Their loyalty to Digital purchased in the form of shelter for mothers and fathers in desperate need.

That protection was gone now. Broderick had stuck a knife in it.

Of the children there was no sign.

He clenched his jaw at the thought of them.

His code. And his list. They were the only things he had.

The code protected children. Those who couldn't possibly be held accountable for the world they lived in. These ones had been born long after the first Storm Season. This ruin of a world was the only thing they knew.

He'd killed their shelter.

The fortress would become a warzone now. High up on its hill with its own power and water, the place was ideal for wintering, and the squabbles over this patch would likely take place year on year from now until it was inevitably burned to the ground or gutted from within.

Broderick didn't spare Digital a thought, any more than he spared for the ten clansmen he'd killed on the way to delivering justice. Work was work. There'd be time to burn the traitor's name into his soul later.

Inside the room the sound was less oppressive, though the wind still rattled something nearby. The three of them stood, already soaked from their brief dash across the yard.

'What do we do now?' Fionnuala asked in obvious fright.

She still clutched at Broderick's arm.

Her grip was disturbingly welcome, her touch felt like something he didn't know he'd missed.

Surely, she hadn't betrayed him...

The way she had looked at him in Bloom, it hinted at something. It was a thought that he knew would lead him further down the road to weakness.

He disentangled her arm from his and stepped clear.

Malley was watching them.

He stared back at her, trying to emulate that cold measuring look she gave that stripped people of their bravery. Looking for the weakness in her that he fought in himself.

The hesitation in Black Stair, allowing Fionnuala to come with them, letting the young woman get under her skin.

How far had it gone? Far enough to betray him?

'We can talk about it later,' she told him, reading his mind in that way she did.

'Who are they?' he asked her.

'I suspect BlueArms.'

'Why do you suspect that?'

'Because we're investigating their leader.'

'The investigation is complete,' he corrected her. 'We're not investigating, we're judging.'

'All the more reason for them to come after us.'

'But how would they know?'

'Digital knew.'

'So, you're saying that Digital ratted on us?'

'I don't know who ratted on us, all I'm saying is that it's not a secret.'

That they spoke the words was a sign of the gulf between them now. Her secrets from him. His from her.

It held there in the air between them.

She wasn't wrong though. Maybe she hadn't betrayed him. Or maybe he wanted to believe that because he too was becoming weak, letting her off the hook, again, because he craved the certainty that she brought to him. The dependability. The righteousness.

'We can talk about it later,' he agreed eventually. As much to himself as to her.

'So, what now?' Fionnuala asked.

'We need a way out,' Malley answered her.

'We could fight?' he replied.

The thought of running away was not something he was comfortable with.

'Two versus how many?' Malley asked icily.

'Amateurs,' he scoffed.

And they were. They had no military training. They bumbled about with their makeshift weapons and shat themselves when they faced the real thing.

He'd seen it.

He'd faced down a charge on O'Connell Bridge during a food riot when the agents had been interspersed with the Gardai to provide some backbone.

Outnumbered heavily, the line had held and the howling desperation of those who had charged them turned to screams of pain and frustration as they broke and ran back toward the

Spire and the shelter of their makeshift accommodation in the hotels and refugee camps.

He'd seen them running in Athenry too, when the BlueArms had first tried to seize a Data Centre. That hadn't been a military operation but a slaughter. His first mission.

A handful of clansmen, BlueArms or not, were easy meat to him.

'It doesn't matter if they're amateurs,' Malley told him testily. 'Numbers count. And there's only two of us.'

He looked at Fionnuala for a long moment. Dead weight to them. Something that would hinder them in every way. But he didn't want to leave her behind. That was the cold truth of it. He didn't want to.

'So, we run?' he asked bitterly.

'We run. For now.'

Her tone was hard and cold, as it should be, but Broderick detected something in it that others would certainly have missed. A note of concern. For the woman.

'How far to the fence?' he asked her.

'Ten metres maybe? It might still be electrified.'

'Someone breached it.'

She nodded at him.

Understanding in things unsaid partially restored. He said, 'someone breached it' and she understood; find the fence and follow it all the way around until you find the breach and exit.

'But we don't know where,' Fionnuala protested.

He looked at Malley again, and she looked at him.

A moment. Fionnuala didn't understand them. But they understood each other. It was enough. For now.

Her head twitched. An invite to get started.

With the alarms still blaring over the howling wind and heavy rain, they made their way back into the floodlit courtyard, back out to Joseph. Two bodies lay on the ground. The losers of the scuffle. Impossible to say whether the victors had been the men of the house or the likely BlueArms who had stormed it.

Malley took point again, peeling out around the makeshift barracks and clearing a low stone wall behind it into a sodden pasture behind.

Fionnuala followed, stumbling a little on the wall, looking about her as she landed in a mixture of fright and anger.

The knife didn't suit her, but the look in her eyes was determined. There was steel there alright.

As Broderick closed on the wall, his head swivelling for signs of danger, he caught sight of another outhouse. A smaller one. Likely where the animals were kept.

The door slightly ajar let a long sliver of light into the building where small eyes watched him in near terror. The children. A handful of them, waiting for their parents to come back to them.

Broderick hoped that they weren't waiting for the bodies in the courtyard.

Then he kicked himself internally for letting the thought creep into his head.

Mentally, he added these men to his own personal list. More responsibility to go around, and if fate allowed it, he'd see them on the end of his knife too.

He cleared the wall without a backward glance, pushing the children from his mind.

Malley led them along the wall, gliding across the sodden earth.

Her surefootedness, and Broderick's, were a product of their training. Drills and exercises in the ruined streets of towns cluttered with rubble or in woodland and forest. They ran day and night in every manner of weather. Speed was everything for an agent.

Then there were their years of experience. They hunted deniers in bogs and valleys, on mountains and in towns. They knew broken and uneven ground instinctively, their feet following that instinct and allowing them to move at speed that even few other agents could countenance.

Not so for Fionnuala.

Despite her upbringing on the side of Black Stair and her forays into the wood, she was clumsy. They learned caution in the settlements as a matter of necessity. All the hospitals were in towns. Doctors worked rough and ready on the edge of civilisation. Caution was king.

She stumbled and yelped as she tripped, the wind thankfully whipping away the noise of it.

'Watch her feet,' he barked at Fionnuala.

She threw a glance back at him, and he was pleased to see the spark of anger still in it. But she did turn back and as she watched Malley, pacing her run to keep Fionnuala close, her footing seemed to improve.

They moved like that around the hill that sat outside the drowned town of Athlone, moving low and quick against the wind and rain underneath the floodlights where the shadows were strongest.

Sounds still seemed to drift to them from a distance, sounds of crashing and calling, though how much of that was imagined in the breaks between the blaring alarms or tricks of the wind couldn't be said.

Eventually, she stopped them with a hand.

In the middle distance, in a dip on the side of the hill, the breach.

The method of entry had been brutally direct.

Covered by the sound of storms, the BlueArms had driven a tractor into the fence.

It had been so long since he'd seen a fully functional tractor that it came as a shock to him.

The vehicle had been heavily modified, with someone attaching the digger part of a dumper truck, signs of the old skills of mechanics and builders being utilised by the old hands of a people who would never leave their homes no matter how grim the times.

In the lowlands, necessity was the mother of both invention and carnage.

Around the tractor, a small group of men and women

huddled. Five of them. They brandished long cudgels wrapped in wire or spiked with nails. One had an old hurley, a rusted scythe attached to the top of it.

Despite the ferocity of the weaponry and the availability of apparent support vehicles, they were still amateurs, shouting at each other over the wind and the alarms, moving in agitation, eager to be anywhere but here where the lights and the sounds would draw danger to them.

Malley looked back at him and jerked her head slightly, ordering him up front with her. She offered Fionnuala a flat stare of admonishment that warned her not to follow. He adjusted the strap of his satchel. She nodded. The packs would stay on. Cumbersome but at least they offered a measure of armoured protection. That was the strength of the agents. Nothing wasted. She slipped her knife back into its sheath and cocked an eyebrow at him. Broderick understood her and reached for his baton. The extendable implement was about a foot long until released, when it extended just over two feet. It lacked the weight or the edges of the BlueArms' weapons, but it could parry and crush a skull if wielded right.

There was no fuss.

No moment of preparation.

That was the way with her. She was always prepared for violence. It was something he had admired in her for such a long time.

They charged then. In that charge, he could feel his control slipping away, a ferocity he surrendered to. Joseph's screams mixed with his own, the crackling electricity of the night sky infecting him, filling him up with a fury bordering on berserk. He screamed his wordless scream, an animal noise as he thundered down the hill at them, Joseph spurring him on.

Halfway to the BlueArms, the alarms stopped.

Though the wind never abated, the noise of it not insignificant, the quiet in the absence of the alarms was felt almost as relief and for a split second the misfortunes, who manned the breach in the fence seemed to sigh, before Broderick's roar reached them and two furies rushed out of the night.

Broderick got there first, moving to the right, letting Malley take the left, to split their forces. The blood pounded in his ears as he casually swatted away a broad stroke from the scythe/hurley. He followed through with his elbow, catching the person on the mouth and the point of their chin. He felt the teeth and bone break underneath his arm as he propelled himself past the falling BlueArm. His follow through caught a terrified-looking woman clean across her crown, the skull yielding underneath the blow and flattening her.

He felt the person behind him, rather than seeing them, and he rolled, the spiked cudgel that was once the leg of a chair passing through the air where he had been a moment before. As he rolled, with one hand he pulled his knife free and spinning to his feet, he tossed it, underarm, the blade striking the man's cheek but not punching through the bone. It didn't matter. The man screamed and threw up a hand to his face and Broderick's wide swing with his baton smashed through the meagre defence.

Malley moved at the other side, bodies falling away from her as she laid about her, seeming to flicker in and out of his vision as she twisted and turned in the rain.

The first of the BlueArms, teeth and mouth ruined, was picking themselves up as Broderick drove a knee into their head. A woman as well. Not that the distinction mattered to him.

All old enough to be guilty, or at least guilty of interfering with an agent of the law if they weren't.

They deserved what they got.

He spun to find his next target and came face to face with a man, shorter than him, but burly. The man had closed on him unexpectedly. Where had he come from? He had a split second only to look at the face of the amateur who had gotten the drop on him as he waited to feel the inevitable blow.

In the moment they were face to face, Broderick saw the

man's triumph turn into something else. Astonishment first, then pain, then fear.

He stiffened up, sucking in a strangled last breath. Then he pitched forward, and Broderick had to sidestep the falling corpse.

Fionnuala stood behind, her face painted in shock and horror. She looked at the corpse as it hit the ground, his long knife sticking out of its back.

She'd seen him. Wherever he'd come from. And she'd killed him.

The plaintive cry she let out was a pitiful thing as she dropped the knife onto the ground.

'We don't have time for that,' Malley told her, stooping to pick it up and pressing it back into her hand.

In the absence of the alarms, through the wind, the sound of men calling out to one another could be heard. There were a lot of voices. No doubt they'd be on them soon.

Fionnuala still stood in shock, the cry still on her lips.

'We have to go,' Malley told the stricken woman.

For a second, Broderick thought she looked satisfied.

He looked at Fionnuala, willing her to be stronger, to be strong enough.

'We have to go now,' he agreed with her.

# CHAPTER TEN

Kelly moved through the storm winds as they raced up O'Connell Street in Limerick. The old Georgian buildings funnelled that wind and created whistles and screams that might make a person believe in banshees. Joseph walked the streets of Limerick, just as all his siblings had done for over a decade, each stretching out a hand to graffiti the city in a different way. Each one scrawling their signature into the very land itself. He tried not to think about when it wasn't so.

The first storm of Joseph's winter reign was mild compared to what would come in the months ahead. He could cling to his memories then. If his plan worked.

He looked about at the people as he moved, more and more pouring into the city in the last few weeks. Their faces bleak. Every year the storms were worse, the faces bleaker. Quietly, privately, he prayed for a tipping point. A zenith for the storms, after which the earth would begin to heal itself. Declining global population and cleaner air surely meant that better days were coming for them all?

Not without a change in politics though. Government still operated like they had Before: small-time, reactionary. Desperately lacking in courage or imagination. The result was a power grab. A totalitarian control, as if they owned what the people had earned, as if all the collective effort was theirs to control, and the collective suffering was for each individual to bear alone. The people of the new world had outgrown this old way of thinking – so the Government rammed it down their throats. Gardai with heavy hands. And agents, they were something else altogether. Something much worse.

The scientific community argued the toss on the 'tipping point'. Some claimed that they had gone too far, setting in motion changes that would get exponentially worse until a new age dawned, while others claimed brightly that next year everything would be fine.

He winced internally at the disparity. There had been almost complete consensus on climate change before the first Storm Season, but the tiny minority of voices had somehow been louder than the majority, and humanity had been allowed to continue destroying itself.

There was no way of knowing what the consensus was now. Ireland was a rogue nation, illegally seizing gas fields that previous Governments had sold, deploying Gardai and agents to brutalise their people, the 'No Movement' orders that kept the population broken up, and their totalitarian grip on the internet and the means of information.

That's how the power grab worked. Keep people in ignorance. Separate the settlements from the cities, divide up the resources, let the people fight over those scraps.

And then scare them.

Stories about people's blood boiling in their veins by the equator, and the hordes of refugees moving like vast seas of people, seeking colder climes, seeking something more than endless misery; these must surely be exaggerations. He discounted entirely the rumour that the whole west coast of America was on fire. There was no way to know if France had really divided itself into city states with each one squabbling over resources, or if that was more Government propaganda designed to instil fear. So little remained of the internet he had grown up with. He hoped such stories were nonsense. But then he never would have believed that Ireland could fall so far so fast either, so who was to say?

But he could fix it... if the plan worked.

The city council followed after him. The elected representatives of the locals had begun to defer to him, accepting his leadership. His national position as leader of a revolution seemed to have garnered that for him. The enemy of their enemy looked like their friend.

He knew that position was precarious though. Both Cork and Limerick, the two largest hubs outside of Government control, were slow to accept outsiders. After all, outsiders had left them to fend for themselves. And they weren't doing too badly without them.

Everywhere else in the country, he was celebrated as a hero. Standing up to the Government. Leading the revolution. The defiance he and Gibson had offered was seen as inspirational. Here though...

Well, here was different.

He glanced back at them as he walked to the chambers they used for public gatherings. It had been an Augustinian Church once. Now it doubled as a hospital and a public gallery. Inside the building, the quiet splendour of the church still had a type of power, the buttressed columns stretching up to the vaulted ceilings added a sense of reverence to the place that was in stark contrast to the hardy, pragmatic people it housed.

It still, somehow, felt like a church.

A feeling he didn't know he missed until he felt it again.

There were too many things like that. Half-remembered sensations, memories that felt alien now because they weren't tainted with a veneer of panic or desperation. Emotions that felt like they should have belonged to someone else, such was the all-encompassing feeling of dread that came from successive Storm Seasons.

He tried to shake that dread off daily, tried to point his brain in the direction of hope and optimism, but he feared he was too coloured by Before to be able. Hope was a young person's game.

The council gathered around the computer monitor. To call them a hard bunch was an understatement.

Each one balanced their role as community leaders with the communal duties assigned to them. Some planted. Some built. Some taught. Some destroyed. Some killed. They accepted these tasks as a part of living now.

Carney and Cummins were his biggest problems. The eldest of the group, with the tinge of red still showing in his massive beard, Carney was almost enigmatic. A stoic, quiet man, it was hard to believe the iron, unbending will he possessed. Cummins was different. Softer seeming and yet her eyes told a story all of their own. Hard as agates. The pupils seemed blacker than anything he'd ever seen. Hilda Cummins was impetuous and fiery, her temper legendary, and her passion somehow contagious to the people around her. The two of them commanded everyone else without ever issuing orders.

Word was coming back from Athlone. The One-Eyed Rook had made his play for the agents.

'They've escaped,' Rook told them the moment his face flashed onto the screen.

There was a fury there in that one eye. As well as scrapes on his skin and fresh bloodstains on his clothes.

Kelly tried not to let his agitation show. The Rook was supposed to be the best. That they had escaped him was worrying.

'We've secured the compound. The local bodyguard are scattered. But the agents are gone.'

'And Gibson?'

He shook his head.

He hoped his friend was alright. He hoped for both of their sakes that he was still alive.

Their old colleague Dr Comber was waiting for him at the end of a long road, and if Kelly had guessed right, she held in her aging hands their entire plan.

'What about the girl?' he asked.

It had been a shock to him that such a small thing as

Fionnuala Regan would turn out to be a secret ace up his sleeve. He remembered her as a fiery child, with a mouth that got her in trouble, always taking an extra step where she knew she shouldn't go.

'Gone as well. Though it seems she's not being held against her will.'

'So, she's with them?' Carney asked angrily.

'No,' Kelly corrected him, 'she's just ingratiated herself with them. We can count on her when the time is right.'

He knew this to be true. Her loyalty and her affection were things he considered inviolable.

They were so close.

To save the country. To save his people. It was so close he could almost taste it.

If things went the way he thought they were going to go, this would be the last winter Ireland would have to go alone. A future awaited them.

Until these agents popped up.

By all accounts, the very worst two that could have been picked.

And one of them the sister of one of Limerick's council. She made no secret of it, though apparently they were as far from each other as sisters could be.

He looked at Hilda. So calm now, but just under the surface… impossible to say where her loyalty lay. She was an outsider too, yet they had adopted her.

'What do we do now?' he asked.

He knew what he wanted to do but telling Carney had yielded fewer results than allowing Carney to tell you.

'I'm going after them,' Rook interjected, his anger palpable even through the screen. 'They've left a trail of bodies. At least six of my own. I owe them.'

'Both of them?' Cummins asked.

This was where her loyalty divided. She was worried for her sister.

'I've sent a harrying team after them, I'm going to take

the M6 as far as Poll Boy, if I can get in front of them and cut them off...'

'Is O'Mahony okay?' Carney asked.

'Yes,' Rook replied, 'we're fine.'

His nod included O'Mahony in that 'we'.

'You can keep the girl alive, right?' Kelly asked.

He didn't want any harm coming to Fionnuala Regan. She'd been through enough. She was an innocent thing really.

'What if they get across The River Suck before you?' Cummins asked.

'You hoping they will?' The Rook asked, and the anger bled into his voice.

'I serve the cause,' she snapped at him, her anger matching his.

'If she gets in my way, I'll kill her,' Rook retorted.

'Enough,' Kelly barked at them. 'We're a team, we serve the same ends, and we are not each other's enemies.'

The last thing he needed was for them to fall apart.

A chilly silence settled on them, made all the more ominous by the howling wind outside that whistled under the door of the great vaulted chamber and swirled about their feet.

'If they get across before you, then you catch them in Galway,' Cummins told the computer screen. 'Gibson is the priority, whatever those Doejays are after is secondary, and you can kill anyone who gets in the way.'

Her face rippled at that. Anger presumably. For her sister who she may have condemned to die.

The One-Eyed Rook returned her furious glare for a moment, his face mottled as though he could hardly contain the anger. If he got them, her sister was dead, no question.

Kelly nodded and tried to look resigned. They had to die.

He just hoped it happened long before they had the chance to ruin everything.

*\*\**

They ran through the storm with trees overhead swaying excitedly, like spectators watching the hunt. In front of Fionnuala, Malley moved, her knife out, running low across the rough underbrush and foliage. Her head constantly scanning through the thin woods.

Behind, Broderick barked at her to keep moving through the night, urging her on.

The wind and the rain and the knowledge they were being pursued had somehow combined to push the man's death from her head as they sprinted through the pitch black of night.

She had watched Malley's feet, like Broderick had insisted before and let her instinct guide her across the sodden, slippery terrain.

A shout behind, so close that the BlueArms must have been right on top of them, caused her to turn as she ran, stumbling as she did. Broderick hit the ground and rolled, coming up suddenly just as the BlueArm burst into sight.

The agent stuck a knife in the man.

'Up,' he barked at Fionnuala, dragging her to her feet and shoving her forward.

They ran until she could feel the exhaustion threatening to overwhelm her, but Broderick was relentless, pushing her forward when she slowed. If not for him, she could simply drop to the ground and let them catch her. She knew the signals she'd need to let them know she was one of them. She'd be safe.

Ironically, the agent thought he was saving her life by driving her before him. The look in his eyes was determination tinged with what she thought might be concern. For her safety.

The tree line ended at the foot of a small hill and then they were moving across farmland, rolling grass fields that were already showing signs of flooding, the turf soft beneath them, the water tripping and tricking her.

Out from underneath the canopy of the trees, the storm welcomed them with hail and wind that pushed her in a sort of vicious joy.

The shouts pursued them in the darkness.

One BlueArm calling to another, tracking them. The sounds were distorted in the wind and they sounded like barks, hounds on their trail, sometimes far away, other times so close she felt like if she looked behind, she'd see them over her shoulder, with their spiked weapons and their face masks and makeshift armour.

They ran and ran, fear pushing her forward. Shouts from behind urging her on.

She didn't even notice the noises dwindling as the pursuers gave up. She didn't have the energy to notice. She ran and clutched the knife that had killed a man and ran some more.

It was nearly dawn when she collapsed, her legs giving out as they crossed a dip in the land between two small hills.

Sobbing slightly, she tried to scramble back to her feet when her legs went but ended up face down in the muddy grass. As she looked up, she noticed the light creeping across the sky. The dawn breaking. And with the light, an end to Joseph's first march through the country.

They stood above her then, for a moment, looking at one another.

Their faces grim but she noticed in them that silent communication that was their way.

Reading each other. Saying everything they needed to with their eyes.

Fionnuala sucked in deep breaths and pushed herself back to her feet, the blood that had been on them washed clean by the rain only to be caked in mud.

On her feet, she still panted as they stood still and looked at one another.

Eventually, Malley nodded.

'Let's go,' Broderick told her, almost softly.

And so they did.

\*\*\*

They moved as fast as Malley dared to push them. As fast, she figured, as Fionnuala's body could take. The younger woman was not strong. She weathered winters indoors, like everyone else. Hunkering down, breaking out in the gaps between storms to get food or Share. A bizarre type of hibernation that Malley had gotten used to when the waves of the coronavirus swept the world in the early 20s.

It toughened them in some ways, certainly mentally. That day-after-day sheltering in place required a type of resilience.

It weakened them in other ways. Leaving them somehow unprepared for when life kept coming and coming. There were times when it was just one thing after another, and the toughness required to keep on keeping on was something Malley felt was lacking in the generation that didn't know how much they'd lost.

She could feel the presence of the younger woman behind her, pushing herself. She willed the smaller woman on. It was a familiar feeling recalled from the first Storm Season, lying on her back, a knife blade in her hands, willing Hilda to run.

She had kept on willing for her little sister. To be stronger. Even as she took her self-defence classes. She got tougher as the flesh clumsily knitted itself back together, leaving the mess of scars that marched up and down her hands. Her sister had not changed, not meaningfully anyway. She went from organising the shelter to organising many shelters. She found new causes and lent her energy and stubbornness and her sharp, pointed temper to them. And somehow, she always found someone to stand up to. She never confronted. She just stood up, shoulders back, chin out as she called them down.

Malley had wanted her to lash out, to show her strength, to take the rage she knew must be inside her and point it at the bad people, but instead her sister had remained sweet and smiling one minute, a defiant statue the next.

In fact, the only time she'd ever really shown her internal fury was the day that Malley had joined the Department of Environmental Justice.

Hilda, she surmised, even as she moved, would like Fionnuala.

She could feel Broderick too, further back. Her thoughts about him were something else – stained. She felt him as an itch between her shoulders. Was her name on the list he'd been given? Too fast they'd unravelled, and it hurt her.

The shifting, changing feelings that had made her hesitate in Black Stair, the same feelings that had spared an old man's life when he was caught harvesting the grid were alien things she hadn't yet figured out. A tangled mess of emotions and motivations that drove her brain in directions she didn't want to go. For reasons she couldn't yet fathom.

Her feelings about Broderick were clearer to her.

It was grief. Or something like it.

She was losing him.

For six years, he'd been a constant. His grunts and his towering fury were things she understood and counted on. They pursued justice together. They didn't have to talk about the things they'd lost from Before. They never mentioned the parts of themselves they'd sacrificed to become what they were now. It was enough that they both understood that sacrifice and loss were common to them both.

Now they stood at odds, and she knew it was her own fault.

She could have just killed Fionnuala the moment she'd found out her secret. If she'd done so, her bond with him would have been untarnished.

But she hadn't done that. Instead, she'd let Fionnuala Regan into her head.

She very much wanted to blame the panting, labouring woman who tracked behind her, but Malley knew that was unfair. She had not only let her live, she had somehow adopted her. She had let the young woman's ridiculous idealism charm her to the point that she couldn't let this world chew up and spit her out. She didn't want the world to force another sacrifice from a young woman.

Even if it alienated her partner of six years.

Now Broderick lurked behind her and the back he had covered for so long, her back, felt exposed to him. There had to be a way to mend their bridges and save the woman, if she could think her way through it.

Still for all that, they moved swiftly, following the old roads, long since reclaimed by grass, that meandered through the countryside.

There was no sign of their pursuers. She worried about that lack of noise. Were they in front already? Were they close behind?

She dared not let Broderick drop back, since it would leave her too vulnerable up front with Fionnuala to protect.

Gibson roamed somewhere ahead. BlueArms hunted somewhere behind.

From time to time as they moved, the M6 came into view. At parts where it rose above them, it could be seen between small folds in the land. Too far away to make out if there were people on it.

She picked up the pace whenever it came into view, the feeling of being watched, eyes on her, of being hunted, it was almost overpowering. Scanning the hard line of the barricades, she looked for a glint on glass or weaponry that would give away their pursuers.

Motorways were dangerous. The fastest form of travel, but difficult to get off in a hurry, often covered in traps. Gardai used to patrol them before the government had surrendered the west. Now they were a no man's land.

They'd eventually have to use it if they were to stand any chance of catching up to Gibson.

She moved them as quickly as they could through sodden ground with a stiff winter wind kicking up now and then to remind them that Joseph was never far. Her eyes scanning for threats, always drifting back to the motorway that loomed to the east of them.

She also glanced back every now and then to urge Fionnuala forward and always met a stubborn glare. She might lack the fitness and conditioning of an agent, but she didn't lack for mettle.

They pushed southward, bending west just a little, heading for Ballinasloe.

It had been a lovely town once. She'd taken a barge up the Shannon many years ago. A family holiday. Her and Hilda and their parents.

The river had taken most of the town now, and makeshift bridges connected properties that still housed people above the waterline.

She'd Pronounced a woman there with Broderick some four years before. It had been after Storm Season then. The loss of loved ones to the winter was still felt by those who had begun emerging from their homes as the storms abated. No one had objected when she'd found the woman.

She hadn't run either.

She had stood on a walkway raised above the river, driven into a tumult by storm runoff and flooding upstream, and she'd looked Malley in the eye as Malley rammed the knife home.

Thusly was she judged.

Malley couldn't remember her name. She was grateful to have remembered the crossing though.

The problem with crossing was geography. Inconstant, ever-changing geography.

The most commonly used crossing point was the Poll Boy ferry. The motorway dipped to the south of the town and The Suck had claimed it. Now that patch of ground was a ferry operated by a local clan. Dangerous at the best of times. Beyond dangerous this close to Storm Season.

If Gibson had aimed for the Poll Boy ferry, he might well be dead, though perhaps his BlueArmband would afford him some measure of protection. For agents of the Government, there would be little quarter given.

Yet she figured that's exactly where the BlueArms would move to cut her off. At least, she hoped it was. If they were heading there, then they were unlikely to be waiting at the far side of the river when they crossed.

The Docker's ferry point was north of the town but required them moving through parts of Ballinasloe that were likely thick with traps, clanspeople, and possible BlueArm ambushes.

As their course twisted them west, away from the M6 and toward the town, she hoped he was still there. She hoped there was nothing else waiting for them.

# CHAPTER ELEVEN

It had been so long since he'd needed words. Now he felt their absence keenly. There was ambiguity between them all now. Terrible, dangerous ambiguity.

There might have been a good reason why Malley wanted to save Digital, enough reason that she'd put herself into conflict with him. Though she had, when it counted, not bothered to challenge him but instead moved to protect Fionnuala.

There might have been a bad reason too. A terrible reason that implicated her as a traitor.

The young woman had gotten into his partner's head. Of that there could be no doubt. She had gotten into his head too. Somehow.

Every look she threw at him as they moved was a mystery to him. Somehow a challenge to him, but with a hint of something else too. And she had leaned on his arm in the barracks back at Digital's. That moment he had felt something, something inside himself. Something he abhorred. Weakness.

What if it was an act, to soften him up, because she had betrayed both of them to the BlueArms who now pursued them?

To save their precious Gibson or Kelly.

The ambiguity. The words left unsaid that meant he couldn't know for sure.

One of them might have betrayed him. It caused his

headache at the base of his skull to flare up and he worked to supress it.

The list he had been given by O'Neill was significantly less important to him than the other list. His personal list. Malley's name had been on that list once. He had removed it. The only name to be taken off the list. Now he feared he was going to have to put it back on there.

Words not said. A dull aching throb in his brain.

He watched her change direction in front of him, angling them toward the northeast of the town. He knew his way in and out of most towns, but the geography changed. Rivers rose and fell and mudslides, earthworks, defences, and perimeters annually shifting made a mockery of maps.

He watched Fionnuala change direction after Malley. She was a quick study. She stumbled less now, found sure footing easier to come by, and her head had started to swivel too, watching around them for threats. It had only been a matter of days and yet she was changing. He could make a decent agent out of her in two years. As long as she was willing to sacrifice.

He threw one look over his shoulder as they moved and caught sight of a glint. The first giveaway. The land stretched out behind him, little hills rising here and there to obscure, but on a raised plateau, the M6 was visible between the hillocks. One of many long, dark snakes that stretched across the country, once carrying the infectious cars that were part of their shared doom. Now desolate looking husks.

The glint was a reflection of light on something at the crest of the old motorway. He pulled his telescope as he tracked the straight line from himself to the spot where the glint had been.

The old machines were the most reliable. The tablets and the internet and all the technology in the world was dependent on batteries and satellites and cables and inconstant governments, but the humble telescope, limited as it was...

He counted twenty. There were more than that, though not by much, but he didn't need to know how many more. That there were twenty was enough. He had been right. They'd sent the bulk down the M6 to catch up to them.

And now they'd spotted them.

The BlueArms were coming. His hand itched for his knife.

He caught up to Malley quick enough, not bothering to try to stifle the rage that he knew must be showing in his eyes, feeling the throbbing in his brain intensifying.

'They're behind us,' he told her when she had slowed to stop at an old gate that led into what was once an industrial estate.

Had her hand flickered toward her knife before she stopped it? Or was he paranoid.

'You were right then,' she told him.

She didn't bother asking how many. She knew he'd have stopped counting at enough.

'What do we do?' Fionnuala asked.

Her voice was steady. She really was learning from them.

'How long?' Malley asked him.

'Minutes.'

'On foot?'

'Yes.'

Clear these words they shared. Clear and unambiguous. He wished they had more of them.

'Then nothing changes. We make for the crossing.'

Broderick looked at her for a long moment, and she understood him, understood everything he asked.

*What if there's no boat?*

'Then we'll head north along the bank and see if we can find another crossing,' she answered his unspoken question.

He really hoped she hadn't betrayed him. He didn't want to put her back on his list. Who could possibly understand him better?

'How long will it take us to get there?' Fionnuala asked.

'We'll need to move through as quickly as we can, but we have to be careful. There's no telling what's waiting for us, but if we move quick enough, we'll stay ahead of them. When we're on the far side we leave the ferrymen there. That forces them to go back down to Poll Boy and cross there. We should be far enough in front to stay ahead.'

The soft calmness in her voice was for Fionnuala. He knew that. The softness was soothing and also awful to hear. Too soft. Too soothing. Too weak.

The words themselves were for him. He knew that too. A plan shared. She was recognising the need for them to close the gap.

He really didn't want to have to kill her.

'Ready?' she asked them.

They both nodded.


They crossed the broken fencing that was the edge of the industrial estate and made their way into the compound. The grass bank they were on descended to a flat space that once must have been a car park. The flooding here covered the area so that the only way of knowing how deep the water lay was by reference to the doors of nearby abandoned buildings. At least, he hoped they were abandoned.

He recognised the shell he was looking at. A data centre, once upon a time. He'd fought here, still in his army uniform, not yet an agent. It had been worse than brutal, it was a massacre. He'd followed orders. He used to wonder if the orders had been different, would he have fought with them instead of against them? But he'd long since given up idling over such stupidity. Things were what they were. All the easier to read in black and white.

They crossed the flat area shin-deep in water, their movements sending ripples and splashes that would give them away. The only sound was the splashes, and somewhere not too distant the rushing sound of The Suck in full flow.

Malley steered them toward the building, but not so close that they'd be hemmed in by it if there was an ambush waiting nearby. Her knife was held in a ruined hand. Broderick slipped one of his free from its sheath. Fionnuala looked nervous, her nostrils flaring as she drew in heavy breaths.

The complex itself was several large hangar-like buildings. Industry had been here. Jobs and comfort. Workers had brought their non-recyclable coffee cups to their shifts and worked machines powered by fossil fuel electricity and parked their diesel engine SUVs and cars.

The whole place, to Broderick, was a monument to failure. Fionnuala's wide-eyed gaze, while still fearful, was almost wondrous too. Likely she'd never seen buildings like these before. Even if she'd been to Dublin, context was everything and those raised in the settlements could hardly have expected to see this in the lowlands.

The buildings themselves were ruined now. What few windows they sported were grimy or broken and showed only evidence of hollow things long since given up, the machinery cannibalised by whatever group had taken it for their own needs over the years.

'Storms didn't do this,' she breathed as they waded past another empty shell.

'People,' Broderick grunted in disgust.

'Why though?' she asked, still disbelieving.

'The storms didn't destroy us,' Malley told her, her head still moving this way and that, watching everything.

There was a hardness in her voice again. A hardness Broderick felt like clinging to. That hardness was their bond. Shared hardness. Shared sacrifice.

'Then what?' Fionnuala asked.

'Like Broderick said, the people did it,' she told her.

Fionnuala looked like she might cry at the words.

'I don't understand…' she whispered.

Their words, though softly spoken, seemed to travel across the water and bounce off the buildings, the stillness of the day amplifying them.

'The storms destroyed the west coast first and fucked up the rest of the country but the worst thing they ever did was stop the boats and the planes from bringing in food and medicine and batteries. We were left to ourselves, for months at a time. When we were left to ourselves, we turned on each other. Everyone decided what they needed, and they took it from whoever had it.'

'Why did the Government allow it?'

'Allow it? They couldn't stop it. The electricity grid was smashed by the first Storm Season. Food riots started after three weeks. Nobody knew where to turn. The breaks in between storms weren't long enough to get the grid repaired so it was three months before power was restored. By then the damage was done. We'd turned on each other. People fled their homes on the west coast. They made for the cities. Not enough to go around.'

'Why didn't they go back to their homes?'

'Not enough money to rebuild them all. The insurance industry collapsed and what was broken couldn't be unbroken. When the BlueArms tried to take back the gas fields, the Europeans cut us off. Once we were on our own...'

Broderick watched the confusion play out on her face. He wanted to laugh at it. She didn't know what an 'insurance industry' even was.

'But there's power everywhere now? We can fix this.'

Her naivete was almost charming.

'Limerick and Cork have stolen their grids. Local government there controls them. Limerick from a hydro-electric station outside the city, and Cork from the windfarms off the south coast. That's clean power and the Government wants it back, but they don't want to give it. So now it's them versus us. And likely will be until there's a winner and a loser.'

And who could blame them? They'd been abandoned by their own people. Now that they had something worth having, those who abandoned them wanted to take it from them? He understood them. Even if they were the enemy.

'We can fix this,' Fionnuala insisted.

There was firmness to her. A resolve.

And something else too. Something more.

The way she said 'we'.

She didn't mean the three of them.

She didn't mean Government.

'We' was someone else.

Broderick's internal alarm bells started to ring.

We.

It felt like a gut punch. So badly he wanted her to not be his enemy.

That was his weakness.

She couldn't be. She couldn't have betrayed them. Surely.

Before he could voice his suspicions, a cry arose behind them. Spinning, he saw them coming, just two of them, rounding a corner at a building they had passed as they waded.

'Move,' Malley barked, no longer bothering with caution.

'There's only two,' Broderick barked.

'I said move,' she told him.

She was right. Two for now, but who knew how close the others were. He only hesitated a second before he snarled and splashed down through the thoroughfare behind Malley and Fionnuala.


Fionnuala panted as she pulled her legs through the water. Now really was her chance. Let herself fall behind, let them power away from her. She could fall into the hands of those who chased them and once 'caught', she could reveal who she was. There'd be safety for her.

They wouldn't let her. She knew they wouldn't. Instinctively, she knew that Broderick would put his life on the line for her rather than let her fall into their hands.

If she let them go, what would happen to Gibson? To Kelly? They'd be out in front of her and closer to their prey.

Those ruined buildings, drowned after successive years of flooding, had been a lesson to her. She couldn't allow this to continue. There was a future for her. For everyone. Even those who clung too tightly to the past.

Kelly and Gibson were that future. She couldn't let them die at Broderick's hand. She couldn't let Broderick do it, as much for himself as for everyone else. There was something inside him that she believed could be saved. He'd shown glimmers of it. The future was his too, if he could be made to see it. A future for them both, together.

The shouting behind urged her on, adrenaline pumping in her ears so that Malley's exhortations were almost drowned out by the sound.

A spray of blood shot out from a corner that Malley rounded, and for a terrible second, Fionnuala thought the woman was dead, only to round the corner and see Malley already moving away from the corpse face down in the water.

She kept pace with them as best she could, but noticed, even as they moved, that Broderick was checking his run, falling in with her. He had two knives out, his eyes hot.

He almost hovered at her elbow, as if he could extend his terrible violence, like a bubble, all the way around her to protect her.

At the far side of the industrial estate, the land rose in the front of them again, a small hill. The sound of the two men pursuing was joined with the calls of other people. They had spread out to cover the whole complex and now they were converging on the trio.

A sound came out of her mouth before she knew what it was. A sob of fear.

Broderick's head swivelled toward her.

'Keep moving,' he encouraged her, 'just keep moving.'

She knew the terror must be showing on her face.

At the bottom of the small hill, she started to climb, her legs burning. Malley was out in front, cresting the hill. A body rolled off the top of the hill and down past them. Her comrades learning the hardest lesson not to stand in Malley's way.

'You can do it,' Broderick shouted again.

She didn't dare look back as she crested the hill, she could hear the heavy panting of them gaining on her.

She plunged down the far side, relieved to see Malley standing on the deck of a type of boat. The boat itself stood next to a small make-shift dock, a thing of recycled bits and bobs from the buildings and old machinery. In spite of its appearance, there was a sense of durability about it. As though it had weathered storms. There was a man standing next to Malley on the boat. A sturdy thing, though older than she expected, somewhere in his fifties she assumed. His face was serene even with Malley's long knife pressed against his jugular.

'Away,' Broderick called, even as they closed the gap to the boat.

The man moved, Malley still hovering with knife in hand, and the boat began to detach from the dock, sluggishly at first. Fionnuala powered her legs into one final sprint and both herself and Broderick hit the dock at the same time, leaping into the boat, though it was less than a foot from land.

She landed hard, certain she'd felt something brush her as she jumped. Broderick rolled as he hit the deck coming up with both knives.

The thump of one of their pursuers landing on the boat was quickly followed by the sound of a low strangled scream and the splash of the corpse being thrown back into the water.

Fionnuala picked herself up and watched as the boat moved away from the dock, the corpse sinking below the eddies in the water. the BlueArms who had been pursuing them looked on in frustration as they realised how close they had come, and how far away they may as well have been. The distance between them was small enough to allow Broderick to look each of them in the face in turn, to show them how little he cared.

A one-eyed man, with long curling hair shot with silver, stared back at them. While all the other BlueArms howled and cursed them, the one-eyed man simply stood, seething.

The Suck was a powerful thing, fat on Joseph's bounty, moving fast. The boat turned in the water, spinning a little as they moved into where the current was strongest.

Behind them, the BlueArms continued to call at them, a string of curses that might as well have been a zephyr for all the reaction it got from Malley and Broderick.

She expected their captain to be looking straight at Malley or Broderick, both equally terrifying in very different ways, and was surprised to notice that the man was staring straight at her.

He was a swarthy type, with broad shoulders to match Broderick's, and enough height that the agent didn't tower over him, even if he was still taller. His shaven head was tanned giving the impression of someone who lived in the outdoors and his pronounced nose and chin somehow conspired to make him handsome for all their prominence.

His fingers flickered. So slight. Hardly noticeable.

She stilled her hands deliberately and tried not to let her face give away her shock.

A BlueArm signal.

'You going to drive the boat or stare at the pretty woman?' Malley asked softly. Suspiciously softly.

'Apologies,' the man mumbled calmly.

He moved to the back of the long boat, a sort of flat thing with a compartment for living or sheltering that seemed to be in the bowel of the vessel. You didn't have to know anything about boats to know that this one was not built for speed, but for weathering.

Malley followed close by, her face unreadable. Broderick had sheathed both his knives and he followed too, engaged in his usual practiced nonchalance, looking at everything else so hard that you'd have to know him to be aware of how closely he was actually watching the man.

His eyes were mostly on the shorelines. The one behind where the BlueArms had begun to pace downstream, following after them, and the opposite one, which looked clear.

Looked clear.

More and more Fionnuala was learning that how dangerous a thing was couldn't be measured by how it looked.

'I remember you,' the man told Malley. 'Couple of years ago you came through. You didn't have half a clan chasing you then. And you didn't put a knife against my neck.'

'I find the knife gets things done faster when I'm in a hurry.'

'I'm sure it does,' the man chuckled lightly.

Broderick grunted.

'Terrible close to Joseph to be venturing down country, isn't it?' the man asked.

'You're still here, aren't you?'

He smiled at that.

'I'm always here,' he agreed.

'Well, we're certainly glad to see you,' Malley told him, standing back a little, easing up.

'Docker,' he introduced himself to Fionnuala and Broderick. He was still smiling, still amiable, despite the presence of the long blade, no longer at his neck but still perilously close.

That was what gave him away. Even Fionnuala could spot it. Two agents on your boat. And some kind of runaway. A knife to your throat. There was no amount of worldliness that allowed someone to take that in their stride the way he was.

He might as well have screamed that he'd been expecting them.

Fionnuala wanted to warn him. There was no way without exposing herself to Broderick. She'd killed a man, and watched others be killed so she could get to this point. Those deaths would be in vain if she wasn't there to save Gibson and Kelly.

The boat pivoted on the water and Fionnuala struggled to stay upright. She noted the way that Docker and both the agents bent their knees slightly, so they swayed with the movements of the boat instead of trying to hold their ground against it.

'I hope you're not planning on heading downstream,' Malley asked him in that deceptively mild voice.

'Well, you're paying the passage, so I'll go where you say. Upstream is tricky though. Joseph has started to have his say already and the storm runoff is going to make battling that current difficult.'

'Over there will do just nicely,' Malley told him, gesturing toward the far shoreline with her knife.

'Nowhere to dock,' he told her mildly.

'Just get us up alongside,' she replied.

'You're the boss,' he agreed, still amiable.

He should have seen them coming. Fionnuala *willed* him to be smarter. He clearly lived down here in the lowlands, where life was terrible and dangerous, and nothing was as it seemed. He should have been able to tell from the too-sweet tone of Malley's voice and Broderick's absolute disregard for him that something was terribly wrong here. That they had seen him. That they had noticed him.

The boat inched toward the far bank. Bits of bushes protruded from the surface of the water, giving tell to the rains upstream that had started to drown the lowlands and would continue to do so until Storm Season Joseph had blown itself out.

Broderick scanned the far bank, behind it the remnants of the rest of the town could be seen. The Suck split Ballinsloe in two and what was left of the settlement on the far side was likely to be just as dangerous as what they had left behind.

The BlueArms behind them had started to break up, some beginning to lope downstream. To what, Fionnuala didn't know. The rest, including the one-eyed man, tracked the boat. None dared to venture into the water.

Mentally, she urged the boat toward the bank. To safety, for Docker more than anyone else. His life hung in the balance. She wracked her brain for the correct signals. She knew how to identify herself, just as he had done, and how to warn of danger. What she wanted to say to him was to stop. Stop talking. Stop messaging her. Stop drawing their attention with his casual affability.

They could sense danger. They wouldn't be fooled by this.

The far bank was almost close enough to jump out when Fionnuala turned to Malley to ask permission without saying a word, just a twitch of her head.

Docker's fingers flickered again. She recognised it as a question, though she couldn't remember what he was asking.

Without thinking, she shook her head at him.

Broderick moved instantly.

A knife materialised in his hand. Malley moved a second later, but somehow it was a second slow as Docker reacted, swinging an arm at her, ducking his own head as he did, so that Broderick's knife sailed by where his face had been a second before.

Malley had to dodge backwards, snarling, her foot lashing out to clip his wrist.

Docker grunted in pain, but didn't hesitate, moving to meet Broderick's charge. The narrow confines of the boat favoured the older man, but Broderick's uncanny speed still gave him the edge. They threw fists at each other, their hands almost blurring, blocking one another so no clean blow could land.

Fionnuala fumbled for the knife Broderick had given her, pulling it clumsily from the small sheath that she had strapped over her shoulder.

She didn't do anything with it, just stood there watching, clutching the blade.

Docker spun, surprising Broderick, and aimed a heavy boot at Malley, who was closing from behind. She adjusted her stance and the boot missed. She didn't bother to counter.

They had him.

Once again, they had moved with one mind, placing themselves so that he couldn't face the two of them at once, and standing so that he would have to commit himself to either one of them.

He chose Malley, his fist flashing out and heading for her throat.

She had a small smile on her face as she deflected the shot.

Another knife appeared in Broderick's hand, secreted in some part of his uniform. He didn't hesitate but plunged it into the large man's exposed back.

Docker jerked upright as the blade entered his kidney.

Malley's knife punched into his chest.

The two agents pulled their blades clear and let the body slump to the ground.

Broderick nodded in satisfaction before turning to face her.

His expression was pained, betrayed. His eyes hurt.

It lasted just a moment before the heat was back in them, burning hotter than she'd seen before.

'You're next,' he growled at her before he lunged.

# CHAPTER TWELVE

The boat rocked as it snagged on something under the water. A rock or a tree or part of a fence now under The Suck's surge. Fionnuala pitched as it shuddered and let herself be carried over the edge.

She hit the water with a chilling gasp. It was cold, unexpectedly freezing. Struggling, she pulled herself to her feet and felt the sodden ground give way underneath her. Her head just above the water, she awkwardly heaved herself toward the bank.

Broderick's hand snapped the water alongside her as he reached for her hair. Fionnuala stifled a scream as she pulled herself away from him, her toes still seeking firmness on the sodden ground underneath.

She was inching toward the bank, imperceptibly, even as she felt the water drag her.

The current was unbelievably strong, frighteningly so, and she struggled to move forward in it, even as her feet scrambled for purchase on the soft ground.

Behind and across the river, she could hear the BlueArms calling and shouting, their indistinct words bouncing across the surface of the water.

The boat was still moving, but it now pirouetted in the water. The front still meeting resistance from something – the back. Where Docker had stood began to twist into the faster-moving middle of the river.

The splash behind her came with a snarl as Broderick entered the water. She screamed a little, allowing a small amount of the river water into her mouth as she flailed, desperately trying to propel herself toward the bank.

A quick glance over her shoulder showed her that Broderick too was struggling, the water tugging at him as the boat twisted in the river behind, Malley still on its deck.

Increasingly she found purchase with her feet as she inched to safety, but the struggle of it was overpowering, the water pulling relentlessly. Behind her, snarling and splashing, the agent struggled toward her, his knife a shark fin in the water.

Her foot made contact with something firm underneath. Stonework of some kind. Old or new, the drowned rocks were a springboard and she pushed herself off them, further away from Broderick, closer to the bank.

The water was only up to her midriff by now and she found moving easier, the pull lessening as she moved closer to the edge, the resistance lowering as she came out of the freezing cold.

Behind her, Broderick was still struggling, only now he was struggling to keep himself in place. He wasn't trying to gain on her but was simply trying to resist The Suck's pull on him. The boat was beginning to move away at pace and Fionnuala could make Malley out as the woman moved swiftly but calmly about the deck.

Not enough time to figure out what was happening, Fionnuala continued to pull herself to the safety of the bank as Broderick continued his fight to keep himself alive. It was a fight he was barely winning, inching toward her with a look of rigid determination, but Fionnuala knew it was sapping him just as it sapped her.

Likely he was sinking deeper into the mud on the bank of the river, his extra weight literally dragging him to his death.

Downstream, the boat began to accelerate, and for just a moment, Fionnuala thought she saw the tongues of a fire begin to leap off the deck.

She stumbled as she moved, briefly submerging herself, but her hands quickly met the bottom and she pushed herself back to her feet. So close to the shore now and moving away from Broderick with every heavy-footed stride.

He was snarling his determination, but The Suck couldn't have cared less for his determination, for all his implacability. It continued to pull at him.

Part of the bank had given way under the pressure of the flood waters and the incline offered a shelf she might pull herself up with. Her breath coming in ragged gasps as she reached for it.

Her hands and arms were numb with the cold. Her clothes were sodden and pulling at her, weighing her down. She managed to pull herself up to safety.

The effort of it was almost overwhelming, her muscles felt as though they'd surrendered to the river and become water. She tossed her knife onto the grass in front of her and had to force her body to comply as she pushed her weight down through her palms and pulled her body from the water onto the sodden, waterlogged bank.

She was clear.

She sucked in breaths in between coughing up the river water.

Behind her, Broderick was still labouring, his face contorted. He was closer now, the water only up to just under his chest, but his feet were dragging, bogged down.

His fury was obvious. As if that alone could overcome the drag of the river.

There was no way that it could. The Suck was going to have its way.

She looked at him for a long moment.

'They didn't teach you swimming in Doejay school?' she asked.

Then, with her breath still rasping, she reached out for a long piece of flotsam, a broken branch thrown up onto the bank, and brandishing it in weakened arms, she turned back to the water and held it out to him.

The furious eyes flickered for a moment. He told so much with that impassive face and those burning eyes. Still snarling and grunting, he reached for the branch.

It slipped in her hands a little as he began to drag on it, but she managed to hold her grip.

He pulled a foot free of the mud that held him and inched toward her again, but with renewed energy. She held the branch as he pulled himself to her, bit by bit by bit, his body emerging from the water as he gained the shoreline.

Finally reaching the shelf, where she had pulled herself clear, he flattened his hands against the sodden earth and she used what little energy she had left to reach under his armpits so that she could help him pull himself clear.

Exhausted, they both collapsed on the bank. The boat, now fully aflame, disappeared into the distance, still firm in the grasp of The Suck.


Malley strode the bank with two knives drawn. She had shed both her own pack and Broderick's when she'd landed on the softened earth.

The boat had been difficult to master, and she could feel the BlueArms on the far side watching her try to bring the clumsy thing under control. She could feel them willing her to fail, willing the boat to move their way across the water. A mere fifty yards separated them from each other, but the river in its flood meant that fifty yards might as well have been fifty miles... unless the boat made its way to their side.

She had moved rapidly then, picking Broderick's loose blade from the deck before scrounging in the compartments below even as the barge began to turn in the water. She could see them struggling for the shore. Fools. Both of them. Strong swimmers would have struggled in those waters, never mind these two. For all his size and fury, Broderick was no match for the swiftly moving waters.

She found the jerry-can; she knew it must have been

somewhere. No doubt it had been hard earned, foraged or plundered. Docker must have paid a price for a meagre jerry-can of diesel.

Such was the way. He had paid for his carelessness too.

She doused the deck and set the fire. Broderick was making no ground on the younger woman. His weight would count against him.

She took the tiller in her ruined hands as she had done once before. Before. When her hands weren't a creeping mass of scars. When she was someone else. She couldn't have imagined that the woman she once was had anything to teach the woman she'd become, but standing there and turning the boat toward the shore she was grateful, for the first time in a long time, for who she used to be.

Grabbing the packs and readying herself, she waited, feeling the flames really take a hold of the boat, spreading where she'd doused it and into compartments beyond. By the time the back of the boat impacted the bank of the river the whole thing was engulfed in flames and the heat of it was threatening to take her.

She leapt then, clearing the river and landing with a thump in the muddy bank. Dropping the packs and pulling her knives clear she moved back upstream as fast as she dared. It would have been stupid to discount potential threats on this side just because the BlueArms on the far side were too far away to hurt her.

But she had to move fast. If he caught Fionnuala, she was a dead woman. Simple as that.

They had both recognised the clumsy attempt to signal her. The BlueArms thought themselves sophisticated, as if the agents didn't know about their little signals. Fionnuala was smart enough to ignore the first one, but the instant she'd shaken her head, Broderick had known what she was. There would be no forgiveness.

He'd kill her.

Malley wasn't going to allow that.

She wouldn't fail. Not again.

Not by their hands.

She almost paused at the thought.

Their hands.

As if his hands were her own.

She broke into a sprint.


She found them sitting feet from each other, both drenched and breathing heavily, both with knives out, both staring at each other.

'Put the knives away,' she told them, composing herself, trying to keep the relief from her voice.

Neither moved.

'I said put them away.'

They still didn't move.

Broderick's typical air of a coiled spring was not new to her. The man lived on that edge. Even when they were in Dublin, safe among their own, the man seemed to be waiting for his chance. Fionnuala's frightened anger was something of a shock though. The young woman sat on the grass, looking for all the world like a drowned cat but the knife never wavered. The resolve in her eyes was visible, familiar to her from her own memories of Hilda, but different now, a hint of violence showing that wasn't there before.

It had been less than a day since she'd used it for the first time in anger and now she sat holding it for all the world as though she was ready to cut the agent's throat.

Broderick flickered a questioning look at her.

*Did you know?*

She pursed her lips at him.

*I suspected.*

She didn't bother lying.

His fury became more evident. If such a thing was possible.

*Kill her then.*

Malley shook her head. Just a fraction of a millimetre from side to side.

He snarled. And offered her a look she couldn't read. It said something about him and something about her. But what he was trying to communicate was unfathomable.

The space between them becoming a gulf in a single look.

'You're slipping,' he growled at her.

'So are you,' she told him.

It was true. He had sat by her side. His hips pressed against hers. It hadn't gone unnoticed.

'What's your excuse?' he asked.

The tightness in his voice hinted at self-mockery.

'She reminds me of my sister,' Malley told him and the simplicity of that truth almost shocked her. That was why. 'What's yours?'

'Old age maybe?'

'Maybe,' Malley replied, knowing fully well what the real reason was.

He grunted a laugh at the implication in her tone.

'She's not your enemy,' Malley told him.

'Yes, she is.'

'She just wants justice. Isn't that what we're after?'

'Pah.'

'She thinks they're not guilty. Just like you thought she wasn't.'

'They are.'

'How do you know?'

Uncoiling suddenly, he surged to his feet. Malley drew into a defensive stance, one knife extended in her right hand, the one on the left tucked up against her forearm.

But he didn't attack. Instead, he looked at her.

It was a new look to her. She suspected it was the look that many of those they'd Pronounced together saw just before they got knives stuck in them.

'We have the fucking evidence, don't we?' he asked through clenched teeth.

'That doesn't mean anything.'

'IT MEANS EVERYTHING,' he roared at her.

'What if they didn't do it?'

'Who fucking cares if they didn't? Look around. It's a little late to be playing the "innocent card", isn't it?'

He gestured broadly at nothing and everything.

'That's not justice, Broderick,' she barked at him, 'that's revenge. I'm not in the revenge game. I don't carry around lists of people I want to murder. I bring justice.'

Him and his list. The list would be the death of one of them. Eventually.

He scoffed at her. 'Justice? You think there's justice? If we could kill them fifty times, it wouldn't be justice enough for them. You think their lives are worth us having to live through this? You think their pathetic fucking existence is fair trade for watching half my country turn into a crowd of howling barbarians?'

'You did that!' Fionnuala suddenly chimed in, her voice hard. 'The Government did that.'

'Pipe down, traitor.'

'No!' she barked. 'You did it. All those lives not worth living, who do you think controls that? Who hoards the food? Who issues the No Movement Orders? Who did nothing when the Storms came? You did. Your Government did. Anyone complains too loud – here come the Doejays to stick a knife in them.'

'We do no such thing,' Malley told her.

It was a repugnant thought, yet a tiny voice inside suggested that the woman wasn't wrong.

Malley had faced charges of hungry, desperate people and killed them. She'd stood in a ruined section of palisade outside the settlement at Tara swinging a long-handled sledge in the pouring rain and dead of night, killing those who had come for food and found the gates closed to them.

She remembered well when the laws had changed and they'd told her that those who harvested the grid be murdered too. For the good of the public. So, she killed them as well.

It stuck in her craw then.

And that was the problem. That was why she'd let an old man with kind eyes go when she'd caught him at the grid. It was why she'd hesitated in Black Stair. And now why she couldn't kill this young woman.

The tiny voice was telling her that what she was doing was wrong.

'Yes, you do,' Fionnuala insisted.

Malley glanced down at the scars gripping the long knife before her.

Those were something the righteous young woman, for all her ideals, could never understand. The scars on those hands. Those scars were earned. She had been given those scars and a lesson at the same time. The lesson was not one that could be learned without taking the scars.

Bad people had brought them to this point. Bad people had brought the world to its knees. Nature wasn't punishing them all, it was punishing the wicked, the rest of them just happened to be in the way. She just mopped up, punishing any of those who nature missed.

She looked up at them in that moment. Drenched. Standing there with fire in both of their eyes. Broderick's unquenchable, since there would never be enough revenge to go around. Fionnuala's the fire of youth and idealism, not yet taken from her by a world that inevitably would grind such things away.

Her hands told her something and her heart told her something else.


Broderick stood looking at Malley. She was staring at her hands again. Right at the edges, where the scars crept around from her palms to the otherwise untouched backs of her hands. Little fissures in her skin where she'd cracked and broken and put herself partially back together. She never spoke of them, but she never stopped looking at them either.

He looked at her looking at them. And he looked at Fionnuala. A little mouse with a knife. Still drenched from the river, she looked like a strong wind would scrub her from the side of the bank, but the way she stood was defiant. He would never have suspected such determination from this little thing when he'd first seen her.

It was beautiful. She was beautiful.

The way she had looked at him that first time…

He wanted that feeling he felt when she looked at him that way.

Malley was right. He was getting soft.

The river would have taken him. That was a difficult thing for him to accept, even if only to himself, but he knew it was true. He had let his anger propel him out of that boat and into the water without thinking.

It had been so strong. It had pulled at him even as he sank. He was less than six feet to the bank when he realised that he may as well have been on the other side of the moon for all his chances of reaching it.

He was a dead man, until she stuck that branch out.

Was that alone reason to let her live?

It couldn't be.

Could he let it be?

He had watched his parents descend slowly into their own private madness. Two scientists. Climatologists. Ignored, derided, heckled, and ridiculed. It was no wonder they'd gone insane – his mother turning to the bottle, his father to a ceaseless optimism that was so far divorced from reality, he might as well have been living in a dream. Right up until Broderick had woken him up.

After that he had begun making his lists.

There were only three types of people in the world.

The innocent, the guilty, and him.

When Malley's name was on his list, it was because she was among the guilty.

When he removed her name, it wasn't because she'd

become innocent. It was because she'd become him. They were one and the same.

Above guilt or innocence. Outside it.

Fionnuala was innocent. Because she was too young to be guilty. She hadn't driven the cars or charged the phones or bought the crap or patronised the airlines. She had inherited a shit world.

Her innocence was the reason he had to punish the guilty.

Until she betrayed him.

To the BlueArms. Those who stood between him and the guilty.

That was reason enough to crush his feelings, to forget the way she looked at him, to add her to the list.

If he still could do that.

'We have a job to do,' Malley's voice cut through the fog.

'You're going to kill him?' Fionnuala accused.

'If he's guilty.'

It took Broderick a second to realise they weren't talking about him.

They were talking about Gibson.

Gibson was still ahead of them. And ahead of Gibson was Kelly.

Their names were near top of his list.

Politicians.

Who was more guilty than the politicians? Who had fought harder than them against the measures that might have saved the world?

'And what if he's innocent?' Fionnuala asked pugnaciously.

So stubborn. And so beautiful.

He had to crush that feeling.

'If he's innocent, no harm will come to him,' Malley told her.

Broderick scoffed.

'He has to say it too,' Fionnuala insisted, gesturing at Broderick with her knife.

She was looking at him again. But not in the way that softened him.

Anger on the surface, but something else too. A disconcerting look, not unlike pity. He remembered what that had looked like. It was how people looked at him and his parents. At protests, at conferences, at the marches when people stopped turning up and it was just a scrawny teenager and his two ageing parents standing in the rain begging an apathetic world to care about its own destruction.

He had almost forgotten what pity looked like when someone was offering it to him.

It wasn't the look he wanted from her. It wasn't the one that made him feel.

'Broderick and I are one,' Malley told the little mouse. 'If I tell you that no harm will be done to them, then no harm will be done to them.'

'I want to hear him say it,' Fionnuala insisted again. 'If he says it, I'll believe him.'

Still the look of pity, and in her voice a change, something soft, the hint of a promise, a temptation in her voice. An invitation even.

A dangerous invitation.

'If he's innocent, I won't kill him,' Broderick told her as he looked her dead in the eyes.

She nodded at him, satisfied.

Malley didn't. Her eyes narrowed in suspicion. Too smart for her own good. Nothing got by her.

The invitation was to weakness. The weakness she'd somehow managed to sneak into him.

His choice was simple. Her, and the weakness she offered, or his duty.

Mentally, he added Fionnuala's name to the list.

He'd kill her when the moment was right.

He didn't owe the guilty any kind of honesty.

# CHAPTER THIRTEEN

Fionnuala trudged through the mucky earth, blinking away her weariness as she followed Broderick's feet. She gripped the knife as tight as she could make herself grip it as she walked in his terrible footsteps. He remained a terrifying mystery to her. There was a human in there, she believed, but it was buried under an almost palpable rage.

Malley followed after her through the marshland on the far bank and into the town of Ballinasloe. There had been a moment when they had left the bank when Malley had gestured at Broderick to take point. His eyes had flashed then. Fionnuala understood what was happening. Malley didn't want her partner to be behind them, where she couldn't see him, and Broderick had felt that suspicion as an insult.

The feeling of immutability that had hung over them like an aura only days ago was gone now, and in its place a sort of feral wariness. They were both on edge. Fionnuala wished she wasn't so tired. All the running and climbing and chasing had drained her and now the wind, picking up again as Joseph gathered his breath, chilled her sodden body.

It was mid-afternoon she reckoned, but there would be no way they'd make Galway by evening. The thought heartened her a little. Gibson would be pulling away with every minute she slowed them down.

Through the outskirts of the town they moved, the sodden marsh giving way to concrete and tarmac. A nursing home, or what had once been a nursing home, stood by the roadside, smoke coming from the chimney being whipped away on the quickening breeze.

In the centre of the town, she could make out taller buildings with makeshift skywalks between them, and the spire of a church. She wondered what it housed now, if indeed it housed anything at all. People might live there. Or the shell of the thing might be all that was left of this place of worship. Her parents had been religious. They'd raised her to be religious too, but she'd let that go when she'd burned their bodies.

She hadn't the depth of faith they had. She surmised that it was because they had seen more good days than bad, and that was enough for them to believe in a benevolent god. But for her, the bad days outnumbered the good, and an angry god inspired no loyalty.

The wind whistling down the long street that was the main route through the town jerked at her soaked clothing as they made their way into its heart.

It was unlike them to move in populated areas. They skirted the outside of those, but the need for shelter as Joseph announced himself was more pressing.

Broderick, still drenched, stalked as though the cold wasn't affecting him. If the stiff breeze was stabbing at his skin, he showed no signs of it, his head swivelling as he walked.

He still moved as she had become accustomed to, as though there was an ambush at every corner. She could feel Malley moving behind her too. No sound came as the woman moved on light feet, not even rustling in the breeze, but Fionnuala could feel her nonetheless.

Broderick stopped and thrust an arm out in front of a building whose façade was a renovated church-front.

It was locked and boarded up, though that was a trifling problem for two Doejays. Broderick pulled a small tool from his belt and set to jimmying at a boarded-up window and turning it slightly so they could climb in, while still allowing the board to hang down and conceal their entrance.

'Careful,' he murmured at them.

His voice was tight with the barely contained anger.

'Problem?' Malley asked from behind.

Her voice was equally tight with wariness.

'Someone was at this recently,' he told them. 'It might still be a shelter.'

Cautiously, he climbed through the window. Knife held low.

Fionnuala stood for a moment, trying to stop her teeth from chattering in the cold, before Malley nudged her. She imagined this is how prisoners being transported must have felt. Nudged in the back to keep moving.

Wearily, she climbed through the window, Malley following close behind.

Inside the damp, cold building, Fionnuala experienced her first ever library. Or at very least the first she could remember. Mouldy and ruined books stacked on shelves above sodden carpet. A patched hole in the roof suggested that someone had at some point tried to rescue the place and its contents. The level of their success told in the number of books still untouched by mould and damp; a hundred or so among thousands of destroyed volumes.

'Here,' Broderick grunted.

A fireplace sat against the back wall. It didn't belong to the building, the makeshift flue looking altogether rickety in places stretching up to the ceiling.

'Still warm,' Malley whispered.

'Since last night,' Broderick told her.

The two of them scanned the place, their innate wariness amplified suddenly.

'Sit,' Malley told her, her tone brooking no argument. 'If you see anything, call out.'

Fionnuala nodded, clutching the knife to her chest closely.

She willed herself to have their energy, but the cold and the wind and the running...

Sitting by the glowing remnants of the fire, she stared straight ahead, only vaguely aware of the two of them stalking about the room.

She sat and stared, fighting to keep her eyes open, and hardly even noticed when she slumped to one side and fell asleep.

Gibson ran.

He let adrenaline pilot him in an uncontrolled sprint. It seemed that was all he ever did now. Adrenaline spikes and crashes. Medically, he understood what was happening. That was his job. But knowing what chemical reactions were happening in your brain seemed to be irrelevant nonsense as you moved through the lowlands. He might have laughed at the absurdity of it all, if he wasn't so frightened.

Kelly had told him to be cautious. Everyone had. Move quietly and stay out of sight, they'd told him. It had all seemed plausible then. Exciting even. The Government was trying to kill them because they were a threat, which meant he and Kelly had righteousness on their side. They were the good guys. And the good guys always prevailed.

That had turned out to be nonsense. At fifty-five years of age, Gibson found himself learning that the Storm Season and the lowlands didn't care one jot for who the good guys were. Late in life to be learning such things.

Not for the first time, he inwardly cursed Kelly.

Joe had been his friend, was still his friend, but there was no doubt who he held responsible for the situation they were in.

That had always been the way with them. Even during Before. Kelly had been somehow blessed, luckier than any man had a right to be. Everything he touched turned to gold and everything he wanted seemed to fall into his lap.

It hadn't been like that for Gibson. All his plans and schemes and adventures seemed to fall apart on him with Kelly bailing him out time and again.

There had been one moment when it might have all changed, in the hospital in Galway when the first Chain of Storms hit. The very first Storm Season. The wind and the rain battered everything, pulled at everything, the violence of it was stunning. Power went. Looting started. Then the violence, taking place even as the elements tried to scour the land, was among the people.

In that moment, lost, frightened, hurt, and confused, leadership was needed in the hospital. It seemed like the entirety of the country's suffering was contained in those walls.

But he had hesitated and Kelly had taken the lead and that moment had cemented their positions in the world. Kelly became the hero. The totem. That was why Gibson was out here in the wild and Kelly was safely behind solid walls in Limerick.

Outside Dublin, Belfast, and Waterford, beyond the reach of Government control, there were no heroes. No 'good guys and bad guys'. There were people. None were more villainous than the next, just differing degrees of desperate or insane.

Digital had been insane, but his insanity was not so far gone that he didn't protect himself at all costs. He played every side. He'd get himself killed for it if he wasn't careful.

By all accounts, those following after Gibson were a different type of insane.

Digital had warned him. Eoghan Broderick and Malley Cummins were murderous savages.

Dispatched by Government, they'd kill him without hesitation.

And they had come so close.

He'd been sitting on the top floor of the library, reading the falsified evidence, wondering if this half-baked plan was going to get him killed, when he'd spotted the burning barge floating down The Suck.

Curious and frightened, mostly frightened, he'd watched as they emerged from the ditch by the side of the river. The agents were obvious. They moved like agents; with the languid grace you'd see in a large hunting cat. The younger woman was theirs apparently. Fionnuala Regan. A spy on the inside of their camp, but she somehow seemed to fit with them. He suspected they'd been double-crossed. She was a Government tool surely.

His death walked slowly from the river toward him as he watched.

Cursing himself for waiting so long, for not moving that morning when he'd woken, he gathered up the falsified evidence and started down the stairs, stopping only to stuff his meagre possessions into his bag.

He had heard the sound of the boards at the front of the building scraping loose as he climbed out the window at the back.

He felt under his jerkin for the 'evidence' while he ran. It wouldn't matter to the agents. They were going to kill him anyway. But it would surely save him and Kelly yet, if he could stay out of their hands. With the people who mattered most. A risky plot to save the day, but perhaps the Government's haste would work against them and they'd be toppled. Then he could be a hero.

He continued his headlong sprint and hoped that they weren't already on his trail.


Malley sat by the small fire in the library watching Fionnuala sleep. Outside, Joseph had begun to howl again, slamming powerful fists of wind and rain against the walls and the barricaded door. Exhaustion had taken the young woman. It was inevitable. What was surprising was how long she had lasted. Experience and training had built her and Broderick for these times, but for the young woman, whose ideals alone had given her strength, there was a limit to how far she could push her body.

She'd been through a lot. Fleeing in the night from Digital's mansion. Killing the BlueArm by the fence. Fighting the torrent of the river as a killer inched his way through the water to her.

Malley remembered the younger version of herself. Before she'd gained her scars, before she'd learned the lesson that had come with them. It was impossible for her to look at Fionnuala and not think of the person she had been Before.

And yet for all of that, it was her sister, Hilda, that she saw when she looked at Fionnuala Regan. It was Hilda's eyes she sometimes thought she was looking into when they spoke. A flash of familiarity that brought a pang of pain and guilt whenever she felt it.

She thought of what they had become after. Her and Hilda. The weeks of not speaking, of nursing their private hurts. Malley becoming hard and cold. Hilda more and more passionate.

'We need to talk,' Broderick told her as he approached the fire.

He had remained distant from her, in every way, since they'd arrived at the library. His face giving away less than its usual nothing. His knife was in its sheath. That was something. She half expected him to come with it drawn.

She nodded at him to sit.

'You thought I was a BlueArm,' she said. It wasn't a question.

'Someone betrayed us,' he told her by explanation.

'She did what she thought was right.'

'She almost got us killed.'

'So did you.'

'How so?'

'Killing Digital.'

'He was on the list.'

'O'Neill's list? You take your orders directly from the Minister now?'

'He was on *my* list.'

His own personal list.

She almost reached for her knife.

If she was on the list, one of them was going to die by this fire.

He tensed too, reading her thoughts again, as he always did.

She forced her body to relax and watched him following suit. Any fight between them was unlikely to last long. They had the measure of each other, and she thought they might be evenly matched. His heat versus her cold. They'd second guess each other quickly enough.

'Who else is on the list?' she asked, trying to sound nonchalant.

'None of your business,' he told her, and she detected the smallest hint of a laugh in the twitch of his mouth.

'You don't think?' she laughed in reply.

They were both good at this. Good at sitting while they decided how someone might die.

'You were on it. A long time ago. When we started.'

'What changed?'

'You did.'

'And now I'm changing again?'

'Yes.'

'So, I'm back on the list.'

'No.'

'Why not?'

'Because you're still not guilty.'

She thought of the man she'd let go. The soft, startled eyes of him, the body-language that suggested an innocence. That's all she had to go on. The suggestion of innocence. If he'd been intimidating in any way, if he'd even hinted at a violent nature, she'd have killed him in a second. But he hadn't. Perhaps it was the eyes.

The old man's eyes were like her father's, Fionnuala's were like her sister's.

If he knew, she'd be guilty again, and if she was guilty again, she'd be back on the list.

Then one of them would have to die.

'Is Fionnuala on the list?'

'Yes.'

'Why?'

'You know the answer to that.'

'What if she wasn't a BlueArm?'

He shrugged at her.

'Do you see the lack of logic here?'

'No.'

'So, her actions don't make her guilty, but her association does?'

'She's preventing justice from being done.'

'What if she's preventing an injustice? What if these men are innocent?'

'They're guilty,' he snorted derisively.

'Guilty of what? Climate denial? How do we know? You'll take O'Neill's word and the word of four snivelling little wretches?'

'If not that, something worse.'

'Like what?'

'Not doing enough.'

'How do you know they didn't?'

'Because I'm sitting in a library burning books to keep warm while another storm starts outside,' he snapped. 'Because every year, Irish people are turned back from mainland Europe bursting at the seams with people trying to run away from the elements. Because everyone is desperate and there's no such thing as the future anymore. That's why.'

'Did you do enough?'

She knew it was both the right question and the wrong question. They never spoke of their pasts. There was no need. It was enough to know they'd both learned the lessons that one had to learn. They had both had something taken from them, something profoundly important, and that loss was the lesson one learned to be tough enough.

'I gave everything. I have nothing left. They didn't give everything. They still have something left to give. Something left to lose. It's our job to take it.'

'And you want me to kill them for that?'

'No.'

She was shocked by that. And underneath that shock was a deeper surprise that she could still be shocked by him.

'So, what do you want me to do?'

'I want you to go home.'

His body changed as he said it, steeling itself, but for whatever reason, it didn't make him seem harder. It made him seem brittle.

She watched him in silence, waiting for him to offer more while the wind screamed in between the buildings. A faint gong suggested it had activated the bell in an old church somewhere nearby.

They both watched each other.

For once, he didn't flinch from her long stare, and she broke before he did.

'Why?' she asked him.

'Because she's made you soft,' he said, nodding at the still sleeping Fionnuala.

'You too, I think.'

'Maybe. But not so soft that I won't do my job.'

'And you think I'll shirk it?'

'Yes,' he told her bluntly.

'You're wrong.'

'I don't think so.'

'You forget something.'

'Oh?'

'I have nothing left either,' she confessed. 'Just this job.'

'Then why not do it?'

'Because the job is about justice. It's all I have left. It's all I can do to make the world make sense. I bring justice.'

'If they're allowed to live, it's not justice.'

'If you kill the innocent, it's not justice.'

He smiled then. Not a twitch of the mouth or a hint in his eyes, but a full smile.

'We're the same, me and you,' he told her.

'You think?'

'I do. So, you'll know I'm telling you the truth when I say this…'

He paused for a second, and the smile faded away.

'I'm going to kill them. And if you come after me, I'll kill you too.'

She looked deep into his eyes and they held together like that, with the reflection of the flames playing between them. He really meant it. He'd kill her.

And somehow, she always knew he would.

'You'll try,' she told him quietly.

And he nodded as he stood. As if he expected nothing less.


Fionnuala woke gradually, a slow rising to consciousness from the depths of heavy sleep, opening her eyes to glance around the room until the moment she realised she was alone which caused her to burst to full wakefulness.

The fire had burned low while she slept and for a panicked moment, she thought they had left her, slipping out of the library in the middle of the night and leaving her with only Joseph for company. Only Malley's pack, propped against the chair she'd been sitting on, told of the presence of anyone else.

There was no sign of Broderick's pack.

She extricated herself from the blanket they'd wrapped her in, and the insulated tarpaulin sheet that they'd stretched over her, it's underside full of sacks of pulverised glass and sand-packs that weighed down on a body but kept the heat.

Her clothes were rumpled and creased, still damp in patches, somehow, but mostly dry. That, at least, hinted that she'd been asleep for more than a few hours, but it was impossible to say for sure. The boarded windows and thick storm clouds outside obscured the evidence that time was passing at all.

Joseph still ran amok down the main thoroughfare outside the door, rattling things as he passed, screaming occasionally at the empty streets. This tantrum would pass, but the next wouldn't be far behind, and it would be worse. They always got worse and worse as winter headed for spring.

A climatologist on the Government's web paper had explained it – something to do with salt in the water, the direction of turn of the planet, and the gulf stream. His words had seemed plausible, but Fionnuala felt an instinctual need for scepticism. They lied too easily.

There was always another level of machination. When the

people most needed direction and leadership, the Government always seemed to be scheming and obfuscating.

She walked among the rows of shelves of books, her hands brushing them as she moved. It seemed so ridiculous, this huge collection of paper, so extraneous, but there was a sort of holiness about it too. Relics of days gone. She wondered what it must have been like for people with libraries of these in their homes. Whole entire rooms dedicated to a collection of paper and print.

These things left behind seemed somehow pathetic now. They were no match for winter, or for the storms. Eventually Storm Season would be successful in tearing the roof off this place and when it did, it would reach a hand in and then these old things would be lost. Pulp and trash, no longer even fit for fuelling the fire.

'We need to talk,' Malley's voice announced.

Fionnuala spun, startled.

Her face was grim. A type of grim that Fionnuala had never seen her wear before. Always it had been Broderick who was grim, while Malley's air had been a sort of pleasant nonchalance.

Not so now, her face was wrong looking, still and stony even though it seemed that something under her skin was seething.

'Where's Broderick?' she asked, trying to cover her fright.

'Why are you here?'

The question was so blunt, the face so threatening. Fionnuala was suddenly aware of their size difference. Was she going to kill her? Where had Broderick gone? Had she killed him?

'Where's Broderick?' she asked again.

'What was your end game here? Follow us and then what?'

'I don't know. I didn't think it all the way through.'

'Clearly.'

'What did you do with Broderick?'

'Would you have killed us? If we decided Gibson and Kelly were guilty, would you have killed us to protect them?'

Fionnuala had asked herself that very question.

She hadn't known when she'd left Black Stair, but their journey had revealed it to her when she'd stuck a knife in a man's back for them. She could kill for a cause. She could kill if she had to. The lowlands were every bit as hard and dangerous as they'd told her they would be and she'd walked into that, to protect a movement of people. For that movement, for the concept of a future she might one day have, she could kill them.

She teased the thought of it out in her head.

'If you try to kill them, I'll kill you,' she eventually told the agent.

Malley's booming laugh was sudden and loud that Fionnuala jumped.

The noise of the laugh bounced off the walls of the library. She laughed loud and long.

'What's so funny?' Fionnuala asked, embarrassed that her voice shook as she spoke.

The laugh was a frightening thing.

'You think you could do it?' she asked, as if reading Fionnuala's thoughts.

'If I had to.'

'That's the lesson that can't be taught,' Malley told her, her voice still brimming with bitter mirth. 'You do what you have to, and you don't know what it is until you have to do it. There's nothing I can tell you, nothing you can read about that will prepare you for that moment. When it arrives, that moment will take something from you, something profound. Something you'll never get back.'

Malley looked at her hands as she spoke. It felt very much as though she was speaking to herself as much as to Fionnuala. The coldness of her was a new depth of temperature that Fionnuala had never seen before.

'I don't doubt you'll do what you have to, when the time comes. You'll do it or you'll be killed. That's the way it works.'

Fionnuala didn't speak.

'Broderick is gone,' Malley said, looking up from her hands.

'Gone where?'

'Gone to kill Gibson, and then to kill Kelly. If you want to save them, you'll have to go after him and you'll have to kill him.'

'Are you coming?'

'Of course, I am. What else would I do?'

'Are you going to kill them?'

'If they did it.'

'But not if they didn't?'

'Only if they're guilty,' Malley told her, her words seeming to freeze as she spoke them. 'This is all I have left. We'll go see this Omega person who apparently has our answers. If they're guilty, I'll kill them. If they're innocent, I'll kill Broderick. This is the decision you must make. We go from here out into that storm and we don't stop until someone is dead. Are you prepared to do what you have to do now?'

Fionnuala thought about Black Stair. It hadn't been a bad life after all that. She had imagined bigger things for herself, for everyone, outside the walls of the settlement, but in this moment, she found herself missing it. Missing the Sharing. The songs. The determination of rebuilding. The celebration of spring, when the storms had passed.

If there was a future for her, and for the whole country, it was out in the storm. And it rested on her shoulders to make it so. There could be no going back. Only forward. Even if that cost her a part of herself that she might never get back.

'I'll do what I have to do,' she told Malley.

Malley nodded at her and handed her Broderick's knife.

# CHAPTER FOURTEEN

Malley moved them quickly through the town of Ballinasloe. The first storms were a curiosity to her every year. In Dublin, Belfast, Waterford, and among the settlements, the weeks preceding Storm Season were filled with a kind of morbid joviality, as though the people were attempting to drag the very last moments of joy that they possibly could from their season while also trying not to panic stockpile on essentials. Decisions were being made for the long lockdown ahead. The black market in the cities and in the larger settlements did a booming trade. Christmas time for traders was no longer Christmas time for everyone else, like it had been in her day. That manic energy in the civilised parts of the country halted abruptly when the first storms came through, and though these would be the weakest storms, these were always the safest, as everyone prepared to hunker down and, well-stocked, took to their homes.

They only started to break lockdown later in the season, ironically when things were much more dangerous, as supplies dwindled or roofs collapsed or families turned on one another in their confined spaces. It was too common, not a year passed where someone wasn't killed in their home during the hard winter.

Now the two of them moved through streets emptied by that early season vigilance. The signs of habitation were here, even alongside the signs of extensive flooding; streets and low buildings under the water table of the now-mighty Suck. But there was no sign of the people. They were behind barricaded doors and windows.

It made for a very unsettling journey through the town. Just her, and Fionnuala, and Joseph.

She felt his absence.

Over their years together they were often separated, sent on errands and missions without one another. She'd gone months at a time without him silently by her side, but inexorably they would find their way back to one another. Silently. As was their way.

Now that was gone.

The gap between them blown open and as near as she could tell, beyond repair.

She didn't blame Fionnuala for it. Though the young woman had asked her before they left the library behind them, if she was responsible. She'd even apologised for it.

'I'm sorry.'

'It's not your fault.'

The words echoed in her mind. Echoed across the years too.

She actually blamed O'Neill for it.

There'd be a reckoning there, if she had her way.

Digital had called the evidence 'contrived'. Fake. Which might have been enough for her, except for his subtle hinting that there was more going on.

'I'm not saying they didn't do it,' he had said to her.

O'Neill and Digital. Gibson and Kelly. Hilda and Fionnuala. Too many players, not enough facts. The solidity of her life had been erased and it started with the Minister.

She pressed on through the town, her cold fury under colder wraps.

They didn't speak as they moved. Joseph would have whipped their words away anyway. So they carried themselves low as they could and moved through old winding streets, past the ruins of old homes, and the tell-tale signs of attempted rebuilding that marked the new ones.

She hoped Fionnuala had learned enough from Broderick, and from herself, that she was scanning their path, and checking their backtrack. Watching their six, as someone had once written.

She didn't have time to worry about it herself.

Speed was key now.

They moved the length of the town quickly and quietly. They passed the old GAA pitch, in the distance the remnants of a long-abandoned hospital. They passed an undertaker, raided shells of former grocery stores and houses. At another time, she would have moved slowly or avoided the town altogether. Each foot would have been placed carefully in front of the other, poking and prodding for potential traps.

Not so anymore. Broderick had hours of a head start on them, which meant that they'd never catch him. On his own, he'd eat the distance to Galway. Accounting for his leaving in the middle of the night, he'd be there by evening, maybe just before dark. Depending on the route he took.

And that was her conundrum. If he was following Gibson's trail, then the motorway was the correct call. No doubt the rebel politician would hug the main roads. Soft living in Before, followed by soft living in Dublin would make the backroads and cross-country too difficult for him. What BlueArms were still abroad would be his allies, so the M6 would be safe to boot. The storm might make it passable for her and Fionnuala too.

But if Gibson was too far ahead and Broderick knew he'd run out of road before he caught the man, then his shortest possible route to Galway would be along the old train tracks. The last train had run in 2030, years before, so most people disregarded them. Broderick would not. Which meant a very real possibility that Broderick would make it to Galway ahead of Gibson, head him off on the way into the town and kill him before Malley could bring justice.

Worse again, he'd get the evidence from whoever this

Omega person was, and he'd be on his way to Limerick. Where Hilda was. Where Hilda would be protecting Kelly.

She didn't dare imagine the consequences of Hilda getting in Broderick's way.

Her options boiled down to two: risk the M6 in the hope of catching Gibson before he got to Galway, or follow the train tracks to stop Broderick before he turned for Kelly.

It was Fionnuala who had decided it for her.

There was a chance to save the man, so they'd take that. To do otherwise was to condemn him to death without even trying. Having made the decision, she didn't feel any better. She had hoped she might. She had hoped that some kind of idealism, some compromise with naivety would energise her and remind her of her old self.

Instead, she just felt the wind, the rain, and the cold whipping her as she climbed the bank that brought her to the M6, the same wind that came every year, that ruined everything, that had taken all of their lives from them and turned their shared home into this hellscape. Fionnuala determinedly trudged behind her.


O'Mahony peered through the rain at the old hospital building. He tried to remember what it had looked like. Even after fourteen years, he was still shocked by the disrepair. It had taken so little for them to destroy what had taken so long to build.

Infrastructure.

One word that covered so much. Roads, electricity, water, internet, hospitals, schools, hotels, airports.

He knew it as well as anyone did. He knew the intricacies of it, the complexity. How each separate aspect leaned on other aspects, how no one thing was built or existed in isolation, but served a pattern. A web.

Infrastructure seemed like a massive thing. A thing too big to be brought down. But it was really just a hundred smaller things. And like a web, it was delicate – more delicate than anyone knew. They'd torn that web apart in about two years and all it had taken was for the people to turn on each other. Then another twelve years or so to really let the destruction marinate.

All it would take to fix it would be for them to turn back toward each other, to start to reconnect the strands, but day by day, winter by winter, and storm by storm that seemed increasingly unlikely.

The No Movement Orders issued by Government entrenched people. The parsing out of resources; a little here and not enough there had those entrenched people huddling over what they had. If you looked at it one way, it was a system designed to make the most with limited amounts. If you looked at it another way, it was a system designed to perfectly divide people.

And divided people were controlled people.

The Gardai and the agents saw to that.

O'Mahony didn't want to look at it either way.

This world was not his.

It hadn't been his Before, when they'd paid him good money to fix their infrastructure, and it certainly wasn't his now.

He was too small, too old, too weak.

He felt weak. He felt it in almost everything he did.

Only when he was fixing or building did he forget how weak he was. Everyone else had additional tasks, that was the way of life in Limerick. The city couldn't afford for people to be just one thing. Except for him. He fixed things, built things and, in doing so, he taught the new engineers. They hadn't even bothered to arm him or train him for militia work.

He was a little ashamed they hadn't asked him. He was old now, but Carney was of a similar age and he still carried weapons and the manner and bearing of a man who was prepared to die using them.

O'Mahony was extra ashamed of how he had attached himself to the One-Eyed Rook.

Though the man had never given him any cause to feel so.

Quite the opposite. They spoke like old friends sometimes. He was a hard, unsmiling, unflinching man, but O'Mahony was of the impression that he had been softer and kinder once. Perhaps before he'd lost the eye – Before.

It was Rook who had him standing on a rooftop in Galway, watching a ruined hospital for signs of a madman.

Or rather it was Rook's unspoken kindness.

'He might be useful,' the man had told them when he announced that O'Mahony was going with him.

O'Mahony was quite sure that they all knew what he meant by that: he's afraid to be here on his own. So I'll take him with me.

They had travelled in convoy, two electric minibuses.

The electric vehicle. A too-little-too-late effort at turning the tide on the destruction they had reaped on the world around them. O'Mahony was ashamed of that too. Ashamed that he hadn't done more. Ashamed of himself as much as everyone else.

He'd only been in Limerick a couple of years. Before that he had lived in the settlements where life had been okay for him. Fixing solar panels and charging stations and mending things. But he'd let that calmness, that sense of place get to him. He'd let the comfort of it, the almost-permanence of it, lull him into a false sense of security.

Then the agent had caught him tapping the grid.

He'd never been the same after that.

She'd just appeared behind him, a spectre appearing out of nowhere. Afterwards he raked through his memories, trying to remember if she'd made a single noise moving across the withered sun-crisped foliage. He was sure she hadn't.

He had assumed he was far enough from Government to go unnoticed. How wrong that assumption had turned out to be.

She had stood over him, loomed even, despite being shorter than he. Her hands were ruined with scars. He'd never really paid attention to people's hands before, but hers were so badly mangled they hardly seemed to be hands at all, and they were impossible to miss. She stood there with her ruined hands staring at him and he'd felt that profound sense of weakness. There was a coldness about her. An almost-terrifying coldness that he felt in spite of the summer's relentless heat.

He'd looked into her eyes and he'd been too afraid of her to even cry or panic.

This, he thought to himself after, is what 'paralysed by fear' meant.

Then she'd softened without moving, without changing expression. It was more the impression of softening than anything else.

'Go,' she told him quietly.

He didn't trust himself to speak.

'I said go, old-timer.' And there was the merest hint of a smile then.

He had nodded at her.

He was grateful to her that she'd given him his life, but she'd never know how much she'd taken too. His mortality was a terrible thing to face, and his fear, and the full comprehension of just how small he was, how weak.

He couldn't go back to the settlement then.

They'd assume he had been killed. Or perhaps had taken the path of the refugee just trying to slip into the capital, already bulging with those who wanted or needed. But he'd gone west instead. Summer had been high then, the world was always less dangerous when the sun was out.

He'd wandered his way to Limerick, stupidly having no actual plan to go anywhere.

And now he was standing on a roof, the driving rain stinging his face, the wind buffeting him angrily, his belt secured to a railing like they did, scanning through the weather, looking for signs of an arrival that might change everything.

Beside him, Rook twitched, the long scar on his face twisting as his eyes narrowed.

He didn't speak, but extended a hand and pointed a finger. A flicker of something. At the edge of the hospital. Movement.

Broderick sat, his shoulder against the wall, peering out through the hole where a window had been. It was a house. Or at least it had been before it became a ruin. He'd followed the railway tracks from Ballinasloe. It wasn't as quick a journey as he might have liked. Flooding. As usual. He'd had to leave the tracks, circle around and find them again. Wading in parts as flood plains became quagmires. The storm interfered too, buffeting him as he moved. Joseph pushing him around.

Still he was confident he'd beaten Gibson to it. All the more so because of the scattering of BlueArms around the hospital. He'd seen them, but they hadn't seen him. And they were still waiting too.

He looked down again at the corpse.

He had been good. Better than Broderick had been expecting. Moving fast, his attack lacking the tentative quality that marked the amateur, full of aggression and intent. Still he'd died with a knife in his chest, and now his corpse lay at Broderick's feet, in the shell of a house within view of the hospital.

His clothes seemed almost reinforced, a sort of lightweight, flexible armour. It was good intel. O'Neill might want it when he got back. If Broderick decided to let him live.

He held that particular rat entirely responsible for what had happened between him and Malley. They had been as one until O'Neill had shown up.

Their concept of justice was close as to make no difference, until Fionnuala Regan, a stranger, had started pulling at that thread, and suddenly the difference seemed vast and too large to accommodate.

Fionnuala was as much to blame, but if O'Neill hadn't brought them a kill list, things would be different now. Better.

Broderick was smart enough to know what was going on. The Minister wanted the job done quickly. Before winter.

If he wanted it done right, it would have taken as long as

it had taken, and the results would have been the results and that would have been that.

But they weren't.

Which meant this wasn't the kind of justice that Malley wanted. She still possessed the kind of purity Broderick knew he had left behind.

His justice was a dirtier thing, more opaque. While hers was transparent, righteous. The differences between them had always been small and compensated for by the balance between his fury and her cold calculation.

Now they were apart, and they'd never be whole again.

Part of him hoped that she'd turn and head for Dublin. She'd leave him to finish this. Part of him imagined them facing The Rat O'Neill together when he'd finished the job. Silently. Then they'd head out into the world again and repeat their jobs, their life's work never done, their justice never ending.

He knew it was a fancy.

She would follow. There was no way she wouldn't. The thought should have made him sad since he'd have to kill her, or at least try.

It didn't make him sad though. It warmed him in unexpected ways.

She would never shirk. She would never back down. He wasn't lying when he told her that they were the same. The drive in him was the very same as the drive in her. While others muddled their way through their lives, living from one disaster to the next, the two of them had learned. Consequences, there's always a reckoning.

They just disagreed on who had to pay that bill. A small thing to fight about. But fight about it they most certainly would. Even if that meant that one of them would die.

It was an oddly satisfying thought.

It was the only acceptable way for them to end.

The corpse beeped.

The noise might have been drowned out by the storm had Broderick not been waiting for it.

The beep was followed by talking:

'Movement near the main gate. Barricade is obscuring. Mac, what can you see?'

Broderick looked at the dead eyes, filmed over.

Mac couldn't see anything now, so he had little to report.

He levered himself up a little and looked out the former window toward the main gate, the rain stinging his face as it hit him.

Movement alright.

Someone clumsy.

And then, her.


O'Mahony strained to see what Rook was pointing at.

Dimly, in the half light of the storm, he could see a figure scurrying.

Other movement followed, almost all around them. In the houses and shells of houses that surrounded the hospitals, heads could be seen poking up from behind walls and obstacles.

Gibson had sprung a trap, and yet no one moved for him.

'Hold position,' the One-Eyed Rook snarled into his walkie-talkie.

'Sir, it's Gibson,' a voice crackled back at them.

'I said hold,' Rook ordered again. 'We're no trap if we spring before the agents show themselves.'

The hardness of the man communicated itself through the radiowaves and the silence from the walkie-talkies was almost apologetic, even with the wind and rain driving and stinging.

Further down the Newcastle Road, there was flicker of movement too. A young woman dashing into the street, but suddenly hauled back.

A brief moment of recognition for O'Mahony made him gasp.

Even at a distance, he knew it was her. Not the woman who had burst into the street, but the woman behind, who had hauled the first one back. The shoulders, the shape of her, the movement, the aura of power she held.

He recognised the agent who had saved him.

Rook looked at him. 'Who?' he asked.

'Someone,' O'Mahony told him.

He didn't want to say it was her.

Rook narrowed his eyes again, the scar wrinkling his face as he did so, scanning the area.

Everything was a threat to him.

It was what had ruined them.

Everyone seeing everything as a threat, so that only the strongest or the smartest outlived the most vulnerable.

O'Mahony relied on being smart to survive, but eventually someone smarter or stronger would remove him too.

'Ground floor positions,' Rook spoke into the walkie-talkie and this time the silence felt like compliance.

O'Mahony stared up the street again. There was no sign of them anymore.

'It's going to get violent,' Rook told him.

O'Mahony heard what the man meant to say.

This was no place for weak men.

He nodded to the soldier.

Rook nodded back.

Then he turned and made for street level. The soldiers would close in on their quarry.

O'Mahony waited as long as he dared for the larger man to move away and then he picked himself up, lamenting his old bones again.

She was down there.

Joseph howled at him, a warning, and pulled at his clothes, but this time he wasn't going to run or hide.

# CHAPTER FIFTEEN

Fionnuala pulled in ragged breaths as they came to a stop inside the entrance to an old house. Malley had pushed them hard along the M6, struggling to make up lost ground. She knew that the older woman had tempered their pace in order to make up for Fionnuala's lack of fitness and endurance, but their journey had still pushed her to her limits.

They'd slowed for traps, obvious ones that even Fionnuala could see, where old cars had been pushed together to make long killing corridors. The husks of them didn't align with the vague memories of cars from her youth, crowding roads, cluttering streets. These were the corpses of her remembered cars. Where had they been going? Who had left them here? Malley had them climbing over the debris in the howling wind and the rain, her grip sure, Fionnuala's slipping on the corroded chassis.

Later, in a shallow dip where a small river had taken part of the motorway, Malley had stopped, signalling with an abrupt hand. She had looked like a painting then, strong and immovable for all Joseph tried to shift her, one hand raised in warning.

She picked her way carefully through the water and then stooping low, pulled up a line of metallic spikes that had stopped just short of the water surface.

She held them in her hand for a long moment, her other

hand hovering at her knife as she waited for the attack that must surely have been coming.

But there had been no sign of people.

If they were smart, they were staying indoors. Joseph seemed to have a hunger about him.

At the outskirts of the city, Malley had pulled them on an unexpected course, dragging them around their target to come at it from the other side. The delay made her push harder again for pace, so that by the time they were approaching the hospital, the tall building dominating Fionnuala's vision, she was breathing heavy.

They stopped in the doorway of the old home. There had been fighting here at some point. Various bits of debris had been jerry-rigged to form a barricade just inside the front door. Someone, at some point, had tried to defend this home long after it had become impossible to do so.

Now all that remained was a mouldy, sodden carpet on the stairs with a row of pictureless hooks to show that someone had once called this home.

'What now?' Fionnuala tried to whisper.

She could have shouted it and it likely would have made no difference, the elements were stealing sound from their lips. Fionnuala watched Joseph take a hold of the world and shake it. There was an awesomeness to it. She couldn't remember a Storm Season where she hadn't spent most of the time indoors, warm enough to almost forget the underlying feeling of dread that pervaded outside. To be walking in it, feeling the exhilarating, almost electrical, energy of it was a giddy experience.

Malley's face told a different story.

Her anger, as she surveyed the surroundings, was obvious. Her eyes scanning for danger, for signs of Broderick, or BlueArms, or Gibson, but all they met was the devastating effects of the ceaseless march of the Storm Seasons.

It was frightening because Fionnuala guessed that this anger, this exact sensation, was what drove Malley to kill. The resentment and bitterness she felt swelled as she watched a countryside she once knew be reshaped by the storms. Joseph just the latest in a line of aggressors who bent the country to his will, and then broke it. This was the reason Malley wouldn't hesitate to slam a knife into Gibson's ribs. Kelly's too for that matter.

'What do we do?'

'Watch,' Malley told her.

Another lesson for Fionnuala in that single word. Keep communication short.

Don't waste words.

The silence between Malley and Broderick that had been so unnerving finally made sense.

She continued scanning, her eyes never resting on one place in particular but always coming back to the hospital, and the top floor.

The main entrance was barricaded with debris and the corpses of cars. There was surely a way to access the hospital but figuring out how might turn out to be deadly.

There was too much ground to cover and, simultaneously, not enough to keep them hidden. The walls of the hospital had been built up with corrugated metal, chicken wire, and barbed wire, but for a few places where one might climb easily over. But these points of entrance were too inviting not to be traps. The buildings all crowded nearby – houses, former shops, and bars – were places where people could easily be lying in wait for them.

Traps, or potential traps – too much danger.

'Look!' Malley barked.

At the crossroads, by the main entrance to the hospital, a figure emerged into the storm.

In a moment, Fionnuala knew it was Gibson, his lanky, stopped frame giving him away.

She was moving as soon as she saw him, making for the long street that led to the barricaded entrance to the hospital.

'Fool,' Malley hissed.

She could have meant either of them.

Fionnuala dashed out into Joseph's embrace as quickly as she could. And an embrace it was, the wind seemed to buffet her, stopping her. Its power immense, a massive hand that closed around her and held her in place. The pure awesomeness of it was intoxicating, exhilarating in so many ways, until it suddenly wasn't. She couldn't breathe properly, as though Joseph's fist had closed on her, squeezing her lungs.

He was so close to her, but she could hardly move for the power of the wind.

Then Malley was by her side.

Fionnuala felt the hand close on the back of her neck, a mother cat's mouth closing on the scruff of a kitten.

'Let me go,' Fionnuala roared, wriggling in Malley's grip.

Gibson was still in the middle of the street. She'd learned enough by now to know the danger he was in, even if he didn't seem to know it himself.

The man was in peril because he was surrounded by people who had something to protect.

The lowlands had taught her that lesson. People protected what they had and Omega, it seemed, had a lot to protect. The agents had their government to protect.

But she had a lot to protect too. Something bigger than any of the rest.

A future.

Malley hauled them back into the shelter of the porch of the old home, the walls offering some protection from eyes, and from Joseph's powerful hand.

'Are you trying to get yourself killed?' Malley screamed at her over the wind.

'We have to save him,' she shouted back.

'By getting yourself killed?' Malley barked again. Even in the half-light, Fionnuala could see the deep anger hiding behind the otherwise stern and unbending face.

'He's a sitting duck out there! You promised me justice.'

It was a stupid, grandiose statement and she knew it, but it was how she felt.

'I don't give a shit about him,' Malley shouted at her.

'Well, I do.'

'Enough to throw away your life for him?' Malley snarled.

The agent would likely not understand. She truly thought that all that anyone could have was what they could hold. For Fionnuala, what was at stake was intangible but so much more valuable. A chance for everyone to take together.

'We have something worth protecting.'

'No, you have nothing,' Malley bit back.

He was feeling out the barricade now, at the front of the hospital. Oblivious. Like he was the only man in the world. As if danger wasn't everywhere, all around him.

She could practically feel the eyes on him. Broderick's among them.

'Broderick is out there,' Malley told her, as if reading her thoughts.

Glancing at her, Fionnuala could see the urge in Malley to throttle her, or slap her face.

'Why do you think I'm trying to get to him? It isn't justice if you let him die.'

'He can die fifty times for all I care.'

Her face was so hard, so brutal looking in the half-light. And it hid something. Fionnuala could almost see it, behind the façade of strength. Like a shadow hiding in the agent's eyes.

'You promised me,' she told her.

'You're a stupid, foolish, naïve woman who shouldn't be allowed out in the world,' Malley told her.

'What about my justice?' Fionnuala shot back.

'I will not allow you to die.'

There it was. Her truth emerging. She'd give up her justice for Fionnuala.

It was absurd.

She'd willingly give up the thing that drove her, the reason to keep going, her motivation for walking into this hellscape and back out again year after year. Just for Fionnuala.

'Why?' Fionnuala asked her.

'There are prices people have to pay,' Malley told her. In her eyes there was something new now, something close to desperation, close to tears.

'What?'

The older woman hesitated for just a moment, the wind still pulling at her, even in the shelter of the porch, her hair slicked against her head.

In that second, she was the same as she'd looked by the fireside in Black Stair. As if the true her was attempting to break out from underneath the stony face that kept her hidden.

Then Malley held her hands up, palms out. The horrific scars that tracked across her skin were a frightening thing to behold. She had stolen glances at those scars but never inspected them up close before. They looked different in every light you saw them in. By the firesides they'd shared, the scars looked like shadows hiding terrible things in their folds. In the daytime, they looked like a landscape that one might die trying to cross. But in this half-light, they looked like dying things, rotting things that might fall apart in the heavy rain, sloughing off the bones that held them until only the hard skeleton underneath was visible.

'This, you fool of a woman. This is the thing that happens when the strong people take what they want from the weak,' Malley told her, her voice reaching depths of coldness that made the storm seem cosy.

'This,' she continued, 'is what you're left with when they're done. And it's not even the worst thing they give you. This is the lesson you learn outside.'

She was no longer trying to stop Fionnuala from getting to Gibson, but her words may as well have been a vice grip for all that Fionnuala could get away from them.

'I'm sorry—'

'You know nothing,' Malley cut her off angrily, 'because you haven't learned yet. There's a lesson out here. You have to lose something. Some people think that if you lived Before, you've lost enough, but that's not true. All those people who talk about Before aren't complaining about losing their cars or their holidays or their coffee machines. They're really talking about the other things taken from them. Important things, things you can't see or hold. That's what they've lost. And it's still not enough. You have to lose more.'

'That's what I'm trying to give them back,' Fionnuala told her. 'A future. A chance to know security and peace. That's what this is about, can't you see that?'

Gibson was still skulking at the entrance to the hospital, his hands probing at the barricade as if searching for something.

The agent smiled at her, ignoring the driving rain, it was a bitter smile.


Malley felt the bitterness inside her as she looked down at the scars… she remembered. Every day they reminded her.

The door frame had splintered under their boots. The weeks of unceasing storms had come to this. Proof that you could shelter wherever you wanted but something would find you. If the wind and the rain didn't get you, the people would.

Neither of the men had seemed so huge when they were banging on the door and she spied them through the peephole. They seemed to grow as they walked into the small basement apartment she shared with her sister.

Their sanctuary, once a damp and spartan place until they'd made it home, comfortable and warm.

The storm charged in through the door they'd kicked down, rushing around the room and laying its cold, wet hands on their belongings, tugging at things, shaking things, breaking things.

Before the power had gone, the radio had told them that this was not one storm, but many, a procession of them marching off the Atlantic to batter Ireland, stripping roof tiles, felling trees, knocking out power, and shaking buildings so that the beautiful, immutable architecture that was once such an indelible mark of the city of Dublin began to feel temporary, precarious. The shells of once homes and businesses corroborated that feeling. This Season of Storms had no romantic notions about Dublin's Georgian architecture.

And if the storm was in a hurry, the two men who followed in behind it were just the opposite, their footsteps slow, ominous.

They had looked ragged and desperate, hair slicked onto their heads, bundled in layers that were sodden and dripping. It shouldn't have been so after only three weeks but there they were, looming, long hunting knives in hand. No planes landing, no boats coming into dock. Food had run out quickly once the chain of supply was broken, and if an aircraft had managed to land in the gaps between the storms, whatever they had brought simply wasn't enough to go around.

Three weeks without resupplying the country had made men into this.

Without thinking, Malley had moved to put herself between them and her sister. Hilda's terrified scream when the door had buckled, now entirely drowned out by the noise of the storm, which roared down their stairs and rattled around their home.

Their eyes had been terrifying. Hungry, not merely for lack of food, but deprived of something else too. Control. A say in their own destiny. The things Fionnuala was so sure she could give people back. They might have been dignified men once, powerful even, but the seemingly endless storm that battered the country had robbed them of that, and left them with these fevered-looking eyes, and no options.

Outside the apartment, she could hear footfalls and rough coarse shouting, a mixture of accents from all over the country and beyond, a people united by desperation and violence, confident that they outnumbered the law.

'We don't have anything you want,' Malley had told them, and she recalled how terrified she sounded, the beginning of her tears leaking into the sound of her voice.

The older one, stocky and balding, had scrubbed the few remaining hairs he had out of his face and took a slight step forward.

She watched those eyes flicker from her to Hilda. Two twenty-somethings. They were little mice to him. Like Broderick weighing up Fionnuala.

The men had come for food, or batteries perhaps, maybe even candles. The things that ran out too quickly and were wanted by too many. The sisters standing before him presented little in the way of an obstacle.

The younger man, less desperate seeming, more dead looking, had flicked his knife at them, a peremptory command to move aside that he might take what was theirs, what they had foraged for in the middle of a storm and pilfered in the dead of night to keep themselves alive. Literally, all they had left.

Malley hadn't moved.

He hesitated and looked at her, his expression curious, as though he didn't quite understand what exactly it was she was trying to do, or perhaps, why she thought she should bother.

He was so much bigger than her.

The balding one, his eyes fevered, twitching and shuddering involuntarily, took another step forward.

She stood her ground.

His eyes turned hotter, and his lower lip began to tremble, a curious mixture of desperation and anger and the fury of impotence, as if his body couldn't contain it all.

The wind continued to whip all about them, just as Joseph was doing now, begging for their attention as if it had somehow sensed it had lost them. The storms always demanded their rightful place.

Hilda's breathing had become deeper, more ragged. Malley tried to keep herself from hyperventilating. To let them take the food might mean death by starvation if the storm didn't end soon. To try to stop them might mean death too, just sooner.

The knife, she reasoned, was the key. Long and silvery looking in the poor light of her basement, the handle wrapped in tape and cloth. If she could get her hands on it, take it from him, maybe they had a fighting chance…

The balding man moved then, no longer merely threatening, aggressive, and dominating, the blade brandished that she might step back from it.

She didn't.

Instead, she reached for the weapon, her hands closing on it, but on the blade only. It bit into her skin, slicing the soft flesh of her unworked hands, even as he jerked back in preparation for a thrust.

Her move had startled him, and for a moment, he did nothing. Standing there with a thin sliver of her blood on his knife, perplexed by her attempt to take something from him.

Desperate to take advantage of his hesitation, she reached for it again, this time grabbing it with both hands and tried to drag it from his grip.

The blade had buried itself in her skin and scraped her bone and she had screamed with the pain. He tried to pull it clear from her, but she held it tight, feeling it slice deep into her skin as he tried to tug it lose.

Angry then, he brought all his weight against her, and it was considerably more than hers. The two of them went down, her hands still clutching, the blade squirming and slicing. The weapon was life to her then. If she could only get it from him.

If not, she figured she might at least buy her sister some time.

'Run, Hilda, run,' she had screamed, even as she hit the floor, her head rebounding off the hard wood. He came down on top of her, his gut pinning her to the ground.

But Hilda didn't run. She crouched down into the corner of the room and squeezed her eyes shut.

The man on top of her held the knife with one hand, the fingers of his other hand trying to prise hers free of the blade. It slithered in her hands and she held it desperately, slicing it with her own blood.

The pain was excruciating, yet she had held on.

She bucked and thrashed underneath him, even as she roared at her sister to run. Clumsily, they rolled together on the ground, his bulky shape sliding off her so that she gained a small advantage over him, pulling still at the blade, feeling it slicing tendons and scraping bone.

'Hilda! Run!'

In her periphery, she could see her sister, eyes no longer squeezed shut, but staring straight at her, in a small ball on the floor. Even at a glance, she could sense the wrongness of that. Small and still and staring straight ahead.

The man stopped prying at her fingers and had instead punched her in the nose. The taste of hot blood filled her mouth, but she still didn't let go of the blade. It squirmed still between them, his pulling and twisting scoring her skin deeper, shredding the flesh, back and forth.

'Run,' she tried to scream at Hilda again though it came out as a gurgle caught by the wind and the rain.

A shadow passed over her as the second man stepped across the brawl on the floor beneath him and reached for Hilda.

She held the blade desperately and willed Hilda to bolt, to sprint out into the storm and freedom. But Hilda merely stood up, her face eerily calm, as she stepped toward the man advancing on her.

She placed one hand on his chest, almost gently.

Her eyes didn't blink. Simply stared.

The man stopped, he seemed to soften too, as if he knew what was coming.

What she was offering to him.

Hilda nodded at him in slight, terrible encouragement.

'Don't Hilda,' Malley heard herself cry.

Then another punch knocked her cold out.

When she woke up, it was done with and the men were gone.

Malley remembered. And every day she lived with it.

In Fionnuala's soft, blue eyes, she saw a replica of what Hilda's eyes had looked like before Malley earned her scars, before Hilda had earned the scars that no one would ever see.

Foolish. Both of them. But with this child, there was a chance. An opportunity to make up for what had gone so wrong with Hilda. A chance to save that innocence. To protect the vulnerable from those who would take. A chance for the child to hold on to some hope.

If Malley herself could be strong enough this time.

Angrily, she spat at her own feet.

'Wait here,' she barked at the younger woman.


'What are we doing?' Fionnuala asked from behind.

Ignoring her, Malley picked through the rubble of the long-abandoned home until she found a cylindrical metal pole among the trash. A bus stop pole at some point, she surmised. A part of somebody's last stand.

She tore up a section of old sodden carpet too. Cutting at it with her knife and pulling it clear with gnarly hands.

Outside the shelter of the porch, Joseph made enough noise that she hoped might cancel any sound they would make until it was too late. She was grateful for that. She'd spotted more than one figure moving among the nearby houses and rooftops. BlueArms certainly. And Omega's security forces. Which were key.

The little princelings and kinglets always had strong men and women ready to fight for them.

Broderick would be hiding out there as well, but there was no way he'd allow himself to be seen. He could be right behind her, or in front of her.

It was a chess game.

The locals wouldn't move until there was a threat, the BlueArms wouldn't move until they could spring their trap, but since Broderick and Malley both knew they were there, it was on them to either provoke that trap into springing at the wrong moment, or to step lightly around it.

At least, that's what they'd be expecting, watching for.

She hoped they hadn't been spotted when Fionnuala had made her stupid dash for the street.

'Follow,' she called back over her shoulder, manoeuvring the long former bus stop as she moved out into the street.

The hospital was a trap too.

The way to beat it was to think your way through it.

If it was her trap, how might she be inclined to bait the unwary?

Gibson had indeed vanished, but if she guessed right, it was because he'd been let in.

If it was her trap, she'd have lots of doors in. All fully functional, but all fully dangerous. Every point of ingress or egress could be armed when she would want it to be, and not if the occasion demanded.

If that was the case, then all the doors were dangerous.

So, she'd have to make her own door.

She stopped where the driveway met the main road and checked one last time.

'Stay close behind me,' she called back.

With that, she hoisted the heavy bus stop, wrapped around the top and the middle with carpet and boldly walked out into the middle of the street.

She could practically feel the surprise all around as she moved, quickly but on certain feet, her eyes scanning the barricade wall until she found it.

A small chink in the panelling. Too small to be a major fault in the defences... unless one had a lance made out of a bus stop.

Without waiting, she levelled her bus stop lance and charged.

The smash of metal on metal rang even in the storm wind, and the barricade gave slightly.

Stepping back, she charged at it again, throwing her anger and her body behind her makeshift pole arm.

It bent a little further.

She heard a shout from somewhere, carried on Joseph's breath: the traps sprung. The BlueArms would move, then the locals would move to protect Omega from strangers, then Broderick would move into the confusion. At least, that's what she was gambling...

Once more she hoisted up her lance, ignoring the incredulous look on Fionnuala's face and she charged straight at the metal.

It buckled entirely, the sheet pulling away from whatever contraption had connected it to the next section. The wall wasn't built to repel attacks. That's what the sentries nearby were for. It was built to funnel people through the doors Omega wanted them to use.

Her door was the hole she punched into the wall.

None of them would have been expecting that.

It was by no means a perfect entry. Even as she pushed a scrambling Fionnuala over what was left of the wall and hoisted herself over it, she could hear the sounds of people calling and shouting.

And then, the sound she had really gambled on. Fighting.

Both sets of soldiers reacted at the same time, pouring from their hiding places so that they came together at the gap she'd made.

If she'd timed it right, she was ahead of the pack, ahead of Broderick, and that's what counted.

Behind the high walls, the wind was slacker, quieter.

She pulled her knife clear of its sheath, as much to feel the oneness with the wrapping in the folds of her scars as for anything else.

'What now?' Fionnuala asked her.

'Now we go find out if he's guilty or not.'


O'Mahony had pressed his body against the side of the old home, making his soaked and shaking form as small as he could. He could hear the sound of them arguing around the corner.

He shivered in the wind and the rain, trying to focus himself. The coldness of it all was hard to take.

One more discomfort that tougher people would have been able to bear lightly.

Rook would have words with him when the man realised

that O'Mahony had gone off on a solo mission, but the woman drew him on.

He'd never been the same since she'd crept up on him. He had always known he wasn't a strong man, but he'd never known how truly weak he was until she'd materialised at his side that day.

It stayed with him. Haunted him. He watched others in this new world making their way, doing what must be done, fighting with that terrible strength people possessed for surviving, while he balked at everything.

Now he was going to have to follow over the wall.

He was too old for walls like this.

That was his weakness talking again. Glancing about in imitation of the furtiveness that was part and parcel of the soldiers he'd seen in Limerick, he picked himself up and followed after them.


Broderick fully laughed, loud and gleeful, when he saw her charge the wall with the 'lance'. The storm winds often made him manic. He had been puzzling the doors in, waiting for someone else to make that first mistake in the game of chess.

It was so perfectly her, to charge like that. He wouldn't have expected it for a million years. For all the closeness of their thoughts.

He watched the soldiers spilling out of the buildings and into the street.

The local clanspeople, Omega's people or their own, were clumsy fighters. They showed themselves in myriad ways; from how they held their makeshift weapons to their posture, to their way of grouping together, too close to use those weapons to good effect.

These BlueArms were a different story. Not like others he'd met in his past, these fought with precision and ferocity. Like soldiers. He'd encountered two of them already since he'd left the house. They'd been just as good as the first one he'd met.

The brawl out on the streets had started already, the locals outnumbering the BlueArms. The numbers wouldn't count. The BlueArms would kill all these amateurs, if they didn't break and run first.

Loyalty bought was usually a fragile thing.

He'd watched Gibson vanish through a small, concealed door at the main entrance. He might be able to access the hospital that way, but it would be tricky enough in the storm, never mind the fighting.

So why bother trying.

Malley had already provided him with a way in.

From inside his jerkin, he pulled out a BlueArmband and slipped it over his coat.

That should add to the confusion.


The Rook could hardly believe it when the woman walked out onto the street with her homemade battering ram, the little rebel in tow. It was difficult to believe that this hardened thing was Hilda's sister. They couldn't look more different. The BlueArm behind her looked more like Hilda, slight with her curly hair.

How he was supposed to keep the two of them alive now was beyond him.

Even hauling the ungainly ram with her, she looked dangerous. It was in the way she moved. Years of fighting had taught him the look of veterans, of soldiers, and of cowards and, most importantly, the look of the dangerous ones. The movement of them.

The most important question was where was the other one? The man agent. The rabid dog. Where there was one, the other was surely not far away.

He didn't issue the order to attack, but once she was in the open and charging at the walls, Omega's people moved. They were clumsy and poorly armed. If the timing had been right, they might have brokered some kind of deal. He wasn't here for their little king or queen or whatever. But the timing wasn't right, and so his BlueArms burst from their cover and converged on them.

The howling wind and rain made the BlueArmbands all important, telling his people from Omega's was damn near impossible in the storm. Racing for the hole she'd made in the wall he was forced to stop, faced by two large axes.

Rook ducked one swing and drove a shoulder hard at the smaller target, twisting his free arm to parry the second. He kicked out a leg, felt the knee break beneath his boots, and turned in time to headbutt the first assailant right between the eyes.

He'd been feeling his years. Each Storm Season that came was harder to cope with than the last, but in this moment, he was himself. The One-Eyed Rook. A silly child who liked birds, grown into a man who would kill and maim for his people.

He reached the wall, hauling one of the local clansfolk back out of the breach and bouncing them hard off the pitted tarmac of the road.

One of his men was approaching.

Moving with the same deadly grace that Hilda's sister had moved with.

The other one.

The BlueArmband was no disguise. The languid grace of his movements, the casualness of it, through a storm and through combat, announced who he was.

Rook turned to meet him.

The rabid dog against the One-Eyed Rook.

He powered himself straight at the younger man, his cudgel swinging as he moved. The agent seemed to spring, even as Rook started forward, their attacks almost simultaneous.

The cudgel whistled through thin air where the agent had been, and Rook felt a blow glance against his head.

He shifted to correct his stance and protect himself, but the agent was already moving. The speed of him astonishing.

Two blows landed on the Rook in rapid succession, drawing a grunt and forcing him back a step.

For a few moments, they twisted and turned in the lashing rain, each trying to land a blow and keep the blows away, both skilled and dangerous.

Not bested yet, Rook probed for a way in, but the blows he aimed, the swings all seemed a split second too late. That or the agent could read his mind.

A heavy boot took him in the ribs, another blow clipped him behind the ear. He dropped to one knee, feigning injury and as the man closed, he surged back to his feet with a roar, burying his fist in the man's gut.

The agent winced, but righted himself and twisted away to his right, narrowly avoiding Rook's right fist. The left fist counter-punch took Rook above his eye, splitting the skin. And that was that.

His lack of depth perception had never been a problem to him against poor fighters, but against this demon with all its speed and power, with his one good eye now clouded with blood...

He didn't even see the knockdown punch coming and he went down in a puddle of rainwater.

The agent vaulted over the wall.

Too easy for the younger man.

He hoped Hilda would forgive him when he got home. There could be no protecting anyone now. It was kill or be killed against these people.

# CHAPTER SIXTEEN

Gibson looked haggard. A battered and bedraggled man, too old to have travelled the width of the country, coast to coast in the blooming days of a Storm Season. His sodden clothes clung to his scrawny figure as he sat, slumped in a chair. He had a gun in his hand, which he didn't even raise, but left both hand and gun sitting across his lap.

He was older than Malley, she surmised, by as many as fifteen years, making him somewhere in his mid-fifties, though he looked older.

She'd seen him in news bulletins, and once or twice in person, when business took her into Government buildings where he was usually found. He had looked grander then, more solid, more real.

Now he looked like a man who'd lived a sheltered life on the east coast, where the water wasn't as high and the storms less terrible. Only that sheltered life was over now. He was tossed out of it and into the real world.

He was paying the cost.

He might yet pay a higher one.

Omega was a surprising sight too. She supposed it must be Omega, a queen in her realm, standing quietly by. She was of an age with Gibson, though she bore it better than he had. Life outside had made her tough. But sheltered in her castle, she didn't lack for warmth or provisions.

Her face was open, her expression bland, her eyes missing the tint of madness that had been so visible in Digital's.

Malley couldn't have said why she expected Omega to be a man. Nor why it seemed so apt to her that she was a woman.

The gun that she held casually, but unshakingly, was pointed at Malley.

Malley tried not to look at the two guns in the room, she tried not to wonder too long if they even had bullets left for them. She didn't want them second-guessing her. She needed them off-balance. Almost every gun in the country had spent its bullets long ago.

'Frank Gibson or Gibson Waters?' she asked him calmly.

Her temper was back under control, though it simmered beneath the surface. There was no room in this place for anger. Anger unchecked typically led to mistakes.

She almost laughed as she struggled with the reins of it.

All this running. Just to find herself here, in front of this ordinary-looking man while a woman pointed a gun at her.

A sorry-looking sight to have given up Broderick for.

Fionnuala hovered anxiously behind her. Her concern for him was evident. But she was aware too that everything now hung in the balance.

'I was born Gibson Waters. I changed my name to Frank Gibson. Don't know why, but I always liked the name Frank.'

'Guilty people hide who they were,' Malley told him.

'Some people just want a fresh start.'

'Most of the fresh starters I ever met used to deny climate change.'

'Occupational hazard, I assume.'

She smiled at that. He had a politician's wit.

Omega cracked a small smile too. She was hard to read. Harder than most, but she gave a little away. She hadn't moved when he announced his name change. So, she already knew that. She was holed up in a hospital and he used to be a doctor. Hardly a coincidence. Likely they knew one another from Before.

'Perhaps,' Malley agreed with him. 'Sort of like having a gun pointed at me. Like your old buddy here is doing.'

That made them twitch. They didn't like that she knew.

'You two know each other?' Fionnuala asked.

Malley tsked at the interruption.

They wouldn't stay off-balance if they were allowed to ramble.

Fionnuala had done some learning along the way, and Malley suspected she might have made a fine agent, but the impulsive streak in her was more than merely annoying.

'We did,' Gibson told her, offering a fatherly smile. 'Once upon a time.'

'Just decided to pop around for a catch up, did you?' Malley asked him sardonically.

'Making my rounds,' he quipped again.

She didn't smile this time. He was too blasé. Too casual. She reckoned herself a smart person, with an eye for detail, and she'd proven herself over and over, but this was different.

The casual banter, the idle chit-chat, the manoeuvring without moving, this was home territory for the likes of him.

She needed to shift him out of his comfort zone.

She cracked her neck with a slow roll of her head.

It was always amazing to her how often that had an effect on people. Omega's small smile vanished and she aimed the gun a little higher, her grip less casual now.

'I'd put the gun down now if I were you,' Malley told her, shifting her focus away from him.

Neither of them would have been expecting that.

'Oh, you would, would you?' Omega replied.

'Under the Offences Against the State Act, it's illegal to interfere with a DOE investigation.'

'Investigation?' Gibson asked with a soft laugh. He patted his thigh with the gun as he spoke.

Too casual by half.

'If I put it down, you'll kill him,' Omega replied.

'Not if he's innocent, but if you *don't* put it down, I'll definitely kill *you.*'

Her tone was pure confidence and had a more profound effect than the sound of popping as she had cracked her neck. Could she do it? Would she be able to get to her before Omega pulled the trigger?

Some of Gibson's cool façade slipped as he swallowed.

Better. This was closer to where she wanted him.

'She's telling the truth,' Fionnuala piped up again.

'Oh, I don't doubt she'll kill me,' Omega scoffed.

'We don't have time for this,' Fionnuala whined. 'Broderick is coming. He'll kill everyone. I'm telling you, she won't kill anyone who's innocent. I swear it.'

Her naiveite was touching. Any other agent could have made the promise she'd made and Fionnuala might still have been inclined to believe them, right up until they plunged the knife into her chest.

That she trusted so much, that she'd invested that trust in Malley was a small but moving thing.

'No,' Gibson protested. 'She'll kill us.'

He wasn't casual now, his gaze was intense, much more like the man she'd seen in the bulletins.

'Not if you're innocent,' Malley assured him.

'Is my word good enough?' he asked.

She pulled the small pamphlet from out of one of the internal pockets. It was sodden, despite the layers and the waterproofing on the wax coat.

'Explain this,' she told him as she tossed the little newspaper at his feet.

He didn't hesitate.

'It's fake,' he replied. 'I've seen about fifty of them.'

'That's no evidence.'

'Innocent until proven guilty,' he countered.

'Some might say this proves you guilty, so convince me that you're innocent.'

He didn't like that. His eyes flickered over her hands, and then the long knife.

'They're faked,' he told her. 'They were printed in Dublin, about two weeks ago. On a Government printer from a Government computer.'

What had Digital called them? Contrived?

'You can prove this?' she asked disbelievingly.

'Why do you think I came here? And Digital's little fortress? The IT people hold the keys to the kingdom, you see? Everything's networked. Digital thought he had it hacked but the information was deleted. Omega has access to backup servers though. She can prove it.'

Malley looked at Omega.

The woman nodded at her.

'I can tell you what printer they were printed from, and that they were sent from Minister O'Neill's computer to that printer. I can tell you the date and time down to the second.'

O'Neill's computer. The Rat.

Malley studied the woman's face as she spoke. She wasn't lying. Malley was certain.

He was innocent then.

'Something about IP addresses and unique IDs for printers,' Gibson told her. 'It's mostly techno-babble, but these are not newspapers written in the year 2020.'

Just like that. All the hunting for nothing.

She stared long at Omega, still trying to read the woman, as she had read so many others before, checking her for signs of duplicity, her in-built scepticism as her last form of defence against liars.

'I can give you exact numbers for printers and computers used. Hell, I can tell you what floor of what building,' the woman told her.

Innocent.

Bodies piled up behind them. A fool's errand to be Government assassins because O'Neill wanted the opposition removed.

'I told you,' Fionnuala almost cried, and she bounded forward.

Gibson beamed at her as she joined his side.

'You've done a good job,' he congratulated her. 'Might have saved my life.'

It didn't fit though. Omega's face was too bland. Too open.

'Why would the Government want to kill you?' she asked him.

'We're the leaders of a revolutionary movement,' he replied with a smile.

Fionnuala stood next to him, her chest out, proud as punch.

Malley wanted to be happy for her. She wanted to celebrate the victory for ideals over a world that seemed designed to crush idealism, but something remained... not right.

Fionnuala could see it in her too, Malley knew, the BlueArm's face frowning back at her.

'You promised,' she admonished Malley. 'You promised if he was innocent. And now you have your proof. The Government printed these.'

Malley wanted to shake her head. Perhaps she was tired. Had she become so cynical and drained that she couldn't accept the proof before her?

'I'm not killing any innocent people. I just want to know why O'Neill or anyone else would think it was a smart idea to make martyrs of two political leaders at the head of potentially armed insurrection?'

'O'Neill's a stupid man,' Gibson replied with a shrug.

Omega smiled when he said it, a knowing kind of thing.

Malley still couldn't stop her eyes drifting back to the gun on his lap.

Something was wrong.

'It doesn't make sense,' she almost whispered.

'The embargo,' Gibson told her. 'We're going to have the embargo lifted. We're going to unite Ireland again. There are new governments in Europe. Governments that believe we can make a future together, and they'll work with us, as long as we end the barbarism. No more refugee camps as towns, no more gangs of desperate people. No more hunger. No more

Doejays wandering the land with impunity. Supplies, trade, technology. The Governments don't want those things.'

'Why would anyone object to that?' Malley asked him flatly.

'Because it comes at a cost. Power. They have it, and they don't want to give it up.'

'I can't accept that.'

'Accept or not, that's what it is. The time has come to look forward, not back. There'll be no more killings for climate deniers or grid harvesters or food rioters. And the Government hates that because the agents are their number one weapon of public control.'

'Bullshit. My job is justice.'

'Yet here you are, with a long knife for me even though we both know that what O'Neill gave you is something he made in his office two weeks ago. He knows the end of the road is coming.'

'So, you and everyone else who ruined the world get to walk away?'

'I did no such thing. But it's irrelevant. The time for blaming people is gone. Pointing fingers at people is getting us nowhere. The time has come to move forward, to build for the future. To do what we should have been doing before the first Storm Season.'

'How convenient for all those people who destroyed the world. Where's all this hope coming from? Industry and manufacturing that poisoned the air? Politicians who voted against climate change laws and fought to line their pockets while the world burned?'

The words were hers but she had heard them before, from Broderick. This was the very thing he railed against. A free pass. A clean slate. For people who didn't deserve it.

'The rhetoric of a Government agent who points the finger at others so they don't have to be accountable.'

'Where's the justice?' she asked him bitterly.

'It's not about justice. It's about moving away from the past and building a future.'

She stared at him, agog. Wasn't this what she hoped for, for Fionnuala's sake? For Hilda's, with all her idealism and impulsiveness? Wasn't this a happy ending?

She looked at Fionnuala and saw the woman's eyes widen.

And that was all the warning she had.

Of course, he had managed to sneak up on her. Broderick was a ghost when he wanted to be.

Spinning, she ducked as she lashed the knife out, but he was already twisting away from her. He didn't hesitate coming at her again, two knives drawn. She parried one, her free hand striking down on the wrist holding the other.

Dimly, she was aware of another tussle happening behind her as furniture was shifted and two bodies tangled in the legs of tables.

A shot rang out. She didn't have time to check it, as Broderick came back at her again.

He was so fast. It hardly seemed natural. He attacked and pivoted and feinted and it took every bit of her to keep the knives from her flesh, while also keeping her body between him and Fionnuala.

She tried to measure him, to judge the speed and weight of his attacks, as she had always done before. She tried to embrace that cold feeling that sometimes enveloped her, helped her to see clearer, to plan better.

Even as they lashed out at each other, their bodies coming together at hips and shoulders, she was satisfied to notice that he was grunting with effort.

She had trained too long to be easy meat for anyone. Even him.

Another shot fired, the bullet whizzing nearby and burying itself in the wall. She could feel the struggle going on behind her, even if she couldn't see how it was progressing.

She desperately wanted to look over her shoulder and check on Fionnuala, but she dared not take her eyes off Broderick.

He struck again. And again. Blades flashing.

Technique wouldn't count here. She'd need to be clever.

She took a chance and double-bluffed, making to feint but following through with her free hand, the heel of her palm striking his chin and pushing him back.

His eyes never left hers, locked in as they were, but he hinged his jaw a couple of times, testing it out. The strike had counted.

He grinned at her. All teeth and no humour.

'Broderick, stop. He's innocent,' she panted at him.

'No, he's not,' Broderick panted back.

His tiredness was a badge of honour. She'd seen him cut a path through a riot, facing half a dozen people without breaking a sweat.

'The Government falsified the evidence. She has the proof.'

'He's innocent?' Broderick barked his bitter grunt of a laugh. 'If he's innocent, explain this…'

His eyes flickered about the room, but she understood the meaning.

If Gibson was innocent, then why were they fighting on the top floor of a former hospital in a once beautiful city ruined by storms and riots in the middle of a winter that would ravage the country.

That was the level of responsibility that Broderick held everyone to account for.

Perhaps even her now.

'What's the point, Broderick? What's the point in killing innocent people for a crime they didn't commit? The Government falsified the evidence. They're manipulating us. You said yourself you're no one's lapdog.'

'They enabled others to commit it.'

'This man didn't cause the storms. Neither did Fionnuala.'

'Innocent and guilty and us. That's all there ever was. They're not innocent and they're not us. No mercy for the guilty.'

'We're supposed to stand for something,' she replied, but even she knew it was lame. A stalling tactic to get her breath back.

'I do. It just isn't the same thing you stand for.'

He tensed and charged at her, and once again she found herself straining to keep him away. He had gathered his breath quicker than her. That was his advantage. Youth. Only by a couple of years but it was enough.

Evenly matched as they were for skill and technique, his superior strength and staying power would win out eventually. She had to try something, roll the dice, sooner rather than later when the action would be much more desperate.

She twisted away from a thrust, but not all the way, instead allowing his knife to score her shoulder.

If he wasn't expecting the hit, he'd be off balance, and vulnerable.

The knife shredded her uniform, tearing through skin, biting into the muscle of her shoulder. But he wasn't off balance, as though he had read her mind, he was anticipating her hip and he stepped into her attempted bump, kicking her feet out from underneath her with terrible force.

Her head bounced on the hard linoleum floor, sending a pain roaring through her skull and dazzling her.

He didn't stop though.

His heavy boot coming down hard on the hand that still held her knife, trapping her under his boot.

For a moment he looked at her and, in that moment, she stole one last look at Fionnuala, in the full knowledge that she'd failed.

Once again, she wasn't strong enough when the powerful ones came for what they wanted.

The young woman was holding the gun, Gibson stunned and on his knees in front of her, Omega cowered in the corner.

Fionnuala, with shaking hand, raised the gun, pointing it at Broderick and pulled the trigger.

It clicked uselessly. The two shots spent were all that it had left. Fionnuala's face changed from rigid determination to hopelessness in one futile click.

Malley lay on her back, her ruined hand trapped beneath

a boot, staring at the face of hopelessness and knew that she had failed her sister again.

They all held that moment, which seemed to last an eternity.

Eventually, he looked down at her.

'It was an honour,' he told her, and there was no mockery there.

She held his eyes as best she could, though she felt dizzy and nauseous from the pain in her head.

Broderick raised one knife.

Then he pitched forward as a small, old, wiry man appeared out of nowhere to crash into his back.

Relieved of his boot, her hand opened and spilled her knife onto the floor.

Then she was being hauled backwards, a familiar-looking old-timer pulling her by her boots toward the door.

She kicked at him to free herself, trying to shake off the daze of her head rebounding.

Broderick looked back at Malley and the newcomer with a grimace.

For a moment, she thought he might come after them, but in a split second, he made his decision and turned on Gibson.

Fionnuala stepped in front of him, her bravery astounding, holding the knife he had given her. He didn't hesitate but swiped it away and lashed out with his own knife, the blade slicing the skin on her face and opening her up from just under her eyeball down to her chin, spraying blood across the room.

She reeled back from him, crying out in pain, her hands going to her face.

Then he slowly rounded on Gibson and, without preamble, drove the knife into his chest.

The shock on the man's face was replaced by a look of terrible fear and then nothing as he slipped off the blade.

Fionnuala screamed a mixture of pain and dismay, and Omega looked somehow satisfied.

Malley's boot connected with the small man's head and

he rocked back. Scrambling unsteadily to her feet, she found Broderick standing ready again, one bloodied knife extended.

Malley blinked at him. There was a feeling of heat on the back of her neck as blood flowed down it. The floor seemed to shift underneath, her vision blurring. She'd hit her head harder than she realised.

Now or never...

She charged at him, summoning the last of her energy as she did.

He tossed the knife at her almost casually.

She tried to raise one hand to block it, but her fogged brain responded too slowly.

The knife bit into flesh and she went down again. Hard.

Fionnuala's hoarse sobbing was the last thing she heard before the darkness enveloped her.

Not strong enough. Again.

# CHAPTER SEVENTEEN

The sound of Joseph outside the window was the only thing she could hear. The violence of a storm using fists of wind to pummel buildings and people with equal ease. The keening and howling seemed to swirl around Fionnuala as she looked down at Malley, then at Gibson. The man she'd tried to save, then ultimately sacrificed because she was also trying to save Malley. All her efforts reduced to two corpses on a hospital floor.

The pain in her face felt like fire, one of her eyes seemed to be filling with blood that she couldn't blink away, and the flow of crimson spilled down over her chin and onto her clothes. In the corner of the room, Omega huddled. By the door, an elderly looking man stood hovering, indecision and hesitation painted all over his face. Weak. Both of them. This, she realised, is what Broderick and Malley had seen wherever they went. Weakness against their prodigious strength. It was no wonder that they felt no fear.

She looked up from them to find him staring at her. A small rivulet of blood tracked down from his nose to his chin before he scrubbed it away with the back of his hand. In his eyes, she saw the ever-present heat, the tinge of furious madness, but he didn't move.

'She was your friend,' Fionnuala told him accusingly.

'She was my enemy,' he corrected her.

That was his way. Enemies all around. And she realised he was going to kill her. Since she was no friend of his either.

If Malley couldn't stop him, what hope did Fionnuala and these other soft creatures in the room have? He was as the storm outside, indifferent to them and whatever defiance they might offer.

That was how it dawned on her. As she watched pools of blood collect under the corpse of the agent who had been her protector, she remembered not only the words the woman had shared with her, but the appalling sentiment behind them.

You survive. Any way you can. Until your moment arrives. Until you're strong enough to do something about it.

'I can give you Kelly,' she told him.

His eyes narrowed at her.

'How?'

'He's my uncle. Not by blood. But I've known him all my life. I can get you close to him. Past the security. Past the BlueArms.'

'In exchange for your life?' he asked.

And there was another flicker across his face. It looked almost like pain.

'Yes.'

She knew it would work. She knew it because his fury, like Joseph still smashing at the world outside, was an elemental thing, a rage without subtlety.

Malley had borne the scars of a fight for survival. Until she was strong. She could be the totem.

If Malley could do it, so could Fionnuala. She could survive, just long enough for her moment to come…

Gibson was dead.

Kelly stood at the window of the Point Tower that overlooked the Shannon and allowed the information to sink in. It seemed like it never would and the more he tried to think about it, the more his mind seemed to wander away from it.

The river was a distraction too.

The Shannon was mighty, unstoppable. It had always been wide and powerful in Limerick, especially at high tide. Now it was a dreadful thing. Any rain at all up-river would send water thundering down through Limerick so that this torrent would often be seen carrying the evidence of the Storm Season's destruction like trophies on its surface, hauling them all the way out to sea.

The Point Tower had once been on dry land, but the river periodically owned most of the ground floor now, and the means of entrance was via the various sky-bridges that connected to the militia barracks that had once been a Garda station.

That made his current base its own towering island, fourteen floors up from the raging river that was one of the city's primary defences.

Joseph was drawing his breath for another scream. The lull between storms in the early part of the season was typically longer than when it was at its peak, but still the clouds raced by, leaden or black, thick and threatening; carrying portents of weather still to come off the Atlantic.

The calm within the storms.

This is not where he wanted to be. He wanted to be in Dublin in comfort where the level of constant dread was pitched lower, still there, but nowhere near as intense as here, but it was part of the plan he'd devised with Gibson. They had known it was a risk when they'd decided to go ahead with it. Everything had hinged on Digital and Omega. What they knew, what they might say, what they could prove and, more importantly, what they could not prove – those were the most important elements.

'What about Omega?'

'Alive,' Carney told him.

'Well, that's good news,' Kelly lied.

He wouldn't have minded seeing her live had Gibson lived too, but with the man dead and her still breathing...

It might still work out, but it was out of his hands now. In a way it always had been, but he'd tricked himself into thinking that he was in control.

'Fionnuala Regan?'

'Unknown, but it's believed that she was taken by this Agent Broderick,' Hilda replied.

Her eyes were slightly red-rimmed from crying.

'They stole a bus,' Carney growled.

'I'm sorry?'

'Rook took two of the electric buses. He left them outside the city under guard. It seems that the agent killed the guards and took one of the buses.'

'So, he could be here already?'

Neither of them answered that. There was no doubt where the agent was heading. And equally no doubt that he'd get there. Taking Fionnuala had been a smart move. She knew the signs and the codes, the passwords. If he had been on foot, they may have had time to change the passwords and nullify the threat, but it was too late now. Smarter again if the agent knew of her connection to him.

He'd be here within the hour.

'Get word to the press. All of them. Tell them the Government has killed a duly elected member of the Dáil and the deputy-leader of the New Democratic Party based on contrived evidence as an act of political sabotage.'

This was the play.

Neither of them moved. Carney studied Kelly from underneath steel-coloured, bushy eyebrows, his ageing face unreadable under the massive once-ginger beard. Hilda, her face betraying the storm of emotions rippling through her, clenched and unclenched her jaw, wringing her hands.

'This is what we agreed, isn't it? Didn't we all agree this was the price of a united Ireland?'

'There'll be riots,' Carney told him.

'They murdered my friend,' Kelly suddenly bellowed.

There was the emotion that had been hiding from him. It had been lurking just under the surface, but it boiled up now.

They'd gone to school together. Before. They'd gone to bars. They'd bought their first cars together, at the same time, so they could drive from Galway back to Dublin along the M6 at the weekends. Racing each other as they went.

They'd begun to make names for themselves as young doctors, young men on the rise. Since they were twelve years old, it had been Joe and Gibson, later Joe and Frank. They'd survived the first Chain of Storms together, in Galway, where they'd tended to the victims of the storms in a hospital that frequently lost power.

There they had learned who they really were. That was the moment when they'd truly become men. He lamented what they'd been Before. Stupid boys who thought they were clever. Who thought they were invincible. He'd learned exactly what they really were when he had to decide who got to live and who got to die, and it was not clever or invincible.

They'd stuck together through that, born again for the first time in that hospital where Gibson was ultimately killed. There was a bitter symmetry to it.

Gibson dead, the agent on the loose, dragging the keys to the city by the hair with him. And now they wanted to balk? Now they were having cold feet?

'Did you think they were just going to walk out and hand us the reins?' he shouted. 'We agreed this. Your council did and those savages down in Cork, and everywhere in between. We can't have these people controlling everything, ignoring half the country, ignoring the people and the evidence. We can't allow them to divide us any more than they have...'

'When this is announced, the riots will divide us just as much, if not more,' Hilda shouted back at him.

Oh, there was a temper there for sure. She didn't bother to try hiding it either, she wore her emotions on her sleeve.

'They carried out a political assassination,' Kelly shouted back.

'He's right,' Carney interjected.

His age carried a lot of weight in the council, but it was the things he'd done to survive that counted the most. They knew he was a pragmatist. A man capable of awful things, but also a community man who took care of his people.

Likely he had been this hard Before as well.

Hilda tried to stare him down. She was tough too. No doubt. But Carney was made of bell metal.

Eventually she blinked. Shaking her head as she did.

'I'll get the word out.'

'What about your sister?' Kelly asked her.

'What about her?'

'Any word?'

'Dead.'

She walked from the room with her back straight.


Malley rose to consciousness as though swimming back into reality.

The pain in her head returning, along with the other pains. Torn flesh on both her shoulders. A fresh wound in her already ruined hand.

It was the first thing she thought about. Her hand. The new scar felt like an insult.

As though it sullied the memory of the old scars. Those scars contained her entire identity, hidden in the crevices of ruined flesh. They were her past and they had no business being impinged upon by the present.

That was her thought before she even realised that she was surprised to be alive.

She opened her eyes, still in the hospital in Galway. Joseph, though still outside rattling windows for attention, had calmed somewhat, a short lull between tantrums that brought people from their homes to wearily eye the devastation before returning to safety lest the season catch them unawares.

She was dressed differently, she realised.

There was whispering in the corner.

'Someone there?' she asked, and it came out in a dry-mouthed croak.

A man leaned over her.

She recognised the eyes. Like her father's. She hadn't recognised him when he'd tackled Broderick and tried to pull her to safety. He had saved her.

'We're even now I think,' he said.

His voice betrayed his age. His tone betrayed his life.

Old and beaten. She'd heard that tone a thousand times. The lifeless sound of someone who had decided enough was enough. That there was no more energy left to give life, save for that expended on not dying every day.

'I recognise you,' she told him.

'You let me live,' he told her back.

From looking at him, that might have been a curse or a blessing.

'Thank you for saving me,' she told him, and in her own tone, she recognised the very same thing.

She wasn't dead but couldn't tell if *that* was a curse or a blessing. She looked down at her bandaged hand, a smidgeon of blood leaking through the fabric. It covered the scars. It would make the oneness impossible to achieve.

'Where's Fionnuala?' she asked.

'Gone.'

'Gone where?'

'With him,' another voice told her quietly.

Omega's voice.

'What happened?' she asked, trying to sit up.

'He thinks he's killed you. It looked like he had. He threw the knife at you, and I swear I saw it go into your chest, but somehow it didn't.'

'Almost caught it,' she told him, glancing down again at the offensive new scar. A new scar, a new knife. 'He just left?'

'She bargained for her life. They're going to Kelly. We're in the building,' the man told her.

It took her a moment to realise he meant the BlueArms.

'Do they know I'm here?' she asked.

Her knives weren't on her person. She remembered leaving them in the tent in Black Stair. How liberating it had felt. Her hands itched for them now.

'We thought we'd just take them off you, as a precaution,' Omega told her, recognising Malley's fumbling for the blades.

'Give them back,' she said as sharply as she could muster.

'You can't go anywhere yet,' the man told her. 'The Rook is looking for him. And the girl. He's furious. Gibson is dead. You have to lay low.'

They were going to hide her.

'Who's the Rook?'

'Leader of the Limerick Militia. A soldier. A very angry soldier.'

'How many are you?'

'Three squads. It's about thirty people.'

'How long ago did they leave?' she asked.

'About two hours ago,' Omega told her.

'If I leave now…'

'If you leave now, someone will eat you for dinner before you get outside my compound.'

She might have been speaking literally.

'I can't let him go. Not with her.'

'Why not?'

'Like he said, the guilty and the innocent.'

There was a long pause then, and the feeling of wrongness she'd felt before Broderick had turned up returned to her tenfold.

'Kelly's not innocent,' Omega told her quietly.

The small old man grimaced uncomfortably. Omega frowned at him.

'What do you mean?'

They were confusing her. Her head pounded. Her scars ached and stung. Still, she pulled herself fully upright and stretched her muscles as much as she could.

'If those stitches come loose…' Omega threatened.

Malley offered her an unfriendly look.

'What do you mean Kelly's not innocent?'

Omega squirmed on the spot.

'He had a gun,' Omega replied, almost by way of some form of apology.

And with that, it clicked into place.

Malley and Fionnuala had interrupted Omega and Gibson. They'd been discussing something. Gibson knew his gun was primed, that Omega's wasn't. He hadn't left it laying on his lap, he'd left it pointing at Omega. She had the evidence needed to exonerate him or condemn him. That's why her face had been so bland. And why she'd looked so satisfied when his corpse hit the floor. He had been pointing his gun at her.

'The evidence? It wasn't fake?'

'Oh no, that evidence is very fake. It's just not the only evidence…'

Malley lurched on unsteady feet to the corner of the room, where a pile had been made of her still sodden clothes. The uniform would be no good, but with some tweaking and alterations she might achieve some form of disguise.

Fionnuala's pack was there too.

She felt a tear coming to her eye. A sting of anger and frustration. It had been a long time since she'd felt enough to summon one of those.

Gibson's gun had worked.

Two shots had been fired.

Then Fionnuala had the gun.

The younger woman had wrestled it from her hero. She'd seen him draw the gun and she'd taken it from him, to protect Malley.

In doing so, she'd left him with no protection when Broderick had come for her leader.

She'd killed another man. Inadvertently sure, but the result was the same. And she'd done it to save Malley.

The agent picked up the pack and pulled the BlueArmband out of it.

'You better start talking,' she told Omega as she picked up her knives.


It was calm when Omega walked her to the edge of what was once the City of Galway. The escorts that came with them stared at Malley balefully. They knew what she was. Malley pretended to ignore them. Her temper was growing inside her. Mollified somewhat by Omega's presence. The woman was soothing somehow. She provided for her people, which meant she was at very least a decent person. But if those soldiers attacked her...

The evidence she carried on her person was light, paperweight stuff, but it dragged at her, because Broderick was right and it would break Fionnuala.

What she carried on her might well destroy the young woman. Malley felt that tug on her conscience as she moved, its presence fuelling a growing anger within her. And anger she always tried to supress. She needed to be cold now, methodical, not smouldering with a latent rage.

'Is Digital dead?' Omega asked.

'Broderick killed him.'

'Because O'Neill told him to?'

'It seems so.'

'Makes sense. I imagine I was on his list too.'

Malley shook her head. If she had been, she'd be dead.

'I think Gibson would have killed me,' Omega told her.

'Why?' Malley asked.

She didn't want to make small talk, she wanted to be in Limerick. Her impatience added to her growing temper.

'Because of what I gave you. But also because I worked with them. I know them.'

'Fuck them.'

'It's funny in a way. They were always assholes when we worked together. Genuinely bad people. Arrogant. And worse, arrogant without cause. They weren't the best at what they did by any means, and they drank too much, and cared too little.'

'Why am I not surprised?'

'Hear me out...'

She hesitated then, plucking at her hood as the wind began to pick up all over again. Joseph had caught his breath apparently.

'That's what they were like before the first Storm Season,' she continued, her eyes swivelling to take in the devastated countryside. 'Arrogant, reckless children. But when it happened, they were different. I suppose we all were. They were heroes during the first Storm Season. I remember it well. I remember the triage and the power failing and constantly being tired and hungry. I watched them turn from arrogant children into brilliant men during those weeks. I think that was why they went into politics.'

'We all pay the price to learn the lesson,' Malley told her.

She was out of sympathy. She didn't have any left to give. Inside her natural coldness, the dispassionate, careful, measured Malley was in danger of being consumed as the heat of her temper continued to grow. She struggled to rein it in.

The soldiers were still throwing her filthy looks, their hands twitching and their movements restless. Amateurs. They gave themselves away with every move. She'd make them regret it if they tried anything.

'I'm not saying any of this by way of excuse,' Omega told her. 'I'm just observing, I suppose. The things you think might last that never do. The things you hope will change, but somehow don't. I never thought we'd end up here. I always thought we'd come together, as a country, as a planet, I suppose, and that we'd find our way out of this. I watched the west coast of Ireland crumble all around me and I just kept on telling myself that at any minute, we'd come together to stop this happening to us...'

She sighed as she trailed off, staring at the ruin of a hotel. Someone had been trying to patch it up lately. Malley almost laughed at the futility. Fixing it up so that Joseph could knock it down all over again.

'Gibson and Joe were like that to me. I never expected them to change either. But they did...'

She stopped where the shell of the old hotel looked down on a roundabout where old roads met.

'I'll leave you here with a request... Ask yourself if their lives are worth the cost.'

The priest had asked a similar question. *Is that justice?* His words echoed in her head now even as Omega offered her variation.

Malley bit back a retort.

A trail of bodies lay in her wake.

Someone ought to have asked them about the cost.

She turned to face Omega, and planted her feet, waiting for one of them to make a move.

Omega seemed to read her body language and the older woman smiled a sad smile.

'No one's going to attack you.'

'Why not?' Malley asked even though she realised the question was pathetically sad. That she would just expect someone to always want to attack.

'For the same reason I gave you all of that,' she replied, gesturing at Malley's tunic, where the evidence was stored.

'Why?'

'Because you were going to save his life when you thought he was innocent.'

Omega understood. She understood that to some people, somewhere, there was still a right and wrong. There were still rules worth obeying. There was still justice.

She wanted to say something, but the anger wouldn't let her. Instead, she nodded at Omega, pulled her hood up for protection against the advancing storm, turned toward Limerick and walked.


She walked through the calm, the moment between the storms. But as she walked, Joseph seemed to step in beside her. Tentatively at first, almost playfully, whipping at her borrowed clothes, toying with her hair, but with increasing vigour as she moved. His energy fed her, almost pushing her down the road to Limerick.

Anyone who had tried to get in her way would have paid the price.

The knife wound in her shoulder hurt, leaking blood that mixed with sweat and the rainwater that spat on her, inhibiting her movement a little, but it was the opening in her hand that troubled her the most. She'd already pulled the bandages off and exposed the fresh scar.

It was different to the others.

The dominant direction of all her scarring on both hands had been side to side, with minimal deviation, and those scars were old, bearing the signs of struggle that had clearly belonged to Before. This new one was diagonal, crossing all the other scars, scoring through them and exposing the flesh in a way that hadn't been done since strong people had come for her and her sister, and had taken what they wanted.

She relived that memory often. Returning to it with macabre frequency. It was almost comforting in its familiarity. Now this fresh scar had ruined it.

She felt at the folds of her tunic underneath the wax jacket she'd been given. There had been plenty of corpses to loot. Plenty of people who no longer needed jackets.

The papers were stuffed in there, she knew that before she reached for them, because she'd reached for them a thousand times already in the hours since she'd hidden them in there.

How long had it been since Black Stair? Four days? Five? They ran into each other.

Certainly, it didn't seem long enough for all the moments that had filled those days, for the cost of those moments. Always the cost. Always what you had to pay. When you thought you were done paying it, you weren't.

She scanned as she walked, fearing that she'd see a body, a small little woman's body with a scarred face, discarded on the roadside. She knew she wouldn't. A product of knowing him so well. Still, she looked.

The anger in her was towering, threatening to engulf her, and as she walked, Joseph seemed to rise all around her. She found herself absorbing energy from the storm, allowing it to drive her onward.

There were so many reckonings coming. She couldn't afford to bring this rage with her, this white-hot thing that seemed to gather energy as she moved, until she was a storm of it herself.

Broderick hadn't screamed.

He always screamed in combat. An animal thing, devoid of any meaning, signifying only that he was possessed with something uncontrollable, unstoppable.

That had never been her way. She measured every blow. She weighted every stroke or counterstroke and every thrust.

Now she felt like screaming. The stirrings of the temper she'd lost with Fionnuala outside the hospital were no longer stirrings, but terrible, huge feelings that she struggled to repress.

Broderick and Kelly.

Their names rang in her head.

Two men who hadn't paid a high-enough cost yet.

She thought of Fionnuala and Hilda until the two of them blended into one another. Her anxiety for them, one long since past, one immediate and present, fed into her growing fury.

If anyone could have seen her eyes, then they'd have seen a heat like no other.

# CHAPTER EIGHTEEN

The riots started almost immediately. Those people who had lived for so long at the intersection where climate change met government authoritarianism found in themselves an energy they didn't know they had.

They had lived from Storm Season Abraham through to Storm Season Joseph with so many names in between that they could no longer separate them from one another. Beaten down time and again, making do with less and less only to be told by their betters that there wasn't enough to go around while well-armed Gardai supressed desperation with the long baton of the law.

For so long they had spent everything they had merely picking themselves back up, accepting rationing and isolation and deprivation, watching with grim satisfaction as justice was served on deniers. But as word spread from Dublin and Limerick, through the only half-tamed internet and via messengers and message boards, they found a spark had hit something that was still flammable.

The word spread first throughout the cities that Frank Gibson, a celebrated leader of the opposition, a heroic doctor who had saved lives in the first Storm Season, had been murdered by the Government on a trumped-up charge of climate denial for which they had fabricated evidence.

The only justice they'd known, abused for political gain.

The end of the people's patience was this moment.

In Dublin, a gang of workers from the flatpack factories congregated first, the tools of their trade now wielded as weapons, and as they moved along the Long Mile Road toward the city centre, their numbers grew. Secret refugees living rough having ignored their No Movement Orders joined with them, as did the documented ones living in the communities. Natives of the city began to gather and the first sporadic clashes between pockets of Gardai had already begun when the factory workers gang, their numbers swelling, like a river in flood as they marched down Dawson Street.

Outside Government buildings they met a double thick line of Gardai, their black and blue uniforms sprinkled here and there with the greens, browns, and greys of the Doejays. There was a brief standoff at thirty or so paces, but the moment an agent by the name of Shields addressed them via megaphone, they erupted in a roar and charged.

In Waterford, a solitary woman stood at The Mall, screaming her frustration at the local Government offices. A crowd began to coalesce around her. A murmuring of support that grew and rippled out from her. Someone inside the office made a stupid decision and a small squad of Gardai were dispatched to arrest her.

As soon as their hands were on her, the volume of the growing crowd increased. When she wouldn't go quietly, one of them struck her across her head with a baton. That spark, that flammable thing that had been dormant in so many of those who were down so long, ignited and justice was meted out to the Gardai.

The reprisal was swift, and soon Waterford erupted in a series of running battles, the brutality escalating on both sides, while Joseph began to shout triumphantly over the carnage.

Word reached Belfast of the unrest and another bad decision was made, as Gardai and agents took to the streets to pre-empt the trouble. The stupidity of that decision became immediately evident when those who refused to clear the streets began picking the fruit of Joseph's destruction from the ground and hurling it at the Government forces.

Fires started in all three cities shortly afterwards. And by nightfall, the reports of casualties and fatalities began to filter out of those places, chasing after the story that began all the trouble in the first place, adding to it, stoking the fury in the farthest reaches of Government writ.

The end of the people's patience was this moment.

In the settlements, the people gathered in the solar-panelled town squares and argued in angry voices. These were smaller spaces, more intimate where every person knew their neighbour, and some of those neighbours were Government-appointed administrators or locally elected politicians.

The black mood filtered through, and many donned their BlueArmbands, only to be remonstrated with by those who still favoured Government control. Those foolish enough to speak on behalf of the Government found themselves outnumbered, and soon people who had Shared with one another, winter after winter, found cracks in their communities. Into those cracks, the violence leaked.

In Black Stair, a man named Douglas found a corpse in the room where the people came to Share; the local circle leader had been beaten to death. It wasn't the only settlement where a corpse was found. In Slieve Foy, a woman was hanged from the gable end of the town hall. In Newcastle, three members of the local circle were put out of the settlement, to face Joseph, alone. They were last seen making their way down Donard, hoping to find shelter in what was left of the seaside town below before the storm got its hands on them. There were no riots in those places, but there was no mercy there either.

A price was being paid.

In the lowlands and the west, the word began to circulate.

In Cork and Galway, Silgo and Letterkenny, the small communities that remained there grumbled among themselves as they checked their homes for damages and shored up what they could in anticipation of Joseph's next temper tantrum.

Some of them talked of heading east, to join the growing rebellion, but those were soon silenced by their elders.

Joseph wouldn't permit them to leave. At any moment he'd arrive ashore again, driving people into their homes and that would be the end of that, as people forgot their politics and remembered the energy they'd need to survive again.

In Limerick, the arrival of the word garnered a mixed reaction.

The BlueArms who were new to town met it with a grim satisfaction that was tempered by the sense of loss they felt at Gibson's death.

The rest of the locals met the news with stoicism.

A city preparing for siege hadn't time to ponder one person's life, much less a Dublin politician.

Still the moment was marked as soldiers from the local militia and the BlueArms who had begun to gather in the city took advantage of the gap in the storm to meet and talk on the streets.

Sheltered from the worst of the elements by the buildings around them, they stayed there even as Joseph began once again to take his hand to the country, running in front of Malley, ready to have his say.


At the edge of the city, Malley took a moment to gather herself. She'd been to Limerick only once. To bring Hilda back to Dublin. It hadn't gone the way she'd expected it to go.

Her sister had returned her calm rationalisation with a fiery refusal to be budged. Her impetuousness, Malley had always regarded a symptom of their respective positions in the family. As the elder she felt she should have commanded seniority, her younger sister railed against that from their earliest moments, but Malley couldn't have expected the reaction she received.

They suffered two terrible moments together in Dublin. Terrible life-defining moments. Malley's scars were external, Hilda's deep inside her. She still felt the moment that the shadow of a man passed over her, even as she wrestled for a knife that was buried in the flesh of her hands, scraping the bones, ruining her, and shaping the next version of herself all at once.

That moment had broken her.

That she couldn't stop it. That Hilda had to give so much of herself.

Malley wrapped herself in cold silence then, the layers of it getting thicker and thicker as she got stronger and stronger. In contrast, Hilda spoke more and more, her temper, her anger always waiting for its chance to show itself. She spoke out against the Government and people listened, they began to seek her out.

Their divergence destroyed them, though neither of them knew it. Malley still thought their future was side by side, hardening together. Hilda carved a place for herself. A place that offered welcome to those who would seek it.

The breaking point was the day Malley had joined the Doejays.

Arriving home in her uniform, all greys and browns and greens, she saw she had become something her sister no longer recognised. To Malley's surprise, she also realised that her sister was a stranger. They fought then, angry words fizzing between them, some striking home, hurting. They talked of weakness and strength as if they each knew it independently, while the other remained ignorant.

Hilda's rage was unfettered. Malley descended into depths of cold she didn't know she had. She weathered her sister's tirade because she felt she owed her that, for her failure to protect her when the men had come calling, but when it became too much, she had slammed the door behind her as she left.

When she returned, Hilda was gone.

By the time she went to retrieve her from Limerick, the damage was irreparable. And once again they met one another in an emotional no man's land, a place neither of them was familiar with and both of them feared. And they'd solved nothing. Malley couldn't find the words, the silence that had been her protection let her down, while Hilda's words had been hard and full of retribution.

She had failed her sister, in so many ways. That moment was the consequence of her failure.

They hadn't spoken since.

On the outskirts of the Limerick city, with Joseph playing in menacing glee and a rebellion brewing, there was no place for the rising temper that had grown within her since Galway. Here she needed the calm that had served her so well for fourteen years, but somehow that calm resisted her.

Her disguise wasn't merely her clothes or Fionnuala's BlueArmband she now wore. It went deeper than that, even her walk had to be changed, the way she carried herself, the way she moved. Her knives were worn on the outside, all four of them, in the manner of the lowlanders, rather than concealed in her clothing.

The only thing she kept hidden was the evidence.

There'd be payment for that too, but Fionnuala came first.

She traced a line from the young woman to Broderick, from Broderick to Kelly, from Kelly to Hilda.

The circle completed itself there.

At her sister's home, she might save at least one woman.

She drew several deep breaths, sucking in the storm-freshened air through her nose.

It always felt fresher, tasted fresher, in those gaps between the winds.

She picked her way along the Ennis Road, past barriers and small clumps of soldiers with face masks and goggles. If they'd had a mind to stop her, the slow-burning temper in her eyes convinced them otherwise, and the body language of a well-travelled warrior dispelled whatever lingering doubts they might have had.

She crossed the only bridge left into the city from the west, hand in hand with Joseph. The other two bridges were long down, whether by storm or design, so that Sarsfield Bridge, named for the leader when the city was besieged in 1691, became a long and dangerous alleyway.

Still she met no resistance, her armband and the fury of her gait granting her access. With Joseph for company, whistling between the buildings as he raced along the streets, the rain spat hard on the road before her. The debris from the last storm hadn't been cleared and so slates and branches, chunks of building rocks and anything else that Joseph might have grabbed littered her path.

Debris seen over and over by those who had lived with nothing but winter Storm Seasons.

The streets were busier than they ought to have been. The people should have taken to their homes in anticipation of the battering that was coming. There was about them an excitement that felt wrong. It wasn't the typical Storm Season energy, but something else, something important enough to spare her from prying eyes, but she hadn't time to investigate. Broderick was already here somewhere near, Fionnuala at his mercy.

Through the city she marched, past the built and rebuilt, past the remnants of what once was, signifiers of things people couldn't let go, past the haphazard repairs that people had made, stoic in the refusal that would never allow them to let go until she was out the far side, into the part of town that was once industrial and commercial. She remembered Before, how the place had hummed with its low-key vibrancy, but it didn't surprise her that it was now a fortress. There was something about this city that had always suggested a readiness to defend itself.

Now the outside was a wasteland. Dublin had survived the worst because of its position on the east coast and its greater population who could maintain and keep the factories running. Here, Storm Seasons arrived to scrub away the weak, buildings and people, and only the strong stood in their aftermath.

She walked it, the bleakness feeding her darkening mood, hoping that she wasn't too late. That Fionnuala was still alive, that Hilda hadn't been killed by Joseph in some ignominious way, that Broderick was still lurking.

She walked it and she gritted her teeth, as if the rising anger within her could be held back physically by tightened muscles and the constant clenching and unclenching of her fists. To no avail, the fury built, as though Joseph exhaled his breath onto the embers of it, feeding it, growing it.

She walked until at last she came to the housing estate not far from the university where she knew Hilda lived.

The houses there formed a natural sort of fortress, which had been reinforced with walls to break strong wind and like Ballinasloe, the signs of life, a newly made public bench, a swing-set in the middle of the small common area, were somehow pathetic in the face of the storms, and inspiring for the defiance they represented.

At a house, she stopped.

At the door of the house, Hilda stood smoking.

They saw one another and for a long moment neither moved nor spoke but regarded each other.

She felt her throat tighten and a hollowness somehow manifested itself in her stomach.

Her sister's face was the same now as it had been fourteen years beforehand as far as Malley was concerned. The eyes showing determination, resignation, and anger all at once.

'Malley,' her sister greeted her bluntly, 'I suppose I shouldn't be surprised.'


Broderick crouched low in the bushes, barely moving.

Ever present, Joseph was teasing them now, moving trees and bushes, waiting for a more spectacular outburst. There were things built here that would be unbuilt by the following morning. The half-light of the growing storm mixed with twilight to throw curious colours on the dark clouds and the air seemed to grow denser by the second.

Broderick watched.

He'd dragged Fionnuala with him. Because she was useful. No other reason. He couldn't allow himself anything else. He needed sharpness.

The memory of her extending him a branch to pull him from The Suck rattled in his head.

And he couldn't forget that she had looked at him differently. Differently even than Malley had. Like there was a part of him that she saw that no one else could.

She had pried something loose in him and for all his fury, he couldn't shake it, couldn't kill the feeling of something dormant inside him.

He should have killed her for that alone.

Now she was behind him, quiet. Suspiciously so. He saw that defiance in her that had been her hallmark since she'd stalked them out of Black Stair. There was no doubt she was tough and getting tougher. She had adapted to the outside in a way he'd never seen before, becoming harder almost before his eyes. The slash across her cheek only added to that hardening. It would serve her, he knew. That hardness.

That was how he knew she'd try again. Without a doubt she'd wait for her moment.

He also knew it would fail, because he was too fast, and too ruthless, and she wasn't hard enough. Yet.

Broderick waited.

Inside the house he watched, there were all the signs of life, but no sign of living. The furniture was spartan at best. The walls unadorned. There was a bowl on the drying rack. Just one. And there were some books on the floor. Initially he wasn't even sure that anyone lived there. Until he'd spotted her coming home.

It was enough to cause another sharp pang in him. Killing Malley was not something he had wanted to do. It was necessary, it was his job, but he regretted it in ways he hadn't thought possible. The sensation of regret was an unfamiliar distraction. A forgotten feeling. Unwelcome and yet somehow bittersweet.

Involuntarily he recalled her hitting the floor with the knife in her chest. The memory caught him when he wasn't deliberately supressing it. It was, he told himself, how she would have chosen to die. Fighting for what she believed in.

The years spent together had made it impossible to keep the memory out. The understanding silences between them. The way she weighed and measured him.

It was a hard thought to dismiss in the middle of his shallow pool of regret.

Broderick waited still.

Hilda was a smaller version of Malley. She looked tough, but slighter, lacking the muscle and shoulders her older sister had. Also lacking in years she seemed somehow frailer. Less permanent. A ghost of a woman in some ways.

Behind him, Fionnuala rustled and he turned.

She regarded him with a long unreadable stare.

She must have learned that look from Malley.

Impenetrable.

He raised one finger in warning and stared at her until she went silent. He counted on fear alone to keep her still. When Hilda left the house, they'd have to move quickly. Wherever Kelly was, that's where she'd be going. Then Fionnuala would gain him his access.

He just needed her to leave her house again, but all she'd done in the intervening time was smoke cigarettes outside her front door, enjoying those last few moments before the new storm arrived and forced her indoors.

People came and went from the house too with an urgency that he found just a little bit alarming. Something big was happening somewhere. He didn't have the time to investigate. As it stood, he'd be running a risk trying to get back to Dublin, he certainly couldn't afford to shelter in Limerick after he'd finished the job.

One doesn't kill two revolutionary leaders in the space of a few days without upsetting some people.

Fionnuala stirred behind him, and he turned on her again,

this time raising two fingers. If he turned around once more, she'd have to be disciplined.

She met his gaze coolly, and he almost smiled at her then. She was tough alright.

The front door to the house slammed in the wind, the sound of it pulling his head back around. He watched through the back window as she came back inside. Something was different. Her face was giving something away...

Before he had time to guess at what it might be, he saw her. Malley.

She walked into the room, with a face like a thunderhead, eyes burning with a fury that caught him off guard.

For the first time in as long as he could remember, Broderick was completely stunned.


Fionnuala had no idea what they were waiting for, but for hours, that was all they did. Crouched low behind a screen of bushes in someone's back garden, they waited. The pain in her face made it hard not to squirm or whimper, but she couldn't show him any weakness.

She had wondered initially if it might be Kelly's place of residence, but all she'd seen through the windows were flickers of a woman she could hardly make out from behind Broderick's broad back.

The way he stared at the house spoke of a terrible intensity.

She steeled herself over and over by remembering the scars that had ruined a pair of small hands.

Malley survived. She'd paid her price to survive. Fionnuala had to do the same. She watched him constantly, never letting her eyes stray off him, hardly blinking, waiting for the moment when he'd give her an opportunity.

She knew he was waiting for it too.

Cat and mouse between them. Lion and mouse really. Only, she hoped, he would underestimate her. His power, his speed, and his fury had carried him so far, and all those who had tried against him had failed. He'd faced bigger and tougher and faster than her before and defeated them. So, he'd be expecting little from her.

And that was why she'd beat him.

She just had to remember the scars.

She adjusted herself on her spot behind him. She didn't need her muscles cramping or sleeping when her moment arrived.

Broderick turned again, his face angry. His look suggested that perhaps he'd add a few more bruises to the hideous scar he'd already given her. He raised two fingers at her in warning.

A sound out the front caused his head to whip back around, and he resumed his intent staring at the house. Fionnuala couldn't see what was inside, only shadows thrown on the wall from the candle flames that danced below the window line.

Broderick shifted then, slumping somehow, so that the rigid, spring-like readiness of him seemed to vanish and for half a second, he dropped his arms as though all that steel that held him together had melted.

Her moment.

She didn't hesitate, but threw herself at him, one hand reaching by his belt as she moved.

He turned, biting off a curse, but was a split second too late.

Whatever had happened in the house was just enough, and she felt one of his knives slide out of his sheath in her unsteady hand, it might have been her knife, the one he'd once given her.

Crouched as he was, he couldn't restrain her properly and with savage elation, she brought her knees up into him, hammered at him with elbows, with the knife in her hand.

She practically exulted when she felt her knee connect with his chin and heard him grunt in pain. His hand shot out, grabbing her by the face. His thumb found her eye, his fingers claw-like digging in and she felt a terrible pressure as he squeezed at her, blinding pain consuming her.

Desperately, she lashed out with the knife and for the second time in her life felt the blade in her hand penetrate skin, burying itself into muscle.

He released her face, crying out in pain and rolling back from her, one hand going to clasp the shoulder where the knife had entered.

It wasn't a killing blow. Too close to the shoulder, but it bought her exactly what she needed, enough room. Enough room to run.

The momentary flash of surprise on his face was enough for her to realise her plan had worked. Desperate people fought because fighting was all that they had. And he killed them for that. She was desperate alright, but not foolish enough to think she could best him.

So, she ran.

She sprinted, not knowing where her legs were carrying her. Joseph whipping her clothing and the nearby trees joined with her heavy breathing to obscure the sound of any possible pursuit. She ran, hoped for the best and dared not look over her shoulder as she bounded away from him through the darkening night and into the storm.

Hilda's home was meagrely decorated. A sharp contrast to the days of their youth. Once upon a time, she had photos everywhere. Some framed, some pinned to things, some stuck with tac. She kept ticket stubs for nights at the cinema on dates or with friends. Her headboard carried the tickets to every gig and festival she'd ever been to. Colours clashed here and there around her room as she abandoned organisation in favour of showing who she was to anyone who entered. Vivacious, engaging, cultured.

Now all that remained were small stacks of books to say who she had become.

Perhaps that was all that was left of the woman she once was. Perhaps in paying the price, her sacrifice had been to cut loose any part of her that she considered unnecessary. It was a sad thing for Malley to see, but the sadness was overpowered by anger and no small amount of resentment. For what had happened to them, but also for what they had done to one another afterwards.

Fourteen years where they should have been side by side.

Physically, Hilda surprised her.

She expected the woman to have grown like she herself had. Muscle and sinewy shoulders. Her body hardening as the world demanded. She expected the world to have forged a new woman from her little sister, particularly here, where the storms lashed the hardest.

Instead, she found the woman largely unchanged. She was still slight of frame with soft, slim forearms and wrists that told Malley that Hilda wasn't training with weapon or weight. Her hair was still long and curly, held back from her face by a hairband. She still held onto her youthful features, even if her eyes had developed the hardness customary to the lowlanders.

The hardness there was itself an almost wondrous thing to see, in that it seemed to make a mockery of the softness of her body, describing as it did a woman who would never relent. And coupled with that hardness was the heat of the younger woman's temper.

That fire betrayed the rashness, the recklessness that characterised her little sister, the same thing she'd seen in Fionnuala.

It jarred her to see such familiarity in a woman that was effectively a stranger to her.

Worse again, it was terrible to think that this woman could ever be a stranger.

And now Malley had to ask of her a favour. To bring her to the man who led her rebellion.

The unspoken words that had hovered between them didn't come any easier as they moved into the house, but Malley's impatience and anger were powerful motivators.

She must speak, she couldn't leave again without saying her part.

She had much she wanted to say, needed to really, and for

the first time in as long as she could remember, it refused to stay inside.

'I'm sorry,' she told her sister.

Years of hurt in those words but they sounded hollow, unfeeling.

Hilda looked at her, silent, and she tried again. Needing badly to say what she couldn't before.

From outside came a noise. A scream or a shout.

The noise triggered something in Malley, a terrible type of déjà vu, as she stood facing her sister while a storm raged outside… as they once had stood before the world had changed them. Malley's knives flashed into her hands.

'A minute,' Hilda commanded her brusquely, holding her hand up for patience.

The sound of her sister's voice was instantly both magnificent and enraging. Malley nodded at her, flexing her hand and testing the wound in her shoulder where Broderick's knife had bitten her.

She waited as her sister went to investigate. A long moment. Still trying to calm the anger so that when she spoke again, her words wouldn't widen the gap between them any further. Might somehow draw them closer to one another.

After a too-long moment, she became aware of the stillness of something gone wrong, even as Joseph dragged his fingers along the outside of the house. Warily she followed her sister, until she reached the back door.

Broderick stood outside, the wind pulling at his clothing, his hair. With one arm draped over her shoulder he held Hilda in place, like a shield, with the other hand he pressed his long knife into her cheek.

Between all of them Joseph moved, and as he did, everything seemed to move with him, swaying, unsteady, impermanent seeming, as if even the buildings feared his attention.

The blade dimpled where it pressed, but didn't cut, the edge of it sat against the flesh creating a hollow valley in her little sister's cheek.

Malley felt a shudder pass through her, and in its aftermath her muscles tightened in pure rage. She fought to supress it, though she could feel her face blanching at the effort.

The knife on the flesh, her sister's eyes determined, defiant, and resigned all at once.

Malley felt she should say something, but the words refused to come out. It was all she could do to hold her entire body together, as if it would burst from the pure rage that filled her.

She tried to focus on the feeling of the knife in her left hand. The oneness where the wrapping met the ridges.

Broderick regarded her warily. Not with his usual fury, but with a calmness that almost surprised her through her blossoming rage.

She scanned for Fionnuala, before she noticed that one of his knives was missing and his shoulder was bleeding.

The little mouse had gotten the best of him.

She might have been satisfied by that but all she could see was the first tiny drop of blood on her sister's cheek and all she could feel was rage.


The wound in his shoulder stung him, but no more so than his pride. She had managed to get away, with one of his knives. He felt his own shame warring with a surge of pride in her. He had known she was tough.

The warring sensations confused him.

Everything confused him. Even as he watched Malley practically smouldering with a fury he'd never seen before, he was glad she was alive. And surprised that he was glad.

The knife must have taken her in the shoulder. Same spot where Fionnuala had gotten him he reckoned.

One feeling rose to the surface, defeating all others. Fear.

This was what she could do to him that none others could. He knew the effect he had on people. He knew what he was, and what he represented to them. An apex predator. Top of the food chain.

Except for her.

His list was doomed people, and she had escaped it. The only one. Yet there was an inevitability to this moment, as though the list didn't care if her name was removed, at some point the list would have its way.

Eventually, all bills came due.

No one escaped.

Not the politicians, not the rebels, not the BlueArms or the lowlanders or the Digitals.

Not Agent Malley Cummins.

Not even him.

The thought hadn't even fully formed when the sky split, a fork of lightning arcing across the thick lead clouds.

He flinched. It was a momentary thing but it was enough, the blade easing on the small woman's face.

She surprised him then with her reflexes, leaping clear of him, rolling as she hit the rain-soaked turf.

He cursed his luck, a bad time for his standards to slip.

It was all he had time for though, as Malley screamed and charged.

# CHAPTER NINETEEN

The scream came loose from her throat almost independently of her.

She sprang at the same moment Hilda rolled clear, but he reacted quickly, as she'd expect of him, his knife coming up, bringing himself into stance.

Their body language mirrored each other as they attacked. Both moving at an angle to keep their strong shoulders out, their injured shoulders hidden, both grimacing in pain as the fresh wounds stretched and tore open.

Broderick's eyes probed for hints and tell-tale rhythms in her stance that would give away her intentions, but Malley didn't bother with tactics.

For the first time in her life, she fought with an unrestrained violence fuelled entirely by the rage that had spent years accumulating in her mind, in her muscles, in every part of her.

She had feared Broderick once upon a time, as she had feared all men for a while, mostly for his physical prowess, his military training, his almost animal qualities that he kept barely contained.

As the years had rolled by, she had begun to fear something else; she feared becoming him. She saw that glimmer of singular madness that had taken him, motivated by his towering anger and resentment at the world, and she abhorred it. She had no desire to leave her humanity behind. Though she hardly knew it, she was desperate to feel something.

For years she had struggled against her instincts, against the parts of her that felt things she couldn't understand or didn't want to understand. All the time believing that her dispassion and discipline were barriers to the kind of animal impulses that drove him. Never realising that those feelings she didn't understand, those feelings that she tried to kill, were the last flickers of her humanity.

All those challenging looks in the settlements, her curious satisfaction at seeing their defiance, her decision to let O'Mahony go – all of them were signs of the last vestiges of her humanity, that she killed, minute by minute.

In this moment, she became something different. Something righteous. The dispassion and discipline were in her way now. The rage, a part of her. The adrenaline that flooded her body, the crackling electricity of her anger were almost intoxicating. They cancelled thought as she opened herself to them.

She couldn't have weighed her blows if she wanted to. There was no room within her for the clear and precise thinking that she had once relied on.

There was only a rage-fuelled instinct that blocked out the storm winds and made the rest of the world invisible to her until only Broderick remained.

And he was a pathetic thing under the blazing light of her anger. His size no longer counted, his cunning and strength, and savagery were puny next to what she brought.

Suddenly, Broderick was a small, inconsequential thing.


Broderick felt the shift.

Too late. He now realised that the moment he'd threatened her sister, he had awoken something terrible.

He focused, controlling his anger, trying to concentrate it into his strikes.

She was out of control and if he was careful, she'd leave a gap. He just needed to see that gap when it arrived and make sure he struck hard enough.

The problem was that as the fight went on, he found it harder and harder to keep her at bay.

They fought with fists and feet, hips shoulders and elbows as much as they did knives. Their bodies slamming together, their movements fluid even as flesh and bone met one another over and over.

He was sweating, or it was raining, he couldn't tell, but the feeling of the rising wind meeting the moisture on his brow was an intense cool that he felt even through the heat of combat.

He clenched his teeth and blocked another thrust with his forearm, dipping his head back out of reach of a wildly swinging elbow.

The sensation of it whistling by where his nose had been, came with the curious feeling that he had never felt before.

A feeling of desperation.

He was losing. And he knew it.

He raised a knee and pivoted on one foot to block a kick, his hand lashing out with the knife, feeling it whistle by nothing. A blind strike.

This is what she had reduced him to. Blind striking, looking for any skin, any bone. Seeking the sound of a scream or a grunt that would tell him that he'd scored a hit.

Stars exploded in his eyes and, reflexively, he stepped back, adopting a defensive stance and slicing the air in front of him.

She'd caught him. High on the top of his head.

He blinked away the spots in his vision just in time to see her snarling and lunging at him again.


She felt the tide of the fight was hers. She had felt it the moment their bodies had met. It was sensory. She was not merely full of light and energy, but consumed by it, as if it had poured into her and now threatened to explode out of her.

He was, by contrast, rigid, responding automatically with the defensive forms they'd both been taught and had learned, the hard way, over the course of many years.

She could feel his desperation as he swung his knife wildly. His face was a rictus of concentration and fear.

In this moment, she now realised, he was feeling what everyone else felt on encountering him. Desperate and doomed.

Countless victims had faced this terrible creature. Hungry people, cold people, people with no futures and a past from which they had become untethered.

And maybe they all fancied themselves to be strong enough, hard enough to do what must be done. In their final moments – small, tiny moments – small, tiny parts of them must have felt what Broderick was feeling now.

There was no escape from the onslaught.


They parried back and forth, swirling around one another in the graceful movements of violence, desperately trying to find, with fingers, fists, or blade, any chance to kill or maim each other.

He couldn't have said how long they surged like that next to one another. That wasn't how combat worked. Hours could be seconds, seconds could be entire lives. In those moments, very little could be known for certain.

Except that he had lost. This was the only thing he knew.

She was landing more blows, and faster. He managed to keep the knife from his flesh, but only just, instead choosing to take the lumps of her fists and knees and elbows to keep what he could of his skin intact.

But he had already lost.

At some point in their journey together, they had changed. He had lost something, or she had gained something, but whatever it was, the change was irrevocable. And it was irresistible.

He fought on, because he had to, because he couldn't allow himself to surrender and he'd die before he'd yield. But he knew that barring some freak accident or divine intervention, she had him.

But he couldn't surrender. Death before that.

His eyes exploded with stars again as another fist connected with his temple.


He reeled as the blow landed on his temple, reflexively swinging the knife in front of him to keep her at bay as he tried to regain his vision.

She didn't step in for the killer blow. To do so would have taken some power of decision-making she no longer had in her savage state.

Instead, still snarling, she punched him in the head again. The blow connected with his cheek, splitting the skin below his eye.

His knife arm wavered and she smashed at it with her fist, still closed around her own knife, blowing his arms wide open and sending his knife scattering.

Without thinking or hesitating, she threw her knife aside as well, and stepped forward, driving her forehead into his nose and shattering it.

He reeled back again, the blood spraying from his face, his arms windmilling as if that pathetic movement could somehow stop her. She ignored his clumsy fists and punched him again, this time with the wounded hand, her own fingernails digging into the wound he'd made there the day before.

He staggered back and lost his footing. Hitting the ground, he rolled, clumsily, slowly, and tried to regain his feet.

She kicked him in the head.

He pitched to one side and came back to his knees again, his fists raised, though she was certain he couldn't even see her anymore through the blood and the ruin.

She lunged forward, one knee touching the ground and smashed another three punches into his face, not bothering to aim, simply hammering at him, softening him.

He dropped his raised fists and tried to steady himself. She had closed both his eyes now, the swelling disfiguring him.

She stepped behind him and pulled him up by the hair, her

fists tightening in his short, sandy-blonde locks. The image of a man briefly flicked in her mind's eye. The man who had invaded her home all those years before, the man who had taken from her sister and left Malley with the scars so that she could never forget. A powerful thing where she was small and little. Now Broderick was the little one.

She drove a fist into his guts as hard as she could, and he sprayed blood out of his mouth as he doubled over.

She took him by the throat in one hand and drew back a fist.

'Enough,' Hilda's voice told her. 'He's had enough.'

That voice reached her, but the rage remained.

His face was mangled.

'He can tell me himself when he's had enough.'

She smashed her fist into his teeth, feeling the lips break and the teeth crack even as they bit into the skin of her knuckles.

Punishment. Justice. Revenge for what was done to them. She had the power now.

His legs seemed to buckle, but despite his weight and size, she managed to hold him up by the throat.

He had dared to hold a knife to Hilda's cheek? To threaten her sister?

Hilda had already paid the price, and he was going to ask it again?

She drew a fist back, and a groan escaped his lips.

'Jesus, Malley,' Hilda begged. 'Look at him. Look at him.'

And she did. She looked at his face. Contusions and swelling and blood everywhere. His hair was matted with it. She'd beaten him bloody.

He groaned something again, as if he was trying to say something.

She let go of his throat and he dropped to the floor. It took her a moment to realise he was laughing.

'I surrender,' he gurgled at her, even as he laughed.

Her fury evaporated as he sprawled out on the grass and dirt of Hilda's back garden.

Slowly she walked to where she had discarded her knife, feeling returning to her, clearing her mind, loosening her muscles.

Joseph tugged at her, to remind her he was still near, and the rain sifting heavily down from the overburdened clouds cooled her skin.

The storm had given them all the warning he was going to give them. His return was at hand.

She picked up the knife and walked back to where Broderick lay. He stared up at her through the eye that remained partially open.

'I surrender,' he said again.

She looked at him lying on the ground, weighing the knife in her hand. Laying there in a pool of his own blood, his ruthlessness and that drive for revenge that motivated everything he did seemed irrelevant. He was weak now, and she was strong.

She sheathed the knife and turned to her sister.

Hilda's face was a mix, part horror, part intense satisfaction, as he passed out at her feet.


They stared at one another over his bound body, lashed to a small cot in a box room in Hilda's house. Her sister had cleaned him up as best she could, but he was still a swollen mess. He had barely stirred as she cleaned the cuts and scars on his skin.

He might survive. He might not. Malley hoped that he did, and she revelled in that moment of humanity. To hope for something was to feel human. She didn't bother trying to freeze the emotion out like she might have, to weigh his crimes against his life and decide if his killing was a thing of necessity. She let that feeling, the feeling of feeling something, bathe her for a long moment as she looked down at the face she had mangled.

'Look at you,' Hilda finally said.

There was a wariness in her voice. A fear almost. Though she had to know that her own sister would never hurt her.

'You haven't changed,' Malley countered.

'Of course, I have. It's called growing up. Years do that to some people.'

The implication was clear enough: Hilda reckoned Malley still had growing to do.

'What do you want from me?' Hilda asked.

'I want to say sorry,' Malley told her.

'For what?'

'I abandoned you. I didn't mean to. I didn't think I was doing it at the time. I thought I was making myself strong for you. To make up for…'

She couldn't bring herself to say it. What her sister had to give up. The lesson she had to learn.

Hilda's face softened, the eyes less wary, less angry. The spark in them, so like Fionnuala's.

'Was that so hard?' she asked with a small, sad smile.

Malley laughed bitterly in spite of herself. Standing over Broderick's prone form, it should have felt wrong, but it didn't. It fit. To laugh at a simple joke.

They smiled at each other then. Like they had done in a different world. The one during Before.

'I suppose you're not sorry for anything?' Malley asked gently.

Hilda never apologised. Hilda doubled down. Even caught, as a child, stealing from the treat-drawer or as a teenager sneaking vodka from the drinks cabinet, Hilda would assume a posture of defiance and dare anyone to condemn her.

'I am sorry,' Hilda replied, her brashness gone, a tentative openness about her, 'sorry for screaming and name calling, and never giving you room to speak.'

The hard words her sister had for her, the lack of words she had to give in return. The terribleness of those moments vanished in that room with Joseph outside shouting for attention.

It was all so familiar and all so strange.

Malley let the moment linger for as long as she could.

Then she broke it. Because she had to. Because it was all she had left.

'I want Kelly,' she told Hilda gently.

'Why?' she replied gently. 'Why do you want him?'

'I'm sorry, Hilda. I am. But someone has to pay,' she replied.

'Pay who? For what?' Hilda asked her, and the sisterly moment was gone, evaporating in the air between them, 'and don't give me that "for the people" nonsense.'

Her sister's legendary temper. It was never far from the surface. Malley loved to hear it. That crackle of anger in her voice, the depth of feeling she could never keep from showing, her heart always on her sleeve.

'It is for the people,' Malley told her, and Hilda smiled. 'But it's also for me. Someone will pay for this...'

She held up her ruined hands.

'Mal, you don't have to keep being their dogsbody. They're not the good guys. You have to know that. Don't be a fool.'

'I called a woman I care about a fool yesterday,' Malley said with a soft laugh. 'A naïve idiot. "A stupid woman" I think I said to her. She reminded me of you.'

The words weren't delivered harshly, but softly, and all the more incongruous being spoken over Broderick's still unconscious form, as Joseph ratted the window, begging permission to come in.

Hilda blinked in surprise.

'I don't mean that in a bad way,' Malley assured her. 'I mean it in the best possible way. She's like you because she thinks she can change the world. But I think this world is what changes us, not the other way around. That's how I think I let you down.

'We both changed way back when. I changed to fit the new world, you became someone who thought they could change the world. Like Fionnuala. I wanted you to change like me, but you didn't.

'I'm sorry I abandoned us. I thought I could give something to you by being tough enough for both of us. I'm sorry for that. I was doing it for me. Not for us. And that drove you away. I'm sorry I'm not the kind of person who wants to change the world…'

The softening in Hilda's face brought a lump to her throat.

'But what if you could?' she asked Malley softly. 'You still can.'

'Because I don't think it can be done. Not anymore.'

'So, what'll you do? Kill your way across the country? Can't you see the damage you're doing to yourself?'

'So instead, I'll deliver justice,' Malley corrected her sister gently. 'Because that's all we can do now that we've burned the house down.'

'Please,' Hilda asked her. 'There's a moment here. He can change things for us?'

She was so like Fionnuala.

'If the country rested on the shoulders of this one person, then we were doomed regardless,' Malley told her gently.

'You're wrong. You can change the world. You can certainly change this little corner of it. For me. For your sister?'

'I'm sorry,' she replied.

'You'll kill an innocent man because the Government told you to?'

And this was the part that was going to hurt her the most.

'Kelly's not innocent,' she told her sister.


Kelly stood in the wide-open room on the top floor of the Point Tower surrounded by the local council. They crowded the room, over forty of them. Outside, the storm winds seemed to drive the river back upstream, turning the tide as it were. Facing out over the river in the evening light, he could still make out the jutting, twisted metal that protruded from the bank to indicate that there was once a bridge directly below him. A relatively modern one by all accounts, now gone.

Joseph screamed a triumphant scream that filled the room, his wind whistled through the bridge-that-was-no-more at the foot of the tower block. The Whistling Bridge they had called it. The room was full of people who remembered that. Or if not that, remembered something else. Before.

Fionnuala Regan stood by his side, her chin lifted defiantly, blood still seeping from the stitching and the bandage that now covered half her face as she addressed the council.

Her story was fantastical and terrible in equal measure. The trail of bodies in their wake, the ambushes and the single-minded bloody pursuit of the two agents. If she could be believed, the man who had brought her here was more animal than person, murdering his own partner in cold blood and there weren't enough soldiers in the country to stop him.

It was coming. As Kelly knew it would be.

Not for the first time, he cursed the suddenness of his plan which had left him here in Limerick, isolated. It had been necessary, but how he hated it.

Their eyes were so hard to read. It was hard to tell what the council were thinking. And they weren't swayed by eloquent talk, or tough talk either for that matter.

They had no time for the former, and he wasn't tough enough for the latter.

Fionnuala was helping him though. He had sold them on the idea that the Government was so corrupt that they'd abuse the concept of environmental justice for the political opportunity to kill their opponents.

He couldn't have sold them on that if they thought he was in any way guilty. The way she looked at him, the loyalty she showed him, the reverence in which she held him reassured them of that innocence.

They didn't have to like him, they just had to believe him.

As he listened to her story unfold, he watched the storm-tossed river and how he prayed that his old colleague Dr Comber, the one they now called Omega, had kept her mouth shut.


Fionnuala fought to keep the bloody tears from her eyes as she explained how Broderick had killed Malley. She could see the knife sailing through the air, the almost casual toss of it that had taken her down.

She had always held to the idea that Malley could protect her, that somehow the woman was a match for Broderick.

She knew differently now.

Looking about the room, she was dismayed by the ages of the people present.

The crowd of faces in front of her, more than she had expected, were all hardy-looking, as weathered and battered as the city that sheltered them. They were from the lowlands. They had to be that way, but they still had *that* look that so many from Before had. As though the callouses they had grown on their way from 2026 to here were unnatural, unwelcome things. Broderick was from Before and he didn't have that look. Malley had never had it either. Their hardness was a thing that they embraced.

These men and women, tough as they were, were older and just a little bit haunted by what they had become. When Broderick got here, he'd eat them up.

And she was certain he was on the way.

It would take something too terrible to imagine to stop him.

She continued to pour her story out for them. Their faces gave nothing away. They didn't even blink when she confessed to killing a man in Athlone. She told them the why of it too, that was the hardest part, to confess that she thought that Broderick was a good man at heart, and she saved his life, admittedly out of instinct, because she thought there was a life inside there worth saving.

Kelly didn't blink either. He stood with his back to them, facing out at the storm.

She reckoned he must have been thinking about the riots in Dublin, Belfast, and Waterford. The loss of life there could only have been cancelled out by the tremendous loyalty shown to him. That people would rise up at word that an innocent man had been murdered, that they would rise up to protest the political assassination of a decent man.

It was the start they needed, though it came at such a terrible cost.

She hoped the weight of what he faced now wasn't too difficult to bear. She would do everything she possibly could to protect him.

Their journeys had so much in common. They'd both walked hard roads. They'd both had to sacrifice. They'd both lost friends. They were both on the side of good, and if they were strong, they would prevail.

That's how it worked in her hypothetical future. The good guys prevailed.


O'Mahony watched the girl talking from just over the shoulder of the One-Eyed Rook.

He listened as she talked about her dead friend, shrinking behind the Rook. She wouldn't have noticed him in the crowded room anyway, small as he was. Out of the way. As was his way.

Rook had admonished him when they'd reunited in Galway in the guts of the hospital. But then he'd clapped him on the shoulder too, and all was forgotten.

No one commented on his being in the thick of the action, because no one could have ever believed that he'd willingly put himself there.

He was proud of himself for that. Proud of himself for saving her.

He didn't mention the agents. Or the fight. Or the woman surviving. Or the evidence.

He couldn't imagine a way in which he could have said it. Who would listen to him? Rook maybe. No one else.

His word against this revolutionary leader? Kelly had the style alright. The sway. A charisma and a confidence that allowed things to work out for him the way they didn't for everyone else.

O'Mahony remembered the likes of him from Before. Senior management types that had achieved promotion without ever having to do the actual work. Men who talked out of both sides of their mouths.

He believed that the man had been heroic during the first Storm Season. He really did believe it. But only because during that first Storm Season, the entire country had fallen into the categories of hero or villain. Too many had been villains, but some were born again as heroes in those moments.

He watched the man watching the river, and he watched the young woman and he waited, because he knew there was a different type of storm coming.


Fionnuala was still pleading with the council to double the guards and bring in more weapons when a voice rang through the room.

It was a familiar voice.

'Climate change remains the single biggest weapon the leftists have, it's just one of many, but it's the biggest one they have, because if you buy it, it means they can put their hands in your pockets and take out your money. They get to frighten you with a lie, and then charge you for the privilege.'

Malley's words cut through Fionnuala's speech.

Through the large double doors, she walked, her eyes ablaze. In one bleeding, ruined hand, she held a small clutch of papers, stained with blood and rainwater.

Her mismatched clothes were a far cry from the pristine uniform she'd worn when Fionnuala first saw her in Black Stair. It had only been days ago, but it felt like months now. There was blood all over her. Her knives were all outside her clothes, long terrible teeth that she could draw in a heartbeat.

Her sister stood beside her, no less angry, no less implacable. A shared aura of menace they both wore, though Malley's was made all the more frightening by the way she moved. A warrior's grace.

There was a kind of beauty in her beaten, battered visage and Fionnuala felt a surge of relief at seeing the woman in front of her. It shouldn't have been a surprise. She exuded permanence. She exuded hope.

'What could make more sense? You invent a monster and then claim that only you can defeat this monster. And what a monster they've invented. The weather. You can't fight the weather. The greatest achievement they've managed to date is to make the unalterable, untouchable weather into your worst enemy. It's a lie so huge they're counting on you to be so impressed with the size of it that you won't bother to stop and question it.'

The only sound came from outside the room. Joseph shrieking his objections to the Proclamation being read out, an angry audience of wind and rain and lightning.

She stopped in the middle of the room, placing herself in front of the council.

Behind them, Kelly watched her arrive.

His facial expression was stern but otherwise unperturbed. His hands clasped behind his back.

One of the council members moved, a one-eyed man with a long hideous scar on his face. He placed himself directly in her path but made no move to interfere with her as she stood before him.

Until they were almost nose to nose.

'They're trying to make the sunshine your enemy, literally. Then when it stops being sunny, they'll tell you the rain is also your enemy. They're lying to you and if you don't resist them now, we'll pay the price later.'

The council member in front of her grew more stony-faced with every word, but he still held his ground, his inner turmoil playing out in the clenching of his fists and the ripple in his jaw that showed how tightly he was clamping his mouth shut.

'Joe Kelly,' she intoned, staring past the man in her path as if he wasn't there, straight at Kelly, 'born Joseph Trench in the Rotunda Hospital, Dublin, 1989.'

A few of the council people shifted their feet as his birth name was given, and Fionnuala moved without thinking to stand directly in front of Kelly.

She was being betrayed.

It couldn't be happening.

Malley had promised justice. She had promised that no harm would come to anyone who was innocent. Fionnuala felt her anger rise with her incredulity.

From Broderick she would expect no less, but from her...

The feeling of hope and relief that had washed through her when she saw Malley walk into the room died to be replaced by a terrible determination. The same determination that had bested Broderick.

If she could beat him, she could beat anyone.

She could beat this traitor.

'These statements made in the year 2019 were made by you. Your location and identity have been a matter of investigation by the Department of Environmental Justice.

'In the presence of the Minister for the Environment you have been accused by two gents of Environmental Justice. The Minister pronounced your sentence.

'You have been deemed guilty of betraying humanity and condemning it to catastrophe. Thusly are you judged and condemned yourself.'

Fionnuala's hand closed around the hilt of Broderick's knife.


Malley let the Pronouncement echo around the room for a moment before she brought her eyes down to lock them with the one-eyed man standing in front of her. He wasn't tall, but he had the manner and bearing of a soldier, and the long scar on his cheek was evidence of a seasoned veteran.

The infamous One-Eyed Rook.

Over his shoulder she could see Fionnuala.

The relief at seeing the young woman alive and well was palpable.

Broderick, beaten senseless, was still unconscious and so she had no way of knowing Fionnuala's fate until she saw her standing before her.

The wounds ached her, her hand stinging as she held the package Omega had given her.

'I deny the charges,' Kelly replied blithely.

The room waited in silence.

'I don't give a fuck,' Malley told him quietly.

Fionnuala's knuckles whitened as she gripped the knife in her belt.

Malley recognised it as Broderick's.

So that's how it had been. Fionnuala had taken it from him and stuck him with it. She felt a burst of pride for the younger woman. The strength and resourcefulness in her were traits she likely didn't even know she had.

She felt a pang of sadness too, a momentary thing. The sweet young woman had become hard. She was learning the price. A price that was always too high.

There was worse to come for her.

'We all know,' Kelly intoned, talking to the council more than her, his life hanging, he knew, on their say-so, 'that the Government invented these charges. Gibson was on his way to acquire the evidence in Galway when he was assassinated by one of you agents.'

Fionnuala was staring at her, the hardness in her eyes was more than just resilience. It was almost hatred; such was her belief in his innocence. As if only he and Gibson had been in on their plan.

'No,' she corrected him, 'he was on his way to destroy the actual evidence.'

Fionnuala's face flickered for a second. A shadow of doubt passing over her before her determined expression reasserted itself.

She was learning the price alright, but she hadn't learned it yet.

'There's nothing you people won't say to get away with this,' Kelly told her.

He was still so sure he could yet convince them he was innocent.

She looked around the room at the council members. If it turned nasty, then she was in trouble. Even the eldest among them, a grizzled-looking man with a long beard that contained only the memory of ginger hair looked like he'd go down fighting and make a game of it.

Behind the Rook, she saw O'Mahony. The wiry old man she had saved, and who in turn had saved her. He knew. She nodded to him. He nodded back at her.

At least one ally.

She looked up at Fionnuala one more time. This would be her lesson. This is what would break her.

'A week or so ago,' she told the room, 'a man known as Digital in Athlone was in communication with a Dr Comber, better known as Omega, in Galway. They traded with one another from time to time. Sometimes food and resources. More often, information. He told her that he had evidence that Gibson Waters, known more commonly as Frank Gibson, and Joseph Trench, known popularly as Joe Kelly, had both been climate change deniers during their college years. They were part of a conservative movement called True Values that felt they were being oppressed.

'Their main vehicle of attack against the so-called oppressors was an online and sometimes printed newsletter known as *Liberal Tears.*'

Kelly's face paled, his eyes taking on a hunted quality.

In front of him, Fionnuala, who couldn't see the change on his face, stared at Malley, her hand still resting on the long handle of Broderick's knife.

The council stood watching. Undecided.

'Digital suggested that Comber, who he knew attended the same hospital as they did during the first Storm Season, might know something about it, and since they studied medicine in Galway, she might be able to recover a server from there, which would verify the sketchy evidence he had.

'Not only did she have the digital evidence, but she also had this…'

Malley drew a sheet from the bottom of the stack in her

hand. A copy of the pamphlet circulated around the college campus.

The mood in the room changed as breaths were drawn and heads began to turn.

Fionnuala's face had grown a frown, but her eyes remained locked on Malley, the knife inching from its sheath.

'Printed in Government buildings, I'm sure,' Kelly insisted, though from his tone alone his guilt was evident.

'Digital offered this information to both Kelly and to the Minister for the Environment, Luke O'Neill, in the hope of starting a bidding war. For O'Neill this was an opportunity, but, a little unexpectedly, Trench and Waters saw it so as well.

'Rather than deny the charges, they decided to print false evidence themselves, hand it to the Department of Environment and then stage a break in to "authenticate" that false evidence. O'Neill being the stupid, opportunistic rat that he is decided it was all he needed to Pronounce both of them.

'Then they fled the capital knowing full well that they could easily disprove the falsified evidence. This would sway the electorate, disgrace the Government, vindicate them, but, most importantly, it would conceal the truth about what they did.

'After all, Mr Kelly, what could make more sense? You invent a monster and then you defeat it, right?'

Suddenly, the room was no longer ambivalent but filled with a growing sense of anger and betrayal.

Kelly took an involuntary step until his back was pressed against the glass, the storm and a swollen grey river swirling behind him.

Fionnuala turned to look at him, her face disbelieving.

'I don't know what was offered to Digital,' Malley continued, 'because Broderick killed him before we could find out. But in Galway, Mr Waters, or Gibson if you prefer, was planning on executing his former colleague. She had the only remaining evidence. Which she gave to me after everyone else thought I was dead.'

Fionnuala turned to face Kelly. She saw the look on his face, the recognition of guilt.

She took a step back from him. Her hand still on the knife.

Malley had been correct. This had broken her. The betrayal was written all over her face.

'There are riots,' Fionnuala almost whispered. 'People are dying…'

'It's too late to kill me,' Kelly told Malley, ignoring the young woman in front of him. 'You'd make another martyr of me. There's already been one. Now you'll have two. And for what? To save this Government? It's too late for them anyway. Times are changing. The people want a future, not a past.

'I wasn't lying about the embargo. We can end it. Can you imagine? When Joseph has passed, we can have boats here, and ships. Food. No more rationing. We can trade and we can rebuild, better than before because we've learned now, not to be so wasteful. We're better now…'

He trailed off as he looked around the room.

The words of the deniers never sat well with those who had lost out on a life.


The Rook stood facing the woman. She was shorter than him, though not by much, but her presence was terrifying. If the one he'd met in Galway was a demon, this one was the devil. The soaked, blood-stained clothes, the solidity of her, the terrible permanence of her.

Was she lying? Did he try to kill her? Was Kelly lying? The taste of betrayal sickened him, but it was familiar too. Hard things were learned in the fourteen years since the first Storm Season. Now a decision would have to be made.

Kill the woman, or kill the man?

A gentle hand on his arm from behind turned his head.

O'Mahony, with his soft eyes, too soft for this hard place.

'She's telling the truth,' the old man said quietly. 'I was in

Galway. She spared me once. I wanted to repay it. I was with Omega when she gave her that.'

She'd saved O'Mahony? And tried to save Gibson? And saved the girl?

This woman, with those eyes. Those dead, cold eyes.

The One-Eyed Rook looked at his small, old friend and made a decision. Standing to one side, he cleared her way to the traitor.


Fionnuala felt her stomach convulse, an almost physical response to having her heart broken. Logically she might have told herself that it changed nothing, but the lies, the machinations, the preaching words that now seemed so hollow... it was her parents' memories that were the most sullied.

Dinners with them. Winking at her. Little in-jokes.

Her parents. The memory of them would always be tied to this man, this traitor, this faker who ruined the world.

With a snarl, she tore Broderick's knife from her belt and dived at Kelly.

The older man dodged to one side reflexively, his face full of panic, and she stumbled through the spot where he had been standing to collide with the window.

Her anger coursed through her veins, pounding in her ears. The betrayal of it all. The filthiness. The destruction of a dream and a future all at once. The end of her hope.

She pushed herself back up from the window and slashed at him a second time.

He skirted back from her, desperately searching the room for support. None came.

Fionnuala snarled again and lunged. This time there was nowhere for him to go, trapped with his back to the wall.

She had him.

A hand caught her wrist as the knife came down.

The younger woman twisted and writhed in Malley's vice-like grip. Her face contorted by the betrayal.

'No,' Malley told her.

'I killed for this man,' she shrieked.

'Killing him for betraying you isn't justice. You kill him for that and you're Broderick.'

Fionnuala writhed. 'Let me go,' she screamed.


Malley felt her heart break just a little, even as she watched Fionnuala's shatter entirely. Her life spared, but this was the cost.

'That's not justice,' Malley told her sadly.

Kelly stood gaping at them for a moment. Standing in the silent room, listening to Joseph howl outside as he tossed the Shannon waters about himself.

Then suddenly he ran. As she knew they sometimes did.

The Rook moved to intercept, but O'Mahony restrained him with a gentle hand.

Malley was grateful.

She released Fionnuala so suddenly that the younger woman yelped in surprise, as Malley took off.

So often she'd only had to stroll as Broderick hunted down the deniers. This time she moved at pace, behind her, footfalls told her that there were others in pursuit. Kelly bounded across the sky-bridge and down flights of stairs, using his slight head start and gravity to best advantage.

Malley moved after him quickly, keeping him in sight, but not tiring herself out. She was fitter and stronger, and patience was her ally.

Down he continued with her no more than a floor behind him, inexorable, until he came to street level where he burst clear onto the stormy street.

Joseph waited outside and the loud howling seemed to increase, as though the storm recognised their arrival. Winds dragged a long, rough hand along Henry Street, pushing the detritus that collected during the storms in front of him, softly bowling the little bits and pieces at their feet as Kelly ran, with Malley in pursuit, Hilda and Fionnuala behind her.

She felt the storm infusing her, as it so often did, but she contained the energy of it, controlled it. She kept pace with him, but never closed the gap. How the early humans hunted, running their prey into the ground.

As the long street sloped down, the older man's legs gave out and he pitched forward.

He turned to look up at her as she closed the gap between them.

He got to his knees only, looking up at her in terror.

Another life to take. For what?

His hands were clasped in a pathetic plea, his eyes pitiful things. For all his political grandeur, it came down to this moment.

'I'm different now,' he shouted at her over the wind. 'You have to believe me. At the hospital, during the first Storm Season, I learned, I swear.'

Fionnuala and Hilda reached her at the same time as he spoke.

Side by side they stood, both wearing their passion on their faces, framed with their curly hair. Malley almost wanted to laugh at the similarity between them. In retrospect she'd never really stood a chance.

Fionnuala gripped Broderick's knife, but she allowed herself to be restrained by Hilda's gentle hand on her shoulder.

'What's it going to achieve, Malley?' her sister asked her. 'We can't change the past.'

Echoes of their long row some years before. Only then she had been the one asking. What would this revolutionary movement achieve? She had her answer now. The slight hint of a future, the glimmer of one.

'You can put down the knife. Let him go, let *them* go,' her sister exhorted, her soft words somehow penetrating the wind and the rain.

Could she really? There was a temptation to that. She'd felt it back in Black Stair. In Bloom. In Hilda's house. Put down the knife. Be that thing that she hoped might still be inside her.

No more oneness, no more holding it by the blade and feeling the edge slip into the cracks of her hands.

'I promise you,' he shouted up to her. 'The man I was is long dead. He was a fool. He died during the first Storm Season, in the hospital right alongside the people who rushed to us for help. I knew then. That's when I knew. I'm sorry. I'm so sorry.'

She looked down at her ruined hands again. The scars new and old standing out. Whatever age she lived to, these scars would adorn her palms and her fingers.

The rain and the wind still drove down on them, soaking them, falling on the just and the unjust alike, as someone had once written.

She looked at Fionnuala. A revolutionary, standing alongside Hilda, another revolutionary. They couldn't stop her if they wanted to.

'If not for you, then for me?' Hilda pleaded, as Joseph screamed his objections all around her.

Could she do that for Hilda? To give back for the sacrifices the younger woman had made for her? Could she abandon justice, *her* justice, if it meant building the bridge back to her sister?

She recalled the words of the priest in Bloom: *Is this what you call justice?*

Her hand wavered then, as if it, independent of her, wanted no part of the knife.

'If I could go back and change it all, I would,' Kelly shouted up at her.

Hilda's eyes closed at his words.

The wrong words.

What was done couldn't be changed.

Malley looked at her hands again. They weren't the only scars. And not all scars were visible. There was no one without scars.

If she could go back, what would she have changed? She looked at her sister for a long moment, remembering the first

Storm Season, remembering what was done to her when Joe Kelly was being reborn in a hospital in Galway.

No going back. The past can't be repaired.

Too little. Too late.

'Thusly are you judged,' she told him.

Then she dropped to one knee and drove the knife into his chest.

He spasmed once, eyes wide with shock and fear. Then he was still.

Joseph's howl felt triumphant to her and the feeling as he smashed the ground with rain and debris was one of celebration. She raised her head to look at them, standing next to one another. Hair slicked onto their heads, clothes sodden in the driving rain, both shifting their weight to keep the wind from blowing them away. Fionnuala's long fresh wound seeping blood.

Her sister's eyes were sad again. More than sad. Pitying. Just like they had been the last time she had come to Limerick.

'Hilda?' she asked.

It was a challenge.

The same challenge she always offered the witnesses to her Proclamation. She knew why she did it now. Because she wanted them to tell her she was wrong, she wanted to know that some people believed killing was wrong. Then she could tell them that she knew that. She was aware it was wrong, but justice had to be done.

Hilda shook her head.

Malley turned to the other pair of eyes that watched her. Steely now. Hard eyes.

'Fionnuala?' she challenged.

The younger woman looked down at the corpse, the blood from her cut mixing with the rain as it dripped off her face.

'Regan,' she replied. 'Just Regan from now on.'

# EPILOGUE

They sheltered in the remnants of a house outside Nenagh. Joseph, all prevalent, had followed them there and was simultaneously waiting for them too. He was fiercer now, as if he too contained a rage that needed out. One of the storms dubbed 'unsurviveable' by the meteorologists; winds too strong to resist, uprooting trees, tearing away roofs, picking up and smashing down.

These had to be sheltered from. Weathered, so to speak.

Malley sat listening to Joseph by the small fire they'd set. Enough of the sturdy old building had survived for them to wake up dry, if a little smoky tomorrow. No words were said.

She ate her rehydrated soup, her mind occasionally wandering back to her sister, gone from her forever now.

She waited for the rattle of his spoon against his tin mug. It never arrived.

Something was broken inside Broderick. Still a swollen mess, he sat by the fire, his hands bound, eating his soup quietly, looking at no one, saying nothing. The air of menace he exuded was gone. She'd beaten the hardness out of him.

And that hardness, needing somewhere to go, had leaked into Regan. The young woman sat in silence, her glance occasionally drifting over Broderick before snapping back. The whites of one eye now permanently red above the wound that marked her cheek, but if it pained her, she gave no sign.

Sometimes, though Malley suspected the young woman didn't notice, she would run an index finger along the length of the cut, tracing from her eyelid down to her jawline.

Every time she did it her eyes would flicker back to him.

Broderick still sat there.

Malley hoped his brain wasn't broken permanently. And was glad that she still held to that shred of her humanity. Her travelling companions were casualties of another Storm Season. Proof that it never stopped taking. Never stopped teaching.

Outside, Joseph screamed victoriously for the new lessons learnt.

Malley stirred her soup and nodded at the younger woman.

*You have first watch.*

Regan nodded back.

*Understood.*

Not a word spoken.

# ACKNOWLEDGEMENTS

I've never done anything worth doing on my own. Anything good I've ever done was with the love and support of the family, friends and communities I'm surrounded by. It would be impossible to list them all here, but since I've got a little page to try...

Ma and Da, you're the greatest. My siblings Ciara, Jean and Paul, you're all a constant source of support and occasional comedy. I love you. My brothers-in-law, and sister-in-law, Mike, John and Tara. The whole legion of nieces and nephews not to mind the army of aunts and uncles and cousins. Thank you for everything you've given me. Christine, for all your constant encouragement and the reading and the listening, I don't have words for how grateful I am.

To Lucy, Liza, Olivia and everyone else at the wonderful Legend Press who keep taking these chances on me, I am so grateful. In particular to Lauren Wolff-Jones whose attention to detail and creative encouragement continues to sort of amaze me. Thank you all for being a pleasure to work with.

To my test readers; Eadoin Shanahan, Phil Shanahan, Cat Hogan, Alex Dunne, Kennedy O'Brien, Emma Langford, Sam Windrim, Ruadh Harrington, Sadb Harrington, Hilda McHugh. Your feedback, especially in the early stages, was so important to me. Most especially to Sheila Killian who badgered me to keep going when I was about to throw in the towel. This book is largely your fault SK.

To all of my other writing group members in Writepace. Too often you guys are the creative kick in the ass I need to stop being a baby.

To my communities in Young Munster, and the Torch Players and the College Players. Thanks for being a place for me to go to shout a little bit.

To the staff and regulars at Charlie Malone's Bar, Mother Mac's and Crew Brewing. You've been a haven for me to work on this book and then a very welcome distraction from it shortly after the work is done. Too often the latter, not enough of the former maybe. You're wonderful people.

Lastly some special shouts out to friends who've literally sat there while I talked at them through all the ups and downs of this book; Liam O'Brien, Sarah Moore Fitzgerald, Grainne O'Brien, Ann Blake, Emma Langford (again), Alex Dunne, Ross O'Donoghue, Will Reidy. Your patience, kindness and generosity could and probably should, earn you a sainthood. Putting up with me certainly should also. I love you all.